"YOU [...] A MA[...] IF YOU [...], MA COEUR, THEN LET IT BE A WORTHY ONE."

Arching her chin with his finger, Laurent bent his head and with delicious languor lay his lips on hers. At the first touch of his kiss, Renée lost all desire to run away. She leaned her slight weight against his taller frame.

Laurent's arms slipped round her, only to have her kiss slip away as she turned her head to gasp for breath. When Laurent's mouth covered hers a second time, Renée felt at once helplessly ensnared and protectively enfolded. The need to speak aloud, to reassure herself with the sound of her own voice brought words to her lips.

"I will be a good wife, Laurent, I swear it!"

The silence that met her statement sent quakes of alarm through Renée and her gaze flew to his face. She thought she saw pity flicker in his eyes before an inscrutable expression replaced it.

"I will not marry you."

Dear Reader,

We, the editors of Tapestry Romances, are committed to bringing you two outstanding original romantic historical novels each and every month.

From Kentucky in the 1850s to the court of Louis XIII, from the deck of a pirate ship within sight of Gibraltar to a mining camp high in the Sierra Nevadas, our heroines experience life and love, romance and adventure.

Our aim is to give you the kind of historical romances that you want to read. We would enjoy hearing your thoughts about this book and all future Tapestry Romances. Please write to us at the address below.

The Editors
Tapestry Romances
POCKET BOOKS
1230 Avenue of the Americas
Box TAP
New York, N.Y. 10020

Moth and Flame

Laura Parker

A TAPESTRY BOOK
PUBLISHED BY POCKET BOOKS NEW YORK

Books by Laura Parker

Emerald and Sapphire
Moth and Flame

Published by TAPESTRY BOOKS

An *Original* publication of TAPESTRY BOOKS

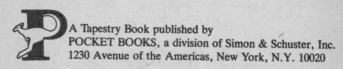

A Tapestry Book published by
POCKET BOOKS, a division of Simon & Schuster, Inc.
1230 Avenue of the Americas, New York, N.Y. 10020

ISBN: 0-671-50684-6

First Tapestry Books printing March, 1984

10 9 8 7 6 5 4 3 2 1

To my husband, Chris

Chapter One

Louisiana, 1797

A FLAME FLARED BRIEFLY IN THE NIGHT, THEN dimmed as the faint crackle of tobacco was heard. For that instant the sunburned features of a man standing beneath a huge oak were illuminated. Thrown in bright relief above the whiteness of his open-throated shirt were sharply etched planes of cheekbones and brow. The lips were set in mild amusement, the stamp of a man who found life a diversion at best, a tolerated insanity at worst. His eyes, large, luminous and onyx-black, held the questioning gaze of a man who once met was never forgotten.

In the distance, beyond the canopy of oaks, stood a large French colonial plantation house. From its open doorways the strains of a Vivaldi concerto rose to an uncertain conclusion at the hands of inexperienced players.

1

A short distance separated the ballroom from the onlooker, yet he moved into the shadow of the nearby *garçonnière* at the sound of an approaching carriage. The floor-to-ceiling shutters of the building opened smoothly to the pressure of his hand and then he was inside.

Laurent Lavasseur scarcely needed the moonlight filtering through the window slats to find his way across the salon of these bachelor quarters. He was not a stranger to Louisiana or to Bonne Vie Plantation. He was home.

Undoubtedly his mother hosted one of her famous soirees this night. Once a month, from late spring until the family's return to New Orleans each fall, the Lavasseur house hosted a party. The names and faces of each and every guest would be known to him. It was just as well that he had chosen not to announce his arrival.

"Nothing changes," Laurent murmured dryly as he found a chair. No, that was not true. Five months earlier he had sailed away in hopes of realizing plans that were now like so many flotsam dreams. He had returned, not as a merchant made wealthy from the safe delivery of his cargo, but as a captain without a ship.

Laurent winced as his hand spread protectively over the tender scar of what had been a serious wound in his upper right thigh. Two grace-filled inches separated the wound from his groin. His chuckle of relief rumbled softly through the night, which was delicately scented

2

with the fragrances of jasmine and rose blossoms. He had so little left; at least he'd been spared the life of a eunuch.

"Laurent, *mon ami*, you are a fool," he said aloud.

Who but a fool would have left a life of certain wealth, to gamble and lose all on a proposition fraught with such risks? The uncertainty of smuggling contraband—brandy and silks, wines and tobacco—from the French to the English colonies of the Caribbean held no special interest for him beyond the exhilaration of the moment, the relief from the tedium of life. As a Creole gentleman, the only acceptable profession open to him was that of a planter and man of leisure.

His ever-present smile deepened into a smirk. What sort of life was that for a man of restless energies and quick, mobile wits? Growing sugarcane required no more than periodic surveillance of one's workers. As a child, he had grown up in the uneasy conviction that slavery was a necessary evil. As a man, he could not accept that he should live off other men's sweat.

His broad shoulders made a restive movement beneath his linen shirt as he murmured, "Laurent, you think too much!"

That characteristic was his bane and his boon. He liked to think of himself as a man with little sympathy for the folly of others. Then why was he sitting now in the dark, like a thief in his own home, unwilling to make his presence known?

"My beautiful *papillon*," Laurent breathed

warmly in answer to the thought of Renée Valois.

Old images returned to him, of rich brandy-warm eyes, shining up at him in silent wonder. He had often felt her gaze when she thought he was unaware. From the first she had not only regarded him with feminine interest but also weighed and judged him with an intelligence that had both surprised and intrigued him. In that gaze he had found open innocence mingled with a passionate streak.

Certainly she was more interesting than the bevy of Creole girls of his acquaintance. Their docile air and serene beauty left him unmoved. Renée's creamy complexion was too alive to be pale. The blood of life rushed a soft effusion of color into her cheeks. Her breath-stilling beauty had the power to mesmerize. To watch her was to follow the gay spiraling of a butterfly: she was sweet and dear, thoughtless and impulsive . . . and as imprudent.

No doubt she was dancing at this very moment, her dark eyes, as wide and mysterious as an Egyptian houri's, captivating her partner. She often wore flowers among her ebony ringlets. Gardenias were her favorite. She was just out of reach, no farther away than the stretch of lawn which separated his rooms from the main house.

Yet, she was the reason he did not move. He could not face her until he came to a decision. He had once thought that upon his return he would propose to her. But as the months passed, he could not allay his reluctance, nay, his natu-

4

ral abhorrence of the thought of marriage. *Ma foi!* He must be mad.

Laurent drew deeply on his tobacco. For nearly a year he had known himself to be in love with the exquisite eighteen-year-old. Certainly his family expected a match between them. That was the reason behind his mother's offer to Renée to share the hospitality of the Lavasseur home. Though it was the custom in Louisiana Creole society for a girl to marry at fourteen or fifteen, Renée was seen by his family as a special case. She was French, a Parisian. And like so many other recent émigrés to Louisiana, a victim of the French Revolution. Together, the two Valois sisters had braved the terror of the old world to begin again in the new.

In the beginning he had been drawn to Gweneth, the fiery-spirited older sister with the emerald gaze. Now *there* was a prize worthy of a man of daring. As luck would have it, he had lost her to his best friend, Raoul Bertrand.

A broad grin broke over Laurent's features. Besotted, that's what Bertrand had been when it came to Gweneth. Watching their adventurous courtship had proved quite diverting. Anyone with eyes or ears had known how it would end. *Enfin*, it was against his nature to resist the temptation to try to woo her from Bertrand. And so he had stolen a few kisses, and would have taken much more had the lady been so inclined.

Yet, in the end, he was glad he had not found himself the possessor of the daunting Mademoiselle Gweneth. Theirs was the rarest of alliances, one forged of pride and desire. But Bertrand had changed. Gweneth had made a proper gentleman of him, settled his roaming ways. In one short year he was the father of twins and the harsh hunger for adventure had mellowed in his blue-fire gaze. Gweneth had done that. Marriage had done that.

Renée would want things too: a house, an ever-present husband, a babe a year for him to bounce on his knee. *Vraiment*? Who needed that? No, he did not want his freedom curtailed, no matter how lovely the bride.

Laurent started as, just outside the door, a woman's footsteps whispered lightly over the brick walkway. Before he could do more than extinguish his tobacco, he heard a man's voice. Intrigued, he moved toward the shutters.

In the milk-white light of the moon the figure of a woman was silhouetted. A moment later a second, masculine form joined hers on the path between the main house and his rooms.

"A tryst!" Laurent muttered, his eyes narrowing as he recognized the pert feminine form.

Renée Valois could not remember ever having been so bored. Seated on a velvet chair in the Lavasseur salon, she negligently twisted the silk tassels of her fan round and round her fingers. What good was a new ball gown when there was no one present worthy to admire it?

Her lower lip quivered as she surveyed the gathering in the salon. Not one of the gentlemen present was worth the exorbitant cost of her new frock. Its daring chemise fit made the most of the perfect proportions of her tiny frame and yet it was all for naught.

"Laurent Lavasseur, where can you be?" she whispered under her breath. For five months he had been absent from Bonne Vie and not one word had reached her of his whereabouts nor when he could be expected home. If not for her certainty that he would eventually ask for her hand in marriage, she would have given up and set sail for England weeks ago.

A secret smile suddenly curved Renée's lips. The reason for her belief that she and Laurent would marry was not altogether a practical one. Not even Gweneth knew all. One never told the full secrets of her heart even to a sister.

A picture of Laurent, as she had first seen him, came to mind. As he stood on the pilot deck of his ship, his long raven-black locks had been lashed back from his wind-sculptured face by a grosgrain ribbon. The gold cross glittering against the polished muscles of his chest, revealed by his open shirt, had been the only concession to civilization in his thoroughly male presence. The very air about him seemed to shimmer with danger and excitement. She had been afraid, awed, and fascinated all at once. He had looked every bit the answer to her secret dreams.

In the beginning, she had kept her wayward thoughts and desires to herself. Laurent had had eyes only for Gweneth. The scattered attention he had shown her, the younger sister, was that of an adult for a pretty child.

But I've known for months how it would end, Renée thought with a leap of her pulse. Unbeknownst to anyone else, she possessed a secret knowledge.

Just as she had predicted a future which had come true for Gweneth, Mama Theo, the voodoo woman of Barbados, had read her future.

Renée flicked open her ivory fan and began applying it against the warmth of the night, but her thoughts were far away. Mama Theo had told her that, unlike Raoul, who was the moth to Gweneth's flame, her love must both conquer and be conquered.

"For de man o' your choice, you be both de moth and de flame!"

Renée shuddered as though an icy wind touched her. In reality, her gown was sticking to her back from the heat. To this very day she had told no one of her fortune, in part because Gweneth had not wanted to believe Mama Theo's prediction that she would win Capitaine Bertrand and in part because she did not completely understand the ominous words. Who could be both victim and lure, both moth and flame?

The opening notes of a minuet drew Renée's attention back to the assembly. She loved to dance but she turned sharply away from the hopeful smile of Phillip Justin, who came striding toward her. A younger son of a neighboring planter, Phillip had spent the better part of the last weeks in active pursuit of her affections.

"Mademoiselle, I thought you had eluded me."

Renée looked up into Phillip's thin dark face

and flicked her fan shut in annoyance. "Phillip, I thought you'd retired for the night," she murmured, and looked away.

Earlier in the evening she had flirted outrageously with him. Anything, she had thought, to relieve the depression of the hour. But now, suddenly, she knew that if he even asked her to dance, she would scream in frustration.

She was no fool, for all he might consider her a lovely feather-head. She knew that Phillip was more interested in the rumors concerning her inheritance than in her beauty. The Creoles were practical people; they saw nothing wrong in a penniless younger son pursuing a wealthy young woman, so long as she was of impeccable pedigree. Whatever Phillip's desire for her might be, she knew it was colored by the gleam of gold.

"Mademoiselle Renée, how could I resist the chance to be by your side?" Phillip murmured, bending toward her as though his commonplace flattery had some special significance.

"Do not breathe so upon me, monsieur," she replied in an icy tone as she leaned away from him. "I'm quite overcome by the heat as it is."

Phillip blushed to the roots of his dark hair, a lock of which had strayed forward across his brow in spite of the liberal use of pomade. "A thousand pardons, mademoiselle. Perhaps a glass of punch would cool you."

Renée bit back the retort that came to mind. After all, Phillip was nothing more than a nuisance, rather like a mosquito who persisted in buzzing about her ear.

Yet, she could not miss the significant looks coming her way. Young Creole gentlemen were not permitted to waste an ineligible lady's time. And Phillip had made it plain by his close attendance upon her at the last two gatherings that he would be a serious suitor if allowed. Either that, or Phillip had heard the rumors circulating about her. No, that was an unfair assumption merely because Phillip wished to please her.

"I would greatly admire a cup of punch, Phillip," she said after a moment's reflection, and looked up to gift him with a bright smile.

To her dismay, she saw that his gaze had been diverted to the swelling curves of her breasts rising from her low-cut bodice. "Phillip!" she snapped, and instantly his gaze was all gentle concern again. But not before she had espied the lustful look on his features. No gentleman would ever have dared look at her like that had he believed her to be a completely innocent maid.

So, Renée thought grimly, her suspicions had ample grounding after all.

She knew Madame Lavasseur had done her best to scotch the inevitable rumors that had sprung up in the wake of her arrival in New Orleans. The true story was incredible enough: her escape from war-torn France, her capture by English pirates, her sister's marriage to an English privateer, and not least her considerable inheritance. It was ample fodder for an active spiteful imaginations.

Except for the embarrassment the situation

caused her future mother-in-law, she did not care what people might say behind her back but she would not endure anyone's open expression of those insulting thoughts. An annoying suitor she could endure, but a lecherous one, never!

Renée rose to her feet, a full five feet of icy hauteur. "Excuse me," she snapped, "I find the company beyond suffering!"

Escape was uppermost in her mind, escape from the noisy crowding and the various smiling, smirking, or sympathetic faces of the Lavasseur guests and friends. Everyone knew that she awaited Laurent's return and his expected proposal of marriage. Week after week, their eyes had followed her every movement. She knew what they whispered now behind their fans as she sped past without a glance. Could not a young lady be expected to sulk when her intended absented himself for so long?

The restlessness that had plagued her for months pricked at her now until her skin began to feel too tight. Tiny flames of unnameable needs abraded her peace, rubbing and itching until she wore the envelope of her discontent like a sheer flame of fever. The longer she endured the restlessness, filled with urgent suffocating desires, the more clearly it found a single focus in Laurent Lavasseur. Anger emptied its bile into her blood at the very thought of the awkward position in which he had left her. Neither Phillip Justin nor any other man would dare to insult her if Laurent were near.

"Libertine! Seducer! Arrogant bastard!" she

11

labeled Phillip under her breath. The last was no more than a whisper of breath, for she knew the words were not supposed to be known to a young lady of good breeding.

But that is the trouble, Renée thought as her kid slippers made whispery noises along the cypress planking of the second-floor balcony. She was no innocent, cosseted and protected all of her life. She knew more than was wise and less than was safe, of the world and its inhabitants. But over and above it all was the longing for something, anything, to break the tedium of Laurent's absence.

The night air still sighed the day's warmth as she descended the main stairway into the garden. Only then did she realize that footsteps followed her.

"Mademoiselle Renée! *Chérie*. Wait!"

"Peste!" she whispered fiercely, recognizing Phillip's voice. Gathering two handfuls of her skirt, she sped across the lush grasses toward the only place of peace she knew, Laurent's unused bachelor quarters. There, at least, no one would bother her.

A lizard scrambled past Renée's feet, its oily body a green flash in the moonlight before it noiselessly disappeared.

Presence of mind kept her from giving in to a cry that might have caught someone's attention and spoiled her escape. She was not so lucky with a tree branch stretched treacherously across her path. The rough bark caught the toe of her slipper and she stumbled, giving in to a cry of fright. Before she could right herself, she

12

was enfolded from behind by a strong pair of arms.

"*Chérie!* I knew you were as eager as I to be alone. Come to me," Phillip whispered softly as he dragged her slight body back against his.

Furious, Renée struggled in his arms. "Let me go at once, Phillip!"

"*Non, ma chère!* Not until you impart to me a kiss for having saved you from a nasty fall."

In consternation Renée heard his passion-rough tone. She could, of course, scream, but she knew that would cause further embarrassment for Madame Lavasseur and certainly bring Phillip a challenge from one of Madame's guests. Never in her life, not even among those of the royal court of Louis XVI, had she ever known such proud people as these Creoles. On any excuse, the gentlemen drew swords and fought. The disgrace of a female, as her cry would deem Phillip's actions, would mean a fight to the death. That she could not bear. There were other ways to escape him.

Inspiration came to her in a moment. "If you will release me, perhaps I shall reward you with a kiss," she promised in the most provocative voice she could fashion. "Only you must promise not to drool upon me."

"A single kiss, it's all I require of you, *ma petite chérie,*" Phillip whispered eagerly.

Phillip's body was so tightly pressed to hers that she could feel its heat, and a wave of nausea rippled through Renée. Steeling herself for a desperate struggle, she gave a gasp of relief as the hard arms about her loosened. It was the moment she had prayed for. In an instant she stepped out of his embrace and swung around to face him.

"Oaf! Poltroon! Here is your reward!" The faint rustle of her skirts was followed by a lightning-swift glimpse of a silk-stockinged leg as she raised her foot and kicked him with all the strength she could muster.

With a yelp of pain Phillip reached out for her, grabbing her by the shoulder. But Renée was too angry now to be afraid of him. She swung the flat of her hand up and delivered a ringing slap to his face and then raised her foot again, the aim higher and still more effective.

With a grunted curse Phillip leaped back from her next blow but determinedly kept a grip on the shoulder of her gown. The thin material gave way as Renée twisted away, freeing herself.

"You fool!" Renée cried as she looked down at her bodice, which was torn open to the waist.

Phillip did not immediately answer. He was bent forward, his hands held over his pain. "I could wring your lovely little neck!" he threatened, the tremor of his voice betraying his discomfort. "When I catch you again, you will not deny me that kiss."

Renée turned away toward the main house, not deeming his statement worthy of reply. So much for gentlemanly behavior! Pausing near the first-floor gallery, she tried to fold the fabric up over her exposed flesh, but it would not stay. She dared not guess what comments the ruined gown would draw from the assembly. What could she do? Giselle, her maid, was waiting in her rooms, and she too, would require an explanation. Renée murmured a disparaging remark under her breath. All she wanted was a little peace and solitude.

Once more the thought of Laurent's rooms came to mind. Perhaps she even would find needle and thread there to repair the damage.

A moment later the green shutters of Laurent's rooms opened to her hand and she slipped inside. Before she could set in place the crossbar to block the entrance, she heard footsteps. Drawing back into the darkness, she saw, to her amusement, Phillip hobbling toward the stables.

Renée watched his painful progress in satisfaction. That would teach him to treat her like some street tart! The racing of her heart made her smile. In spite of her momentary fear, she was pleasantly excited. At least Phillip's roguish behavior had supplied her with a momentary relief from boredom.

"*Adieu*, Phillip," she whispered in laughter.

"*Pardon*, mademoiselle," a deep voice intoned from the room behind her. "You would seem to choose poorly your choice of trysting place. May I suggest the barnyard."

Startled by the sudden voice, Renée jerked around. "Who are you, monsieur?" she demanded across the space of the night-darkened room as she self-consciously attempted to hold her bodice closed.

"I cannot see that it matters," the man replied amicably. "Particularly since you have much more grave concerns at the moment."

"Such as?" Renée demanded.

"Unless my eyes deceive me, mademoiselle, you have just possibly been compromised."

"You insult me, monsieur!"

Low rich laughter answered her indignation. "No, you do not have my leave to go," he added when he saw her move to open the shutters. "You, mademoiselle, must explain your behavior to one who would save you from grave folly."

For the first time in months Renée felt a strangely familiar pang of recognition. The odor of tobacco wafted and registered in her senses. Other, more subtle but more persuasive clues resonated in the air. Before she could gather her vague impressions into firm belief, he moved toward her.

"Non! Stay where you are!" she cried. Her torn gown forgotten in a gesture of self-protection, she raised both hands. "I have no intention of remaining in the presence of a man who is so uncivil he will not even identify himself."

"Know that I am not so much a fool as young Justin," the man replied. *"Oui.* I know the name of your would-be love, and yours as well, mademoiselle, though you should prefer to remain in ignorance of my identity."

"Laurent!" Renée choked out, no longer in doubt of the owner of that steel-veined voice.

"The same," he agreed coolly.

Chapter Two

IN QUICK STRIDES LAURENT MOVED TO THE NEAR-est table. A moment later he set a spark to the lamp wick and the darkness retreated to the far corners of the room. Satisfied with his handi-work, he lowered the globe.

"Now, mademoiselle," he said pleasantly, turning to face her. "You will explain exactly what you intended in luring a man to my private quarters!"

The fiery glare of Laurent's black eyes bespoke the mood of a man who often dared all and gave little quarter. In the face of such bold challenge, a genteel Louisiana lady would have swooned. But Renée had known her accuser too long to be daunted by his angry tone. Still, she did not rush up to embrace him as she had dreamed of doing a thousand times in the last few months. Now that he was before her, the strange tingling

17

excitement of his nearness dazzled her, rooting her to the spot with indecision.

He wore a riding coat of dark blue to which the dirt of the road still clung. His shirt was open at the throat, a style he preferred to the Creole habit of the black cravat. Greatly daring, she glanced at that portion of him from waist to knee, and what she saw pinkened her cheeks. No other man of her acquaintance wore such a scandalous cut of breeches. The soft leather hugged every bulging contour of his long thigh muscles, stretching the limits of decency to the utmost.

Her gaze flashed up again to his face and Renée forced herself to study him more closely. His skin was darker, burnished by the tropical sun, throwing into sharp relief the familiar planes of his face shaped about pronounced ridges of nose and cheekbones. There were changes, too. His mirror-bright ebony locks had been shortened to *en brosse* and now willful curls made their shape against the uncompromising masculine brow. Gone was the sable mustache that had hidden his straight upper lip and drawn a woman's gaze to the full lower lip with its deep sensuous cleft.

Mesmerized by those lips, Renée heard herself speak as if from far away. "Laur . . . Monsieur Lavasseur, you're home at last."

Breathlessly aware, she watched his gaze move from her face to the scandalous expanse of her bosom revealed by her torn gown. Earlier in the evening she had despaired of proper admiration. Now she felt this man's regard bringing the color of wild roses to her cheeks as she tried unsuccessfully to gather the pieces together.

Laurent's smile broadened and she wondered with deepening unease if he were imagining, just as she was, what it would be like to have his hands cupped around her exposed flesh. Then she recalled that his consuming gaze was wont to alight on any woman of fair face. That thought fanned her temper.

"Do not gape so, *mon cher*. It is not polite," she observed with a twitch of her shoulders as she turned from him, eclipsing his view.

"So, in my absence, you've come to fancy yourself quite the Delilah," he said quietly.

Renée heard the warning in his voice, but the nettling discontent of the evening had not yet subsided. He did not seem particularly glad to see her, she noted in pique, when she, with so little encouragement, would be in his arms.

Deliberately setting out to provoke some response from him, she turned. One shiny ebony ringlet swung forward over her shoulder, perching saucily on the full swell of her breasts. She had practiced that movement often enough in her mirror to know she presented him with a picture of thoroughly desirable womanhood. Yet, much to her annoyance, he did not seem moved by her beauty.

In static silence that gave no clue to his thoughts, Laurent studied her. He had known too many women of beauty and more skill to be awed by her flirtatious manner. Yet he was not unmoved. She was a tiny thing, no higher than his heart, but every inch was perfection. How quickly he had forgotten the fresh dewy luster of her skin, the way a lamp's flame could play upon the moist redness of her softly parted lips, the rich amber gaze of her dark eyes. Now they all worked their effect, rushing a quick downward stroke of desire to stir his groin in spite of his resolve of only moments before. His gaze moved lower to skim her luscious womanly curves and he felt an urge to sweep her up in a welcoming embrace that would leave her in no doubt of her desirability.

Observe the proprieties, Laurent, he counseled himself. He was in his family's home, not aboard the quarterdeck of his ship the *Christobel*. You must play the gentleman even if the mademoiselle herself appears to have lost her scruples in that regard.

The memory of Renée in Phillip's arms flashed to mind. Now she stood before him, every yielding line of her lovely body begging his caress, and he could not say he was immune.

Irritated that he should be so affected by the actions of a girl he had no wish to marry, Laurent said, his voice brimming with mockery, "Do you so tempt and flatter every male in the parish? 'Tis very effective. I doubt there's a bachelor in all of Louisiana who has not yet fallen under your spell!"

The glib sarcasm found its stinging mark on Renée's pride. He was laughing at her! Renée glared at him, a barb of her own at the ready. "I daresay that's true. But surely there are one or two I've overlooked."

"No doubt!" Laurent answered gently, but to

his astonishment he realized that he was growing angry. He knew Renée to be a natural co-
quette, yet it had never occurred to him that she
might not be pining away as she awaited his
return. And to think he had just been sitting
here in the dark, at a loss to fashion words which
would free himself from an unofficial engagement to her while sparing her pride.

"I should have thought a lady of your tastes
would find Phillip's inept fumblings tiresome,"
he jeered. *Ma foi!* Do you care so little for
propriety? . . . Well?"

Renée nibbled at her lower lip as she recalled
the revulsion she had felt in Phillip's arms.
Surely, if he had seen them, Laurent knew that
their meeting was not of her design. Perhaps,
she admitted begrudgingly, she had flirted with
Phillip more than was proper, but she had not
seriously encouraged his affections.

Glancing up through her lashes, she met
Laurent's wicked black stare with plummeting
spirits. She had not yet won the heart of the man
she desired most. With so little encouragement,
she would gladly have given and received
Laurent's kisses. Yet, in the months they had
shared a roof at Bonne Vie, never once had
Laurent sought to press his attentions upon her,
steal even a kiss. It didn't take much effort to
guess why. Surely it was because of her sister
Gweneth.

She had not forgotten a single minute of
Laurent's infatuation with her sister. His eyes
had followed Gweneth's every movement. It was
as if he could not view her long enough. She had

seen them walking, heads bent together, aboard his ship, and later beneath the oaks which marched along the road of her uncle's mansion in Barbados, where they had lived for a short time.

Squirming inwardly, Renée recalled the times the sting of the green-eyed monster had left her lying awake far into the night, lest Gweneth climb from the bed they shared in their uncle's home and flee to the arms of her lover. Not even the fact that she knew Gweneth was in love with Capitaine Bertrand could ease her jealousy.

Indignation fired her gaze, and golden flecks sparkled in her soft dark eyes as she looked up at her inquisitor. If Laurent could have a past which included many women, certainly she was entitled to a few innocent flirtations.

"I am a woman!" she announced, and was pleased to see Laurent start. "Why should I not wish to be treated as one?" she continued boldly. "At least Phillip is not afraid to demonstrate his desire for me."

The challenge had been spoken before she realized its full import, and suddenly Renée knew she had uttered one provoking remark too many.

"You want to be treated as a woman?" Laurent inquired softly, his black eyes like twin flames as he came toward her. When he paused, only inches separated his lean well-muscled tallness from her tiny frame. "Any man can make you feel like a woman, mademoiselle," he whispered. "Shall I prove it?"

The entire assembly of the ballroom would

have been brought running by her cry, but Renée said nothing. There was a tiny, reckless voice within her whispering: Let him do as he desires. 'Tis what you want, what you desire most!

With one hand, Laurent reached to massage the delicate column of her neck, so slender that his fingers nearly encircled it. "You long to know a man's caress? So, to have a man touch you and to touch in return?" he murmured deep in his throat. "If you desire a man, *mon coeur*, then let it be one worthy of appreciating that delicacy which is his opposite. Kiss *me*, Renée!"

Arching her chin with his fingers, Laurent bent his head and with delicious languor laid his lips on hers.

At the first touch of his kiss, Renée lost all desire to run away. So sweet, so soft, her mouth seemed to melt beneath the smooth warmth of his. And then the melting sank downward, disconnecting the fright-tensed muscles of her body and emptying liquid desire into her veins. The melting weakness continued through her limbs until she thought she would sink to the floor. Instead, she leaned her slight weight against his taller frame. Her legs met hard thighs and her breasts filled with the heat radiating from the flat contours of his masculine chest.

Laurent had meant to do no more than frighten her, but the tremors of her body registered within his own with an unexpected intensity. His arms slipped around her to capture the sweetness of her, only to have her kiss slip away as she turned her head to gasp for breath against his coat sleeve.

A smile of victory warmed his face at her response. "Again," he commanded.

Renée buried her face deeper in his shoulder, afraid of the tiny sparks dancing through her body at his mere touch. Without proof, she knew Phillip's kiss would be nothing like this. In Laurent's arms she was aware only of the ragged drumbeat of her heart and the heat of the body enfolding hers.

Unwilling to heed the rational part of his mind which warned him to content himself with one snatched-away kiss, Laurent again turned Renée's face to his.

When his mouth covered hers a second time, Renée experienced a surge of heat that began in her middle and spiraled dizzily outward through her tingling limbs. She felt at once helplessly ensnared and protectively enfolded. His kiss seemed to take her upward and outward, making her soar higher and more recklessly with each heartbeat. When his lips opened, parting hers, she whimpered and clutched at him for fear that he would snatch away his magic and leave her to plummet winglessly back to earth.

He is too potent! she thought wildly. He will consume me! And yet she could only tighten her embrace.

Laurent proceeded slowly, deliberately exploring her mouth with every nuance and shade of expertise of his thirty-two years. There was innocence in her taste, not unlike the sweet tartness of strawberries. And yet, as his tongue swept

24

with maddening thoroughness over the dew-soft lining of her mouth, he knew he could persuade her to give up that innocence to him. It did not matter that his desire for her did not make marriage any more appealing to him. All that mattered was the satiation of his hunger, the capture of the lure held out to him, the need to be consumed by the fire that raged within.

Renée did not think of protestation when Laurent scooped her up in his arms. She went willingly, reaching out her arms to grasp his neck and laying her head on his shoulder.

Laurent tenderly kissed her crown of curls as he carried her up the steps to his bedroom. He did not speak as he carried her across the floor and lowered his precious cargo onto the high wide mattress. But he watched her as she lay in the white slats of moonlight pouring through the shutters. He studied every line and curve of her face for some gesture or flicker of reluctance.

Renée, her mind a maze of wonder and excitement, looked into his face, taut and pale in the moonlight, and realized that he was as uncertain of her as she was of him.

It doesn't matter if this comes first. We are to marry, she assured herself. The joyous knowledge of her love for him burst upon her. Impulsively she sat up and reached for him, wrapping her arms about his neck.

It was the gesture Laurent had waited for. He murmured words of thanksgiving against her hair and then his lips found hers as he followed her back onto the bed. The perfume of gardenias filled his nostrils and he breathed deep of her favorite fragrance. He kept his kisses tender, nibbling gently at her lips until they opened to his entreaty and her tongue licked through shyly to touch his.

Feeling her surrender, Laurent deepened his kiss, burying his tongue in her, seeking and tasting, filling her mouth as completely as he longed to possess her body.

With a whimper of half-pleasure, half-fear, Renée dug her fingers into his shoulders, surprised by the warm smooth-muscled flesh under her hands. At some point he had shrugged out of his jacket and shirt. Dregs of doubt made her uneasy as she felt his hands move under her, his fingers seeking the buttons of her gown. His lips seemed to be everywhere: on her mouth, her cheeks, her brows. Then white-hot pleasure scorched her as his mouth found the crest of a breast exposed by her torn gown. Waves of passion broke over her, stilling the fear, and she moved naturally under him, pressing her breast upward for the stroke of his tongue.

After a moment Laurent leaned back from her, pulling her opened gown down to her waist. The moonlight flooding over his shoulder revealed full young breasts, rosy-tipped and quivering to her rapid breath. "Exquisite, *mon coeur*," he whispered in delight. "No . . . don't," he begged when she reached down to cover herself.

Renée drew a shaky breath, cut off in mid-action by the incredible feel of his mouth once more upon her. He took a soft nipple between his lips, rolling his tongue around it until it tautened and the torment of that sensation made her grab two handfuls of his hair and hold him close.

For an instant exultation ran like wine through Laurent. She wanted this as much as he. All reasonable argument against feeding the glorious hunger raging within him was nothing compared to the need to possess the woman beneath him.

Caught in the grip of emotions which threatened to overwhelm her, Renée could only moan softly her pleasure. It was as though he were reaching inside her to touch some secret core of her being, and she did not want him to stop, never for the conflagration to end. Her head rolled back and forth on his pillow when his lips left her breasts to trail hot wet kisses over her stomach and thighs. Finally she set her teeth into his shoulder to keep back what she knew would be a shameless cry of pleasure. But the need to speak aloud, to reassure herself with the sound of her own voice, brought words to her lips.

"I will be a good wife, Laurent. I swear it! I lo—"

Her words jolted Laurent like a splash of icy water upon a flame. *"Mon Dieu!* I must be mad!" he whispered hoarsely, and pulled away from her so abruptly her nails raked deep scratches across his shoulders as he tore free of her embrace.

Sitting up, he dropped his head in his hands as the grim reality of what he had nearly done sank in. A gentleman—and he counted himself that, no matter what else he might be—did not seduce and then desert an innocent lady. And yet he had nearly done just that because a kiss had lured him beyond the bounds of reason. He desired her. God, yes! He felt even now the pressing demand of his body's response. But she was not an island girl to be taken in joyous seduction to ease the clamor of two eager bodies. Renée was a gentle woman—and under his own mother's protection.

"What is it? What's wrong?" Renée begged, frightened by his abrupt desertion and yet unable to resist reaching out to him.

"Enough, enough!" he muttered thickly, pulling her arms from his neck and then rising from the bed.

Renée hid her blush of shame with her hands. What could she have been thinking of? *Mère de Dieu!* She had wanted the dizzying madness to continue forever! "Please, please, don't look at me," she whispered in shame as she tried to gather her bodice back together.

Laurent felt the sting of shame under his skin. Damn his lust! He had lost all discretion when she inflamed his senses. He had come to Bonne Vie to break his tie with this girl, but now that task would be so much more difficult.

Anxious to find an excuse to move about the room, he went to a nearby table, picked up his jeweled snuffbox and flipped open the lid. He wasn't partial to the habit but it was a safe, civilized thing to do with his hands—much more civilized than ripping off her gown as his hands itched to do and making love to her beneath his family's roof. Then, too, the doctored tobacco erased from his senses the perfumed fragrance of her body.

No real harm had been done, he reflected grimly as he returned the box to its place. If only he could persuade Renée of that. He had often rid himself of mistresses, but never before a bride-to-be. Perhaps, if he treated the situation lightly, she could be cajoled into reasonableness.

He turned and looked at Renée, and what he saw did not reassure him. She stared at him with tear-filled eyes, the wet imprint of his lips still clinging moistly to her passion-smeared mouth. The urge to move back to her, to make love to her and damn the future, rose up in him, making his muscles tense as he fought the impulse. He must not do that. The temptation to make love to her would pass. He had not lost his aversion to marriage, he reminded himself. He must not allow lust to doom him to an alliance he did not want.

But he could not resist drawing closer. He bent and picked up his jacket and went to wrap it about her naked shoulders. *"Ma chère,* you look chilled," he murmured as the scent of gardenias rose from her body. His hand accidentally brushed the lush curve of a breast as he pulled his coat together over her, and both of them started at the touch. Annoyed, he dropped his hands to his sides.

"Cease your tears, mademoiselle," he pleaded. "No harm's been done you. Now you understand what your kisses do to a man," he continued, watching her closely for signs of panic. "And I understand that you come to passion quickly, too quickly for your own good." His lips smiled but it was not reflected in his gaze as he mentally added: And my shaky grip on self-control!

"As much as I'm tempted to teach you the art of love . . ." He shrugged. "I feel honor-bound to limit my tutoring. You must wait for additional lessons from your husband."

Renée clenched her teeth until they ached. A myriad of conflicting feelings tumbled through her as the giddy sense of arousal ebbed. The eddies of receding desire made her weak and she sagged back against the head of the bed, but she made herself sniff back the last of her tears. She should be grateful that Laurent had stopped them, she told herself. How foolish and empty-headed he must think her, crying because her virtue had been spared. Perhaps he thought she should have been the one to stop them, and was appalled by her wanton behavior.

She ventured a glance at him, but her gaze fell away from his face when she saw the stern disapproval etched there. Well, if she must, she would speak to the subject that was of most importance to both of them. "Perhaps I should have objected." Renée knew she blushed, though it was too dark for him to discern. "After we marry it will be permissible for you to finish the lesson, *non*?"

The silence that met her statement sent quakes of alarm through Renée and her gaze flew back to his face. Perhaps it was a trick of the moonlight, but she thought she saw pity flicker in his eyes before an inscrutable but implacable expression replaced it.

"I will not marry you."

Renée stared at him in disbelief, certain she could not have heard him correctly. He loved her. Hadn't that just been proved by the passion they shared and the fact that he had saved them both from an enormous mistake? Yet her heart's heavy pounding as she locked gazes with his magnificent black eyes hammered home the sincerity of his remark. "But you must!" she whispered, feeling as though the earth was slipping from beneath her feet.

"*Je regrette*," Laurent said simply, wishing not to hurt her but unable to save her that pain. "I cannot."

"Your mother—" she began.

"Maman knows that I always do exactly as I wish." He was long accustomed to the female penchant for creating scenes. Nonetheless, Laurent found it impossible to meet the tear-filled gaze accosting him. *This is what you came home to do. Finish it!* he ordered himself. "I do not wish to marry you . . . or anyone, mademoiselle. I wish to remain a bachelor, responsible only for myself."

"What . . . what of my reputation? The expectation of your friends? Everyone knows . . ." Renée's voice faded away at the humiliating pictures her words conjured up. This could not be be happening, it could not!

Laurent nodded, prepared for that inevitable question. "I will concede to you a few embarrassing moments, mademoiselle. Believe me, you will survive and thrive."

"I will not be jilted!" Renée shrieked, giving up all pretense at self-control.

Alarmed by the rising note of hysteria in her voice, Laurent whispered with a cautioning finger to his lips, "Gently, mademoiselle." If they were discovered here and now, everything would be lost. "Of course you are not jilted. If you maintain your composure, none will ever know of this conversation. You will broadcast the story that you refused me."

"I hate you!" Renée sobbed, tears slipping unheeded down her face onto her breasts, glowing like white opals in the moonlight.

"Yes, I know," Laurent replied in an even voice that did not betray his sympathy for her very real misery. If only he had not touched her, her shame would be so much less. "You may say of me anything that comes into your lovely little head. Only, I beg you, remember Maman. For myself, you may blacken my name at will. But my mother should be spared a little, I think."

Like an unexpected slap that begins to sting only seconds after the act, Renée became aware of a sensation of rage unlike anything she had ever known. He had used her for his amusement and she had nearly given him her body as a prize. Fury quaked through her, making her tremble, and then it erupted in words.

"I thought you cared for me, monsieur, but I was wrong. You hold me in contempt, *n'est-ce pas*? You forced your kisses on me only to humiliate me. And yet I've never done anything to you to deserve that. I despise your wickedness, monsieur, but I will find a way to repay you in kind. That I promise!"

Renée ran past him and down the steps of the *garçonnière* and out into the night. Finally, a stitch in her side made her stop as she reached the back stairs of the main house.

"I hate him! Hate him! Hate him!" she repeated over and over like a curse until she choked on her tears. For months she had loved him and had waited patiently for him to return her love. Now he had rejected her, and because of her impulsive desire to please him, she was left without a shred of pride.

"At least I never told him of my love," she whispered, but it gave her no satisfaction. She had wanted him; the taste of his kisses was with her still. He had made her heart beat furiously when he touched her. How that must have pleased him, to know that she was so eager for his embrace that she had brazenly bared herself to him.

Shame pounded through her, its force making her groan aloud. Mama Theo had been only half-right. He was excitement and she had been drawn to him like a moth to a flame. But he had felt nothing, not even the tiniest spark of affection.

"I do not like singed wings," she murmured, wiping tears from her cheeks with the backs of her hands. "I will find a method to pay you back, Monsieur Lavasseur. I will!"

* * *

Laurent watched her go without a word, the arrested urge to call out to her causing pain in his chest. There had been no way to refute her expectation without hurting her.

Still, his conscience smarted as he lay in the dark, the faint but pervasive fragrance of gardenias rising from his sheets, the sheets on which Renée had lain. She had been like a flame in his arms, all warmth and light and yielding to the slightest breath of his passion. Until this night she had never before seemed so lovely, so desirable.

Was it only that he regretted giving her up? Laurent frowned. He did not like to think of her in another man's arms, kissed by other lips. But marrying her was the only way to prevent that, and nothing was worth the loss of his freedom.

"So be happy, *mon ami*. You are free." But the words made hollow empty sounds in his room, and Laurent had the feeling that the harm he had done this night would somehow rebound on him.

Chapter Three

THE STRANGER WRINKLED HIS NOSE IN DISGUST and sidestepped an open sewer. As he moved along the narrow banquette of the New Orleans street, he wondered at the perversity of human nature which allowed splendid courtyards to be backed by ditches where the daily waste of kitchen and chamber pot was thrown.

Here on the riverfront the streets were muddier even than those which ran above them in the city. The cooling breeze from the river vaulted over this sunken stretch of town behind the levee. It was, he reflected in grim amusement, as if nature herself took exception to the lowlife on the quay.

Human debris of every sort found its way into port with the ships that traded here. It seemed to him that the rotting timber and unrelieved stench heated by the late-summer sun were enough to turn most men's hearts toward malicious forms of entertainment and release.

The laughter and music that were peculiar to every port city he had ever known filled the street he walked. It bespoke a sailor's philosophy. Life was good today. Yesterday was gone. And tomorrow? Tomorrow belonged to those who would be there to meet it.

"Mayhaps there's the answer to what brings me abroad tonight," he said to himself.

He slowed before the tavern specified by a weathered sign spinning dizzily on its single unbroken hinge: Azar.

He pretended not to notice the open stares of the customers as he stepped into the hazy, ill-lit common room. His eyes roamed insolently over the crowd of leather-clad Kentucks and stripe-shirted sailors. His own seaman's garb seemed to mollify them, yet no one could make out his features beneath the lowered brim of his hat.

He moved quickly to the back door, following his instructions. The door opened onto a small patio, and a short path of bricks led to a wooden staircase.

For a long moment he stood in the shadows pondering the step he was about to take. The morality of it did not disturb him. He had long ago thrown away that useless shield.

What more could he bring upon himself? He was a man wanted, two hundred guineas alive or dead. What matter the number of extra nails he put in his coffin? They would be bought with gold and that gold could buy him a little of the heaven he would be denied in the end.

"You're certain he's coming?" testily questioned one of the two Englishmen sharing the dark of the shuttered upper room. "He's late."

"He'll come," his companion answered calmly.

"He's late," the first repeated. "I don't like it. We're strangers in New Orleans. Someone may have tipped off the authorities."

"You worry too much, George. Have another glass of brandy. Damn, if it ain't fine brandy at that. No wonder our citizens encourage these French privateers. If we don't succeed, I may myself try a hand at the trade."

His chuckle was not shared. "Be at ease, George. We've a grand future before us. My aspirations for a governorship in the West Indies will be assured once I've proved my ability to run a smuggler aground. The Navy has been thrashing about for years with little success. They're playing by the book. No imagination. I've the imagination and the daring. Success is within our reach. And we won't even dirty our hands. Our informer will point the finger. We'll simply spring the trap."

"How do you know we can trust this informer? He may take our coins and flee."

"Weak stomach, George, that's your trouble. A man in the spy business cannot afford queasy digestion."

"Does that reference include me?"

Both men started as one of the long shutters

opened and the city lights below threw the shadow of the tall man across the room.

"You'll be the man we were told would aid us?" the braver of the two occupants inquired. "Come in, come in and sit. 'Tis abominably warm but we'll suffer through. Brandy? Good. Will you honor us with a name?"

The man did not reply as he seated himself.

"Very well, if you insist upon secrecy. Mayhaps 'tis best. You speak English—are you a British citizen?"

No answer.

"See here! You must hold a part of the conversation if we're to deal together."

The stranger sat still so long a time his shadow seemed to become a part of the dark. Finally, his voice slurred by liquor or some deliberate act, he said, "You're looking for a man with a stomach." He paused to chuckle low. "With the stomach to bait a trap for a privateer."

"That's so," the spokesman answered. "A French privateer, to be precise. My government's interests are of no concern to you, but it may help to tell you that we're determined to stop the smuggling trade of the British West Indies. We need an example to be made, a warning to those who are gentlemen by profession, smugglers by whim. Nothing short of a well-publicized trial and a public hanging will do. We want to run the amateurs off the sea before we take on the professionals."

"Didn't you English have a spot of luck a few months ago?" the slurred voice inquired.

"He knows something," the quieter of the two now said. "He's probably one of them!"

"I might be. What of it?"

"Now, sir," the spokesman said with dampening force. "I am not overly squeamish about your proclivities for wrongdoing. But I must know, sir, if you're the man for the job."

"I am."

"We believe, at last, we have the means to trap one of these devils."

No comment.

"A ship, sir, a smuggler's ship!" the other man continued with glee. "We've learned the identity of a French smuggler and we intend to bring him to justice."

"If you know his name—"

"No proof!" the first man answered, pounding the table before him. "The authorities must have proof. You will provide us with information that will give us the proof we need."

"Who's this scapegoat?"

Now it was the spokesman's turn to hesitate. "Laurent Lavasseur," he pronounced very softly.

The stranger did not move, but some new intensity of manner seemed to make his shadow vibrate.

"You know the man?" his interviewer questioned.

"Not well."

"Excellent! That will make your task easier."

"So thought Judas."

"What?"

"Nothing. How much am I to be paid, and when?"

"A hundred pounds sterling. Half now, half when Lavasseur is in irons."

"Five hundred pounds . . . sterling. Two and a half now. I am a man of expensive tastes."

"See here!"

The stranger rose. *"Au revoir, gentlemen."*

"Wait! Five hundred it is. If you fail . . ."

"I'll try not to lose too many nights' sleep over the matter. The money." A bag of coins was put into his hand and he weighed it thoughtfully. "Close enough. *Merci.*"

"Here is the plan. Lavasseur lost his ship during a British raid on a smugglers' cove near Jamaica this summer. Unfortunately his crew escaped and when Lavasseur turned up he claimed that some of his crew had mutinied a few days earlier and he had lost the *Christobel.* Damn! It's as good a lie as any, and we've not been able to disprove it. Rumor will not serve justice, I'm sorry to say. But we've baited a trap for our fine French friend. His ship, the *Christobel,* will go to auction in Tortola next month. We know that he plans to be there, with enough funds to purchase his vessel. The sale will be rigged his way.

"Now, to your part. We need a man in place who can keep an ear open, learn of Lavasseur's next smuggling venture. When your word reaches us, we will be there to greet him."

"A simple enough plan."

"That's the beauty of it. It's up to you to make his acquaintance by any means you can. By your dress you're a seaman. Perhaps you might seek a place in his crew."

"You needn't worry. I know this much about Lavasseur. He's a sea captain. He will do anything to gain back his ship. Until Tortola!"

In a flash the stranger was gone.

"Can we trust him?"

"Do we have much choice, George?"

Chapter Four

"Laurent has gone, madame?" Renée's face reflected all the astonished disbelief of her words.

Madame Rosalie Lavasscur's shrug was expressively French as her concerned eyes watched the young girl. "I myself am bewildered by the behavior of my son. Scarcely home, and then gone without a word. Had I known how intolerably Laurent would behave, such barbaric behavior . . ."

Her voice faded away in faint shock as she heard herself railing against her own flesh and blood. But then, Laurent's behavior was nothing short of shocking. She had expected her son to propose to the girl upon his return. Now he had returned and then departed all in the same night without so much as a greeting to his mother.

Had Armand been alive, he would have beaten some sense into his eldest son.

Rosalie slanted a thoughtful gaze at Renée. Dressed in yellow sprigged muslin, her unbound hair flooding her shoulders with carefree curls, Renée was the picture of youthful beauty. Her features were perfectly formed, her dark brows winged away from enormous dark eyes ringed in thick jet-black fringe. If her rosy lips drooped in the corners it was from disappointment rather than imperfection of molding. She understood Renée's attraction for her son. What amazed her was that he was not Renée's choice. Perhaps she had hoped for too much when Laurent had brought the girl home. Indeed, it seemed she had.

"I've been encouraged to expect an eventuality over which I had no control," Rosalie said gently, her mind racing on to the next points of the speech she had begun preparing the moment she learned of Laurent's abrupt departure. "Do not be uneasy in my presence, child. I no longer expect you to marry my son."

Surely Laurent has not told his mother the truth! Renée thought in dismay. What had he said? What could she say? Her gaze fell before the woman's sharp gaze. "I . . . I don't understand."

Rosalie smiled approvingly at the girl's modest behavior. Regardless of the rumors, she knew Renée was no hardened flirt toying with a man's emotions. She must feel she had good reason to turn down Laurent's proposal. Perhaps, without asking, she could extract those reasons from the girl. "There are many ways of obtaining a husband. We have many excellent families with eligible young men from which you may choose. I will arrange something, never fear."

As Renée moved away from the older woman, the skirt of her gown scattered faded rose petals which had been blown from the trellis during the early-morning rain and now lay on the flagstone path of the garden. What should she say? Could she confide in this woman? "One doesn't arrange love, madame," she said softly.

"And you do not love my son?"

Renée flushed deeply. After the words and deeds that had passed between them the night before, she should hate Laurent Lavasseur. Indeed, she did despise him! The other, the strange confused emotions she had felt in his embrace, they must be forgotten.

But even as Renée willed them away, stray sensations filtered through the barrier of her anger. Laurent's kisses had made her feel hot and strange, so unlike herself that she thought she would have caught fire and burned had he continued.

But that was not the same thing as love, she reminded herself. Laurent had used her, nearly seduced her, when all the time he had no intention of marrying her. If some vestige of decency had not halted him . . .

Renée's cheeks flushed with anger at the memory. "I cannot say what I think of your son, madame, without incurring your displeasure and proving myself to be the most ungracious of guests."

"So, it is as Laurent's letter says." Rosalie reached into the fichu of her gown and produced a page of folded parchment. "*Oui*. You may look surprised. You thought you would not be forced to tell me that you refused Laurent's proposal of marriage last evening. His letter does not go into the circumstances of your meeting, only informs me of your refusal and begs me not to be angry or upset. He tells me that he holds you in very high esteem and that he quite understands your reservations." Rosalie unfolded the letter and handed it to Renée. "Read for yourself."

Bewildered and feeling she had been outmaneuvered by a superior force, Renée took the letter and read it. It was as Madame Lavasseur said. Laurent's letter advised his mother of a proposal—which he had not actually made—and of her refusal!

Confounded that Laurent had felt so supremely confident that she would not tell his mother the real events of the night before, Renée crushed the note between her fists. But of course! No matter how it was phrased, she could not tell of Laurent's betrayal without embarrassing herself and encouraging Madame Lavasseur's pity. He knew—damn him—that she was too proud to so humiliate herself.

"Scoundrel!" she murmured. He was free and away while she had to bear the burden of her jilting silently.

Rosalie patted the empty space beside her. "Come and sit with me, Renée. We have things

45

to discuss." When Renée was seated, she took the girl's small hand between hers. "I must speak to you now as your own mother would if she were alive. Every young girl must marry. And, to be most candid, love seldom enters into the choice. One does not marry for love, one marries for . . . for position, for comfort, for respectability."

Renée smiled at the older woman, a mischievous dimple winking at the left corner of her mouth in spite of her misery. "But you, madame, you yourself told me you married Monsieur Armand for love."

Madame Lavasseur blushed prettily. Of course she had married for love. No woman could have been long in Armand Lavasseur's presence and not felt herself drawn to him. He had not been as tall as his eldest son, but his shoulders were proudly squared and his blue-black hair and eyes had held the same velvety depths that were Laurent's. As a girl of thirteen she had gone to the altar and then to Armand's bed with the awed regard of an innocent maiden for the embodiment of a Roman god.

Still, she could not allow Renée to hope that something as unlikely as love before marriage would be hers, not when it was spoiling her chance for happiness.

"It's a rare alliance in which love takes the lead," she said gravely. "Most ladies learn to love their husbands after their vows are made. That kind of love is no less real for all it follows the ceremony."

Renée folded her arms resolutely across her

bosom as an expression close to stubbornness marked her features. "I fear your example and my sister Gweneth's have quite spoiled me for the other sort of marriage. I will marry no man I do not love." She added more gently, "There is only one thing I wish to do now, madame, and that is return to France."

"Return to France?" Madame Lavasseur's hand tightened on Renée's. "But, *ma chère,* you know no one. You have no family there."

Renée tossed her curls in a valiant display of indifference. She wanted no one's pity. Her pride was hurt, that was all. Pride soon mended, she told herself.

"The Valois family had many friends before the revolution. Some of them, surely, will remember me and offer me hospitality. You do understand that I cannot stay here any longer, not after . . ."

Aware that the drawing together of Madame's brows signaled the barrage of argument to follow, Renée pressed on quickly. "I will hardly be alone, madame. Of course Giselle will accompany me."

For the first time both women acknowledged the perfectly still form of Renée's quadroon maid.

Giselle Latour sat in the shadow of a nearby oak, far enough away not to overhear their conversation but close enough to be called if needed. Slender and quite pretty despite her drab gray gown, Giselle was the closest thing Renée had to a true friend in New Orleans, and the girl was devoted to her. Even now her kerchiefed head was bent over the volume of poetry which Renée had been using to teach her to read.

The signs of displeasure crossed Rosalie's features. "I hardly consider Giselle sufficient chaperon. Why, the girl is two years younger than you. She knows nothing of the world. Before you chanced upon her in the streets, she was merely a modiste's assistant."

Renée ignored this eroding of her defenses. The problem of Giselle was an old one. She knew Madame Lavasseur disapproved of her association with the pretty young quadroon. Instead she forged ahead with her ideas. "I shall go to Gweneth first, of course. She will know what to do. May I not go to England to visit my sister?"

Rosalie Lavasseur found herself suddenly disarmed. How could she refuse Renée's desire to visit her sister? It did not lie within her power to do so. Besides, what could be better for the girl than a change of scenery?

She reached out and fondly patted Renée's cheek. "It grieves me to think of losing you. You are such a delight to have about the house. I never really knew what I had missed in raising sons until you came to us. You must know we will all miss you."

With a quick squeeze, Rosalie withdrew her hands and rose. "There are always ships sailing for the Continent from New Orleans. When we reach the city we shall make immediate inquiries."

"Why, you filthy wall-eyed bastard!" Adam Breedon jerked away under the sudden dousing, sputtering back the flood of water that ran into his nose and mouth. All arms and legs, he floundered on his soggy bunk like an overturned crayfish.

"I warned you that the potables of New Orleans are more lethal than those in other ports," Laurent responded in lightly accented English. The tiny cabin smelled of stale tobacco, boiled shrimp, and the sickly-sweet odor of Oriental incense. Laurent picked up one of the vials on the captain's table and lightly sniffed the white residue. Laudanum. Grimly he turned back to the bunk, where he lifted an empty bottle of rum from Adam's side and sent it skittering across the floor. "It's nearly daylight, *mon ami*. Time to be about one's business."

Adam grunted and pulled himself upright, flicking damp blond hair from his eyes. "Damnation, Lavasseur! I near about drowned."

"A fine seaman like you? The first time we met, you had swallowed more of the Caribbean than most men live to tell of, and still *you* live."

Adam rearranged his long frame so that his bare legs stuck out before him. "A man could get used to having you for a friend if it didn't cost him part of a night's sleep every time you come around." He cocked his head to one side, his red gritty eyes focusing with disgust on his laughing friend. "Well? Aren't you going to apologize?"

"And spoil your perception of me as an arrogant, self-centered, class-conscious Creole?" Laurent looked about and, lifting a pair of breeches from the cabin's only chair, sat down. "So tell me, after two weeks in my city, how would you describe it?"

"Hell!" Adam began divesting himself of the shirt he had slept in. Six feet tall and big-boned, he was a match in size for his companion as he padded about the captain's cabin of his ship, the *Pelican*.

"Those little ladies on the street don't understand my lingo and you know I don't hardly know enough French to call a bastard a bastard." Adam reached for the water pitcher, poured a bowl of water and then began lathering his face and upper body.

"That's your misfortune," Laurent replied without sympathy. "I advise you to use your abominable excuse for the Spanish language when approaching even the easiest of Louisiana women. *Finesse, mon ami.* Even our harlots expect it."

"Uh-huh. I hear you. Only I figure to stick with you. I want myself one of those fancy Creole women." Adam aimed a wink at Laurent. "You ever going to bring that little gal to town, the one you've had tucked away with your mother at Bonne Vie? I've got a powerful itch which needs scratching. Maybe we could do some sharing."

"I don't think I heard you correctly, Breedon. Would you care to repeat that?"

Adam paused in his washing and slowly turned toward his friend. It was not often that Lavasseur used that tone. As he had expected, Laurent was watching him with a steady black gaze that had the power to melt most men's courage. Two months earlier in Cuba, he had been witness to a Spaniard's belittling of the marksmanship of the French. That man's gravestone was now a marker to this Creole's expertise with a dueling pistol.

Adam smiled inwardly. If he had to face this man, he would just as soon the reason be a better one.

"Sorry. Must be the rum talking," he said with a weak grin, and went back to washing.

"My apologies, Adam," Laurent replied with an easing of his own anger. "I am in bad temper today. Leave it," he added in warning when it seemed that Adam was about to question the cause.

Laurent drew out a thin cigar and clenched it between his teeth. He knew Adam had not been serious, just as he had not meant his own words to become a challenge. He couldn't name the feelings that had sparked his wrath, but it was lit by the thought of Renée allaying another man's lust.

Adam broke into a boyish grin that denied his three-year seniority to Laurent. "What you need is a woman. Don't go setting your back up again. What we both could use is a . . ." and he veered off into such graphic profanity that Laurent laughed.

Whew! Creoles were like gunpowder, Adam thought. The tiniest spark could set off fireworks. Well, he guessed he would be short-tempered too if he had lost his ship.

"How's your luck running these days?" Adam asked as he pushed his arms into the sleeves of a clean pullover shirt. "You quit gaming early because you were winning, or because you had a streak of bad luck?"

Laurent propped his feet up on the table, careful not to disturb Adam's work. *"Eh, bien.* I must not appear too eager to win a fortune or someone may accuse me of cheating."

Adam's wheat-blond head poked through the top of his shirt as he said, "Why'd they do that?"

"Perhaps because I *am* cheating," Laurent suggested pleasantly.

Adam's brows rose above the fringe overhanging his forehead. "You cheating? I don't believe it. I've seen you bluff a man when you were only holding a prayer. You don't have to cheat."

Laurent accepted the compliment with a slight inclination of his head. "I hope you have not been repeating tales of my feats in the rumshops of the city. A man's sporting ability is profitable only as long as his reputation remains small."

"I won't give away your secrets, not even with a gallon of rum in my gut."

"What of opium?" Laurent questioned softly, his eyes hard on the other man.

Adam swore under his breath and shoved the tail of his shirt into his hastily pulled-on breeches. "I don't owe you any explanations for my behavior, Lavasseur. What passes in my cabin is my own private business."

Laurent was silent so long that Adam finished dressing and then turned to face him, hands on hips. "Well? Say something, dammit," he urged without heat.

"I suppose I should say you may go to the devil any way that pleases you." Laurent realized that this was not the moment to press Adam. There would come another, better moment. "Perhaps I would—if I were not in need of your services to retrieve the *Christobel*."

"Damn straight!" Adam replied.

Laurent did not answer this. Instead he said, "It still grieves me to realize that I had my ship taken out from under me. *Ma foi!* It seems an impossibility."

Adam grinned, hunkering down next to his captain's chest. "You were caught unawares. Who could have known De Fasse would squeal like a stuck pig when caught? He had a price on his head the size of a king's treasury. Don't know what he thought talking would do for him. Giving away the location of that lagoon sealed his fate."

Something in Adam's voice intensified Laurent's interest. "What?"

Adam dug out his logbook and roll of maps, then stood up. "De Fasse didn't get out much more than the name of that lagoon before one of his own men jumped him right there in the magistrate's office. By the time they pulled the seaman off De Fasse, he had bitten his captain's jugular clean through. The poor bastard just spilled his life's blood out before the authorities' eyes."

"My God!" Laurent whispered. He had known many desperate men in his association with

53

those who sailed the world's seas, but some depravities still had the power to astonish and sicken him.

"Not for every ear, that story," Adam agreed, but he was a little surprised by the Frenchman's reaction. In his own life he had witnessed worse atrocities. "Didn't think you'd heard it. Now at least you know why the English were lying in ambush for you at Juan's Cove. It was pure luck you managed to escape."

Laurent nodded. "I was ashore with most of my crew when the English swept in on us, but several of the smaller vessels ran for open water." Laurent's expression became suddenly rueful. "The rest of us hid until the English left. I suppose I should be grateful that they were so puffed up by the size of their booty that they didn't think it worth the effort to hunt each of us down.

"Que diable! To be forced to sit in the sand with a leg wound and watch her being handled—and badly—by English hands, I could have torched the *Christobel* myself!"

"But now you expect to get her back, at open auction," Adam finished, his gaze speculatively on the man.

"Why not? The English have nothing to link me with smuggling." Laurent pointed to Breedon's logbook. "I carry my private papers on me whenever my ship carries illegal cargo. The English may make any assumptions they choose. They cannot prove anything."

Laurent smiled. "Fortune still shines on me. Did you not come to New Orleans with the news of the auction in Tortola just when I had given up hope of recovering my ship?"

Adam, not answering, spread his hand over a fresh paper of his logbook. "When I got a cargo signed on this page, that's when I'll set sail for Tortola, no sooner."

Laurent nodded. "You'd better advertise if you expect trade. You're new to New Orleans merchants. You have no reputation, so to speak."

Adam looked up, the irises of his red-rimmed eyes suddenly silver-bright. "I'd as lief my reputation not precede me, Lavasseur. Those who've looked into my heart and know me for what I am would be of no aid to me."

The slip of the tongue that alluded to the American's past did not happen often, and once more Laurent was confronted with the enigma that was Adam Breedon. They had known one another nearly two years and he accounted the American a good captain and ally. Yet Adam, the private man, he knew not at all. That wide grin of his hid a sea of secrets and Laurent knew without being told that he was never to probe those dark depths. In time, if he chose, Adam would speak of the private fears that drove him to seek the senselessness of an opium dream.

"What cargo do you prefer? I may be able to steer some small business your way," Laurent said after a moment's silence.

"Any damn thing but pigs and sheep!" Adam responded readily, an oddly grateful expression coming and going in his face before most men could have registered it. "Might take a passenger or two, if the money's good."

"You'll have me as your passenger," Laurent reminded him.

"Then I'd best make it a pair of womenfolk. You and me still got some whorin' to do!"

Laurent was not surprised when he lost Adam to the deep curving smile of a dusky-skinned girl. They had just stepped out of a café off Rampart Street when she appeared, barefoot and her head tightly bound up in bright yellow to match the castoff frock she wore.

"You like me?" she asked in Spanish, and twirled about to give them a full display of her charms. Not a single petticoat lined the thin muslin that clung to her hips and the inward curves of her thighs. Only a provocative smile answered Adam's gasp when one sleeve slipped from her shoulder and a pert brown breast, rouged nipple and all, popped into view.

Adam was hooked, snapped up like a big-mouth bass, but Laurent shrugged off her offer to send for a friend. Too many thoughts chased about in his head, answers to be found in the tidbits of information he might glean from the patrons of the cafés on the street.

He had yet to learn the fates of his entire crew. Most of those who had escaped the British had already returned to New Orleans in hopes that their captain would return with a new ship. But there were others who had not made it, and information about those men captured by the British was scarce.

The thought sat uneasily on Laurent's shoulders that they might have been hanged or pressed into service aboard British Navy ships. He was their captain and as such responsible for them. He would not rest until he knew one way or the other their fates. He had failed them at Juan's Cove. He would not fail to help them now if he could.

Half the men on any voyage were always new, but his core of seamen, men he had grown to trust and those who trusted him—they were the ones he sought.

Chapter Five

RENÉE PULLED THE COLLAR OF HER CLOAK UP under her chin, pretending not to notice the unwavering stare of the keelman just behind her. Little more than a week ago the river had been impassable, clogged with debris from a storm upriver which had delayed their departure from Bonne Vie. Now the wide muddy river ran free again.

Her eyes moved to the pile of baggage beside her in the rear of the barge and then on to Madame Lavasseur, who sat ahead under the canvas shelter. Her hostess had continued to extend unfailing kindness but Renée knew that things would never again be quite the same between them. While that was an accepted practice in theory, no mother easily understood why a girl would find her strong, handsome son unacceptable marriage material. That was one more reason why she longed to leave Louisiana.

Renée fingered the letter in her pocket with nervous anticipation. It was addressed to Monsieur Chasson, her lawyer and financial adviser. By Louisiana law, she did not have the right to administer her own money. At Laurent's suggestion Monsieur Chasson had been chosen and the gentleman had performed admirably, never declining to pay even the most extravagant of her wardrobe bills.

Certainly. It costs him nothing. Every penny came to me through the inheritance left my mother by her English family, Renée reflected with a sigh.

Even so, it was not considered proper that she should visit Monsieur Chasson's office. Therefore the need for the letter. The letter informed the lawyer of her desire to leave Louisiana and directed him to make ready her finances so that she might take the money with her to England. With her share of the inheritance she would be able to afford a house in London, perhaps even a carriage and liveried servants. How easily plans were laid when one had money. And past mistakes were as easily erased. Or were they?

The trickle of warm tears on her cheeks surprised Renée. She had thought herself long past mourning the plans that had formed in her head as she lay enthralled in Laurent's embrace.

"Forget!" she murmured angrily. "Forget him!"

"Coffee, ma'am?"

Renée looked up into the face of the American keelman. He held out a battered tin cup clouded at the surface with steam. She gratefully accepted the cup with a nod of thanks, trying not to notice the missing teeth in the man's smile nor the peculiar odor of his buckskins. He meant to be kind, she told herself. Probably he had seen her tears. Yet she hesitated to put the cup to her lips.

The decision was made for her when her maid reached out and whisked the cup away. With lips set in disapproval, Giselle tossed the liquid overboard and then glared up at the rangy riverman as though she had the advantage of height.

"Mam'zelle use her own possessions," she said, using the English that Renée had taught her. "Come with me. I give you a cup for her. *Yanquis!*" she added disapprovingly under her breath.

Renée shared the surprise on the man's face and then his arrested look creased into a grin and she realized that he was young, probably no older than her own eighteen years. The man followed Giselle forward to where a small fire had been lit in the shelter of the canvas blind, a look of admiration on his face. It was not the first such glance Giselle had inspired, Renée mused. After all, Giselle was a pretty girl of sixteen. The gown she wore flattered her narrow waist and emphasized the graceful arch of her spine. Her hair, when not tucked up under her *tignon,* fell in thick, coffee-dark waves to her hips. No wonder the young *Yanqui* was impressed. Only the delicate tint of her complexion, a lustrous butter-cream with a blush of rose, gave a hint to her ancestry. If not for the silk scarf covering her head, a "mark of station" demanded by law, she might have been viewed as just another pretty French girl.

Renée frowned thoughtfully. She had met Giselle on the streets of New Orleans eight months ago. The frightened thing was being accosted by two young Creole gentlemen who were teasingly trying to relieve her of the packages she carried. Outraged that no one else on the street would come to the girl's aid, she had ordered the Lavasseur carriage halted and had made the coachman bring the girl to her.

Stephan, the Lavasseur coachman, had warned her as he helped Giselle into the carriage. "Ain't none o' our business, mam'zelle. Besides, Madame Lavasseur ain't gonna like us messin' in the doin's of no quadroon," he had finished in a voice of doom.

Madame Lavasseur had not been pleased. But after discreet inquiries revealed that the girl was from a suitably genteel background, Madame had relented and allowed Renée to employ the girl as her personal maid.

Renée shook her head. Though she had spent two full years in the New World, she could not understand the social complications of slavery. The laws of Louisiana that were used to separate white from African, Indian from a person of color, slave from free—*Mon Dieu!*—they made no sense at all. Yet, because Giselle was the result of a liaison between a Creole man and a mulatto woman, she was destined not to marry but to form a similar alliance, a *plaçage*.

Of course, Renée mused, she had not been told any of this by Madame Lavasseur. She had had to pump bits and pieces of it from Giselle. When such subjects were discussed, they spoke in English. That was one of the reasons Giselle's knowledge of the language had progressed so rapidly. Creole ladies were not supposed to know of, let alone discuss, the less-than-honorable-deeds of their menfolk.

That was the problem, Renée thought. She always wanted to know, to experience more than she was told was wise. It had led her to the brink of ruin in Laurent's arms.

Renée jerked her thoughts from that direction, looking out over the river. It lapped lazily at the sides of the great rectangular barge, its yellow-gray tinge the only color beneath a lead-colored sky. A sudden breeze skimming over the water brought a chill with it and Renée nuzzled her chin lower in her cloak, impatience chafing her nerves. Would they never arrive in New Orleans?

The scent of flowers filled the air as the Lavasseur carriage turned into the courtyard of one of the better houses on the Rue Royale. A fountain gurgled in the shadows of the flagstone patio where huge wide-mouthed jars spilled forth ruffle-leafed geraniums of scarlet hue.

As soon as his coachman was dismissed, Laurent crossed the brick walkway, thoroughly familiar with his surroundings. Every night for the last two weeks he had been a participant in a game of cards at the home of Monsieur Pascal.

Laurent snapped a cluster of geranium blossoms from a plant as he passed and stuck the bright red spray into the buttonhole of his dark green evening coat. Though the air was cooler with the coming of fall, the invigoration coursing through him was more than the freshening of the season. He expected to win tonight. It was the sort of luck a man could pocket. The knowledge lightened his step and tugged a smile from his lips. His grandfather had often said that a man could tell when the gods' cup had been placed before him. And when it happened, a man was honor-bound to grasp it in both hands and drink deep, accepting the full consequence of the act.

Five hours later, as the faint light of early morning streaked the sky, Laurent patted his pocket and smiled. His eyes ached from the smoke and his head was fuzzy with an abundance of French brandy, but he was happy. A sharp eye, a calm expression, and his gamester's luck at *bourée* had won him enough this night that, when added to his winnings of the last two weeks, ensured his purchase of the *Christobel.*

"If the bidding remains reasonable," he said aloud. That was the one plaguey concern that would not leave him. He might be outbid. If that happened, he did not know what he would do. It was within his power to wait a few days more, gamble again and hope to enlarge his winnings, but he knew he might just as easily lose. It was better not to take any more chances. Now that he had the funds in hand, he would make immediate arrangements with Adam to leave the city. He had tired of New Orleans and longed for the sea. It would be best for Adam, too. The city had a bad effect on the *Yanqui*. Not once during his entire shore leave had Breedon been sober.

Laurent cursed under his breath. There was another reason for his haste. During the course of the evening, one of the gentlemen had mentioned that his wife was pleased to learn that Madame Lavasseur had opened her town house the day before.

"Diable!" Wrinkles of annoyance creased Laurent's brow. The last thing he wanted was to meet his mother and Mademoiselle Valois on the street. If he meant to avoid that, he must leave soon.

Laurent shook his head in bewilderment. He had never been a man to dwell on past mistakes. Most often his anger was a sporadic, easily forgotten emotion. The separation from Renée was of his own choosing. He had freed himself from an entanglement he did not want. Why was he not happy? In recent weeks he had been in the company of two beautiful women eager to offer him a night in their beds. Why had he not accepted their invitations? What exactly was wrong with him?

Images came to him—of lips flushed with his kisses, of an inky flood of hair upon his pillow, of dark eyes wide and unfocused with the pain of betrayal. The scent of gardenias wafted through his thoughts in this unguarded moment. He had not expected an innocent girl to be capable of the passion Renée had shown in his arms. He had thought her too inexperienced to match him in desire. He had been wrong.

Thoroughly given up to reverie, he ran into a saber-leafed yucca stationed at the end of a passageway. Its needle-sharp points thrust into his arm, making him gasp in pain, and he jerked free, uncaring that he snagged the thread of his coat. He needed quiet surroundings . . . and peace of mind from the haunting memory of Renée Valois, a memory from which he gleaned only shame.

"I don't think it wise of you to insist upon going yourself," Rosalie Lavasseur repeated for the third time that morning. "The riverfront is a terrible place, even in broad daylight. To think that we must walk among those savages!"

Renée exchanged a smile with Giselle but did not reply until they had stepped into the Lavasseur carriage, which had been drawn up in front of St. Louis Cathedral as they exited from morning Mass.

"With Giselle at my side, I'm perfectly capable of seeking suitable accommodations for our voyage to England, madame," Renée assured her hostess as she made room on her seat for Giselle. "After all, we shall be weeks at sea. I want to make certain we will be both comfortable and safe. You need not distress yourself by accompanying us."

Madame Lavasseur shook her head firmly. "I wouldn't think of neglecting my duty to you. We will go together. Ah! The vendors are abroad," she exclaimed in delight as they crossed the Place d'Armes. "Let's have a glass of *eau sucre* and a ginger cake or two before we attend to our business."

Smiling, Renée nodded.

The cries of vendor and buyer filled the morning, a mixture of French, Spanish and African tongues flavored with the occasional English or Indian voice. *Yanqui* buckskin and blue homespun mingled with French striped silk and taffeta. Black skin contrasted with naked red men sporting hand-painted breechcloths. Spanish uniforms of the present colonial government mixed with seamen's rags.

To Renée's eyes, the rare view of the old square was like a glimpse of a city on a fair day. Fascinated with the display, she sniffed the aromatic air as they rode past the collection of sidewalk booths boasting oranges, bananas, wild grapes and pomegranates from the Caribbean as well as local melons and yams, peanuts and pumpkins, and assorted fish and seafoods.

When Madame Lavasseur directed the carriage to halt before a particular vendor, Giselle climbed down to purchase cups of orgeat and cakes. Upon her return, the three women consumed the barley water flavored with orange blossoms and ginger cakes with relish as their carriage moved on toward the quay.

The riverfront itself presented the slatternly

facade of an aged courtesan who, for all her flamboyant display, could not hide the ravages of her excesses. Where the broad flat-topped levee divided the city from the river, the streets were muddy, oozing fishheads and garbage along with the occasional bloated rat carcass.

"*Mon Dieu!* The stench, it's unbearable," Rosalie murmured as she applied her fan at a feverish pace. "If only we had a gentleman with us, someone . . ." she finished in a wistful voice that left Renée in no doubt that she was thinking of Laurent.

Flushing with a mixture of guilt and resentment, Renée looked away. It was Laurent's fault that his mother's wishes were thwarted, yet it was she who was left to silently endure Madame Lavasseur's censure. If only there was some way to frustrate his fondest wish as he had hers!

The carriage rolled along the levee road, past the rows of shanties stacked carelessly alongside one another. Finally the rough planks of the docks built out onto the river came into view. A forest of ships' masts, their sails tightly furled and lashed, rode smoothly on the river's current.

Laughter and music flowed along the boardwalk. Women sporting scandalously cut gowns and plumed hats that had made them the talk of the New World strolled barefoot on the arms of men whose nationalities were as diverse as their features and speech.

The world of rope and sail, sea and men infected Renée with the excitement of a child. "Oh, look!" she cried, impulsively poking her head out of the carriage window for a better view. A pianoforte of pecan wood and ivory inlay rode the backs of three black men who followed a mule-drawn dray piled ten feet high with massive pieces of furniture.

"Lookin' us over, lassie? McTavish'll meet yer price!"

Before she could react, Renée felt her bonnet dragged from her head by a heavy hand. A split second later fingers closed over her shoulders and she was nearly hauled headfirst through the carriage window. The reek of alcohol reached her on a fetid breath as she screamed in fright.

She did not see her rescuer but all at once she was free, the weight of callused hands lifted from her. She did catch sight of a beefy red face beneath a thatch of dirty hair, a huge purple tattoo on a massive forearm, and seaman's nankeen trousers as her assailant was dragged backward from the carriage and sent sprawling by a well-aimed fist.

And then she saw her savior. He was shrugging out of his black captain's coat, a dangerous wide grin on his hard mouth. Sunlight shone on his fair head, turning it the color of cornsilk. When he realized that she was staring at him, he turned incredibly blue eyes on her and winked.

Before she could decide how to react to this insolence, Renée was pulled back inside by Giselle, who had tugged on the skirt of her gown.

"Come on, then, if you want a fight!" Renée heard the blond stranger challenge her attacker as the seaman rose from the boardwalk, a stream of curses spewing from his blood-smeared mouth. She and Giselle exchanged glances. *"Yanqui!"* they pronounced in unison.

A cry of glee went up along the levee, followed by dozens of others as men, both black and white, came running. Within seconds the two men were ringed in by avid onlookers shouting words of obscene encouragement to each of them.

"Stephan! Drive on! *Mere de Dieu!* We shall all be killed!" Madame Lavasseur cried, falling back against the carriage squabs, one hand to her heart, the other at her throat as the carriage moved away.

Renée and Giselle reacted immediately. Renée reached out to fan her hostess while Giselle closed the curtains to shut out the terrible sounds of the fight.

"I don't know, I simply don't know why I allowed you to talk me into this," the older woman murmured, and then gasped as Giselle waved a vinaigrette under her nose. "No, no, do not stop!" she cried in alarm as she realized the carriage was slowing once more.

"This here is the ship Mam'zelle Valois is asking after," Stephan called down from his perch.

Once again Renée poked her head out of the window, this time slowly and after a careful look around. The ship rode the swift river current calmly, her decks a tangle of canvas, hogsheads, bales, and rope as her crew worked to lash down the last of her cargo for an outward voyage. On the bow in fresh paint was the name *Pelican*. *"Oui, merci,* Stephan. This is the ship."

"You're not going out! Not after all that's occurred?" Rosalie Lavasseur's voice was keen with horror.

"Certainly," Renée said firmly, and reached up to adjust her bonnet, only to remember that it had been snatched away. A moment of dismay touched her. No lady ever went abroad in daylight without her hat, parasol and gloves.

"Well, there certainly won't be any gentlemen to see me here," she murmured, and tucking a stray lock of hair behind her ear, reached for the door latch. "You will remain with Madame Lavasseur," she directed Giselle. "I shan't be long. The advertisement for passengers is weeks old, they may be full."

"But no!" Rosalie Lavasseur sat forward suddenly, revived by the extremity of her concern. "You must not go without this." She reached up and pulled out the long pearl-headed pin anchoring her veiled black straw hat. "You must be properly attired, and Giselle will accompany you. I insist."

Reluctantly Renée donned the broad-brim bonnet with its heavy veil, which entirely hid her face when Giselle had arranged it. *"Merci, madame.* I won't keep you waiting."

A few moments later Renee stood on the *Pelican*'s middeck while Giselle went in search of the ship's captain. The slight rocking of the deck was a motion at once familiar and strange. How long ago it seemed since she had been at sea. Though not the hardiest of sailors, she had grown to love the smell of salty spume and the gentle swells of a calm sea.

Curiously she looked around, wondering if this ship would carry her to England. Finally her gaze came to rest on two men. The pace of her heart did not alter but the subtle rhythm suddenly became heavy thuds against her ribs. The taller man's back was to her, his head bent in conversation with a seaman, but there was something tantalizingly familiar about the set of that curly black head. He did not look her way but turned after a moment and disappeared down a ladderway that led belowdecks.

"Laurent!" she whispered, and a current of shock as sweetly surprising as a cool breeze on a summer's day coursed through her. Even as she turned away, her heart beat a gladdened pace in a way that shamed her.

At the riverside railing she threw back her veil for the fresh cool wind from the water to touch her feverish cheeks. She had never expected to see him again, had told herself that she did not want ever to see him again. Yet here he was, and the mere sight of him had the power to melt the thin hard shell of her hate and flood her with love.

What has he done to me? she silently lamented.

"Mornin', ma'am."

Renée dropped her veil back into place and turned to face a wizened scrap of a seaman whose features were nearly lost in an unkempt bush of beard and hair. Giselle was at his side. "Name's Ben, the *Pelican*'s steward. You be lookin' for the cap'n?"

Renée threw a wild glance at the ladderway down which Laurent had disappeared. No! Laurent would have told his mother if he had purchased a second vessel—wouldn't he? "Your capitaine's name?" she asked, willing herself rooted to the spot until the name could be pronounced.

"Here he be now," the seaman replied, pointing a gnarled finger in the direction of the dock as he let out a whoop of glee that made both women back away. "Looks to be the cap'n were a-bloodlettin' this day, and not all of it his own!"

Eager to have her fears annulled, Renée swung toward the gangplank. The sight which greeted her eyes made them widen in relief mingled with revulsion.

The tall *Yanqui* who had saved her from the rough grip of a seaman was striding toward her. The once golden hair was now plastered to his skull with sweat and blood. From one eye a bright red stream coursed down his temple to his cheek. But his step was light and vigorous and his grin bared a full set of teeth as he came toward her. "I believe this is yours, mam'zelle," he said, and stretched out his hand.

Renée looked at the ruined concoction of velvet and silk that had been her bonnet and shivered. *"Merci, capitaine.* But I do not—"

Before she could finish, the blond giant sent

the crushed soggy material flying over the railing of his ship.

"Didn't want it anyway," he said. "Only kept it in case I needed an excuse to find you, ma'am. And here you are awaiting me." His expression held laughter and a hint of mockery as he placed a fist on each hip and looked her over from crown to toe. "You've come to give Adam Breedon your thanks? Here I am."

Renée bristled indignantly beneath his bold regard, but it was Giselle who took action.

"Yanqui parvenu, do not stare so at the mademoiselle. Look, you bleed on your jacket. It will be ruined." Turning to the old seaman, she wagged a finger at him. "You, find something to stop the bleeding."

Surprise showed clearly in the old man's face, but after a quick nod from his captain, he hurried away.

"Well now, aren't you the spitfire." The *Yanqui*'s gaze moved over Giselle with the equal thoroughness he had shown Renée. "You're a mite stingy in the carriage for my tastes, but what there is is nicely formed."

To Renée's astonishment, Giselle did not respond with the hauteur she had shown the keelboat man. Giselle's eyes sparkled as she looked up into the reckless smile on the man's strong-featured face and her cheeks pinkened prettily. It was like watching the helpless chagrin of a small bird trapped by the mesmerizing gaze of a blue-eyed serpent.

Indignation fired Renée's speech as she

stepped between the man and her maid. "You may not speak to my maid in that way. I forbid it!"

The American's eyes narrowed until they were slits of blue between spun-gold lashes. "You own this girl?"

"Of course not!" Renée responded. "Giselle is a paid servant." Then, summoning her dignity, she asked, "Are you the capitaine of this ship?"

"Giselle?" he repeated softly, seemingly satisfied with the sound. His manner relaxed. "None other. Captain Adam Breedon at your service," he answered, and dabbed at the swelling of blood at the corner of his lip with his shirtsleeve.

Renée's gaze followed his action and she was immediately stung by shame. Despite his ill-mannered behavior, this man had rescued her from a very unhappy situation and at no small cost to himself.

"Capitaine, forgive me," she said, holding out her hand to him. "I am very rude to keep you standing about when you have injured yourself in my defense. You should sit, no?"

Breedon enclosed her small hand in his huge one but did not salute it with his lips as was the custom. He simply held it, trapping Renée to the spot. "Glad to be of service to so beautiful a lady," he said warmly, squeezing her hand before releasing it. "But I'm not fool enough to think you came aboard to thank me personally. You've got some other reason for boarding the *Pelican*."

His sharp reasoning surprised Renée. Everything she had ever heard about the Americans had led her to believe them to be the worst of savages, without manners, taste or wits. "You are correct, capitaine. I saw your advertisement for passengers. I would like to secure passage to England."

Adam's brows rose. "My bill didn't say anything about passage to England. Don't expect to go any farther than the Leeward Islands this trip."

"Oh." Renée frowned. Few ships in the harbor advertised for passengers and most of those provided no special accommodations for them. The *Pelican* had promised private quarters and two meals served daily. This called for an extra effort on her part. She moved forward, laying a gloved hand lightly on his arm. "If I could afford it, would you not take me to England, capitaine?" she asked in her most persuasive voice.

A bellow of laughter erupted from his chest. "Dammit, mam'zelle, but you beat all! I would like to think on your proposition." Surprisingly, his eyes slid sideways to Giselle once more. "But I've got other plans this trip out. We're headed for Tortola. After that?" He shrugged; then his gaze came to rest on Renée once more in bold regard. "Just what kind of payment did you have in mind?"

Renée lowered her veil back into place, considering the action to be safer than to continue to flirt with the *Yanqui*. Obviously the man did not understand a thing about the art. "You have other passengers?"

Adam nodded once. "Sure do. That doesn't mean I couldn't take a few more, provided they were interested in seeing Tortola."

A thousand thoughts flew through Renée's head. Tortola was a British possession. Perhaps she would be able to find a ship bound for England there. After the shock of seeing Laurent, the need to escape New Orleans had become an overriding need.

"Here go, cap'n," announced the grizzled old seaman as he came forward. "Got bandages and water for the cuts and a bottle of spirits for the bruised soul," he said with a wink.

"Excuse me, ladies," Adam said as he took a strip of linen and dipped it in the basin the seaman held. He applied it to his temple but the water merely mingled with his blood and sent rills of pinky fluid streaming onto his shirtfront.

"Give that to me." Giselle took the cloth from the startled man's hands. She dipped it into the basin and wrung it out, careful not to splash a drop on the deck.

"Sit there," she directed, pointing to a barrel. The American did as he was told without a word, but his mouth was curved up in amusement.

In a mixture of amusement and consternation, Renée watched her quiet little maid bathe the American's face. Giselle had never shown any interest in men in all the months they had been together. She kept to herself, offering little of her private thoughts or desires. Madame Lavasseur thought Giselle was allowed too much freedom but Renée was grateful for her quiet friendship. She had never been any trouble. Certainly no one had ever accused her of an undue interest in the gentlemen who visited the Lavasseurs. In fact, Renée thought, she had decided Giselle was too shy ever to be interested in a man. Yet, here she was offering this intimate service to a complete stranger.

After thoroughly cleansing the wounds, Giselle poured a little of the whiskey onto a clean cloth, despite the vocal protest of both seamen. Undaunted, she applied the liquor-soaked linen to the first of the open wounds. The American fell quiet, gritting his teeth, and for the first time Giselle smiled at him.

"There you are at last, *mon ami!* I . . . But excuse me, mademoiselle."

Renée turned slowly around at the sound of the masculine voice at her shoulder and then lifted her veil to look straight up into the black gaze of Laurent Lavasseur.

Laurent's mouth fell ajar. "Renée?" he whispered incredulously. The shock that went through him was so complete he did not even realize that Adam spoke to him.

A curious mixture of dread and pleasure churned in her stomach and shot color into her cheeks as Renée stared up into his face. He was as surprised as she by the unexpected meeting, and that knowledge made her brave.

"*Bon jour,* monsieur. *Oui.* Your eyes do not deceive you. I trust you have found suitable amusement to occupy you since our last meeting?" she continued with an icy calm she could scarcely credit in herself. But his effect on her nervous system could not be long contained. Here was the man who had jilted her. Rage boiled up from the core of her being, an eruption of hurt pride, shame and frustration which made her tremble. *Never! Never will I forgive or understand your cruelty!* her heart cried.

"Lavasseur, you know the lady?" Adam inquired for the second time.

"I know the mademoiselle," Laurent replied, his gaze never wavering from Renée's. He saw the flush of her skin and the tense muscles of her face as she fought to maintain her dignity. I would have spared you this, he thought in sorrow.

"Thanks, darlin'," Adam said to Giselle as he reached to take the end of the bandage she had wrapped about his head and tucked it in place. Afterward, he reached for her hand and brought it to his lips for a brief kiss, a gesture so gentlemanly and unlike his previous conduct that Giselle merely stared at him with wide eyes. "Life's full of pleasant surprises, huh, Lavasseur?"

At last Laurent managed to tear his eyes away from Renée's face. "I beg your pardon?"

Adam's knowing grin went from Lavasseur to the young lady by his side. "Why, the mam'zelle was considering booking passage with us."

"What?" Laurent turned back to Renée. "Why?"

Renée eyed him coldly, wishing that she did not have the absurd desire to tame the black curl that a sudden gust of wind had lifted from his brow. "I find myself in an awkward position in the home of my hostess," she stated stiffly. "You, above everyone, should understand why."

Once more Laurent found himself without a ready reply. He had not thought that his mother's reaction would be to turn Renée out of her home. "But Maman would never . . . I will speak to her. Shall I go with you now and see her?"

"No!" Renée put a detaining hand on his arm. The effect was like touching a boiling pot and she hastily drew the hand away. "I assure you, my desire to leave Louisiana is against your mother's wishes." She lifted her chin. "I find myself no longer enamored with the pleasures of your quaint colony. I am going to England and Gweneth."

"But that's ridiculous!" Laurent protested, shaken out of his calm by yet another unpleasant jolt. "You cannot sail to England unaccompanied. You have no family, no one to see to your well-being, no—"

"No husband to shelter me?" Renée ventured in acid politeness.

"No one . . ." Laurent stuttered to a halt, his eyes widening in amazement. He had expected Renée to be crushed beyond all reasoning. Memories of her tear-blurred face had half-convinced him that he had done her irreparable harm. Yet, she stood before him now, delivering volleys to do proud the most accomplished of sophisticates. With growing annoyance he realized that

that did not please him as much as it should have. It left him with the irrationally irritating conclusion that his refusal to marry her had not hurt her as much as he thought it had.

Adam had been watching the pair with increasing interest. There was something here of which he was not aware, and he meant to discover what it was. "I was just telling the mam'zelle that I'd be happy to take her to England, provided she has the fare."

Renée turned a bewildered gaze on the American, for he had said nothing of the sort. "I have the funds."

Laurent started to protest and then smiled. "So you do. I had forgotten. But perhaps you will reconsider when you learn that I, too, will be a passenger on the voyage."

Minutes ago Renée had resigned herself to finding another vessel, so eager was she to flee Laurent, but now, standing before him, she knew a new desire. The unpleasant start her appearance had given him moments before gave her a new focus on the situation. Being near Laurent would afford her many opportunities to make his life as uncomfortable as possible. To make him pay in some manner for his callous treatment—yes, that is what she wanted. She might as well test that theory here and now. *You owe me my revenge*, she thought. *I will have it yet!*

She turned to Adam, laid a hand on his arm and gave him her best smile. "Capitaine Breedon, I ask you, is it too terrible of me to wish to book passage on the same ship as the man whose proposal of marriage I have recently rejected?"

Adam's expression, compounded by Laurent's murmured depreciation, put the seal on her determination. Oh no! She could not let this opportunity pass.

"If you insist on sailing with the *Pelican,* mademoiselle, I will withdraw," Laurent announced, his sardonic smile slipping back into place despite the sense of unreality that coursed through him.

"Oh, do I frighten you, monsieur?" Renée inquired most innocently. "Then perhaps it's best I concede defeat, Capitaine Breedon. I would not wish to be the object of Monsieur Lavasseur's *mal de coeur.*"

"Nom de Dieu!" Laurent muttered, his amicable expression momentarily dissolving. Then suddenly the humor of the situation got the better of him. She was not the only one with barbs at the ready. "I believe I'm equal to a few days' dose of your charms, mademoiselle. And you may be assured I will give neither of us cause to nurse a broken heart."

Renée did not miss the implication of his words. And if that were not enough, she had but to see the wicked twinkle in his eyes. She had nearly given herself to him once, with very little entreaty on his part. He did not even want that of her now.

"Well, then, we've got a deal," Adam declared with a gleeful look at Giselle. "We sail in two days' time. Can you be ready?"

"I can be ready," Laurent returned, and then

his voice lowered: "Will you be ready, mademoiselle?"

Renée regarded his black eyes, brimmed full of humor and challenge, with a coolness that did not reflect the galloping of her heart. "I am ready now."

Chapter Six

THE UNRELIEVED HEAT OF MIDDAY MADE ADAM restive. His shoulders itched beneath the shirt which clung damply to his back as he sat at his desk. Finally he shoved away his noonday meal of sweet potatoes and peas with pickled pork and went to open the stern windows of his cabin. He pushed them as wide as possible but only the stagnant warmth of a calm met his sweaty cheek. The last thing he had expected was a becalmed sea.

"Damn heat . . . damn calm . . . damn sea!" he muttered as he stared out over the glassy smoothness of the gulf. After a moment he put a hand to the dirty bandage at his brow and winced. The wound was four days old but he had not allowed the bandage to be changed.

His thoughts drifted from his cabin to one of the passenger cabins forward. He had not seen his female passengers since they boarded two days earlier. He had been too busy launching the *Pelican* and navigating her down the Mississippi to the mouth of the gulf. Now his mind filled with brief memories of a piquant face, of small hands with exquisite tenderness in their touch, of dark eyes wide with quiet curiosity. Giselle was the reason he had not changed the linen set on his brow.

"Because you hoped, like some besotted jack-ass, that she'd offer to change it for you," he mused aloud. Damnation! The very thought made him feel like a fool. He could imagine how much amusement it would have caused Lavasseur.

He could not quite credit the feelings running through him. It was not just the swift current of lust. He was not above satisfying that urge with any female, his tastes having been broadened by indifference and availability. And, he suspected, the little quadroon would run screaming if he laid a hand on her. So what was the point of this quickening in his groin at the thought of her? Why did he speculate at odd moments on the taste of her skin, on the texture of her thighs, on the ripeness of cocoa-tipped breasts? She would never come and spread herself upon his bunk, lifting her skirts in invitation. She would not come to him in any manner. He was an American, a white man to be feared. No, she would not come to him.

Yet he wanted her, wanted her so badly he was content to nurse his aching since the day they had met on the dock. But now, out at sea, he knew that had been a stupid gesture, a gallant's sacrifice worthy of the kind of man he had never been.

So, Breedon, what will you do now? he mused with a sardonic grin. Will you find some excuse, any mealymouthed reason to lure her into your cabin, where you'll force—

"M'sieu?"

Adam spun around at the sound of the feminine voice. She stood with her face in the shadow of the portal, her form backlit by the noonday sun.

"I knocked, m'sieu, but there was no answer," Giselle said quietly in French.

Astonished by her sudden appearance so quick upon his lusty imaginings, Adam could only stare, and the silence stretched out until she turned to leave. "No, no, come in," he said, hurrying toward her. "*Entrez-vous, s'il vous plaît.*"

Giselle turned back to him. "M'sieu speaks French?" she questioned in surprise.

Adam reached around her and quickly closed the door. His proficiency with languages was one of many secrets about himself he preferred to keep. Yet when he turned, he grinned at Giselle. He did not doubt he could trust her with the knowledge. "If you will keep my secret, I will speak any language you choose."

Giselle looked up at him. He was a head taller than she. His shoulders filled the doorway. It was as if he had grown since her last glimpse of him. Then her gaze fell with fascination on the crisp curls of gold glistening with sweat where his shirt had been unbuttoned.

"What may I do for you?" Adam inquired, eager to learn the reason she had sought him out.

Giselle's gaze again moved to his face. "You must have your bandage changed," she announced firmly. "I tell your man so. I tell him a good servant takes care of his master whether the master wants it or not. But he is a lazy rascal. He says for me to . . . to . . ." She paused, frowning, trying to recall the exact English, which she had not understood. "He says, 'Keep your plaguey yaller arse outta de cap'n's biz'nuss.' I say it correctly, no?"

Adam's laughter was heard well beyond the confines of his cabin.

"I will tell Ben to mind his manners when next I see him," he answered. "You've come to change the bandage yourself?"

Giselle nodded, her eyes moving from his face to gaze curiously about his cabin. She had never been aboard a ship before and she wasn't at all certain that she liked it. The captain's cabin was grander than the cramped quarters she shared with Mademoiselle Renée, but the heat was no less. "I don't so much like the sea," she ventured.

Adam sat on the edge of his desk and silently allowed her to unwrap the filthy linen. While he did not speak, his mind was busy, noting that the blue-black lashes lying along her cheeks were long and straight, that the perspiration dampen-

ing her bodice traveled the natural cleft made by
her bosom, that the full swell of her breasts was
revealed beneath the thin bodice of her gown
when she raised her arms. When he grunted as
the last of the bandage stuck and pulled at the
sore edges of his wound, he saw her full nether
lip catch between her teeth in sympathy.

"No one has cared for my pain since I was a
lad. Nothing you could do would hurt me,
mam'zelle," he said warmly. "Nothing." Reaching out, he dragged her lip from between her
teeth with the pressure of his thumb.

Giselle shrank from the intimate touch of that
callused finger at her mouth and he quickly
drew it away.

Despite a conscious effort to the contrary, her
gaze wandered back to his sea-blue eyes. They
were unlike any eyes she had ever seen before.
Surrounded by a thick tangle of golden lashes,
they rivaled the blue jay's wing in intensity.
Looking at them was like staring into the
strange blue-green waters upon which they now
sailed. She swayed a little, to be steadied by a
hard hand gently catching her shoulder.

"Gently, *chérie*." Adam's fingers curled more
tightly on the slight shoulder under his hand. "I
doubt you've gotten your sea legs yet."

Giselle shook her head, bewildered. "Me, I
don't much like the sea," she murmured again,
as if that explained her strange reaction to him.

Adam smiled, his hand moving from her
shoulder to her waist, where it lightly rode that
inward curve. "Do I frighten you, Giselle? I
should."

Giselle's lip found its way back between her teeth, and Adam noted the slight overlapping of one upper tooth. The tiny imperfection made him smile. He was glad for it. It made her real, more real than his vague imaginings. His wide masculine smile broadened to its limits as she tried to knock his hand from her waist.

"You will let me go!" Giselle said forcefully, as fear began rising in her. She had come to the *Yanqui*'s cabin without permission but she could not bear to see him wearing that horrid rag on his head any longer. "Please, m'sieu," she begged softly.

Adam saw the clouding of her mink-dark eyes and knew the cause, but he wanted the victory of her reply. His hand rose to cup her chin, raising her face up to his. "Why did you come here today, Giselle?"

"I wished to repay your kindness to my mistress," she answered shyly.

Adam's grin grew wider. "Liar," he whispered, and then again, "Liar. This is why you came."

The hand at her chin moved behind her head as his other arm snaked around her waist to pull her forward. He jerked the silk *tignon* from her head, giving no attention to her squirming protest, and was rewarded by the spilling of long dark waves about her shoulders. His free hand dived deep into the lush tresses to bring her mouth to his, where he sucked in her lower lip and set his sharp teeth into that tenderness.

"Please! M'sieu!" Giselle pleaded, her words

forming whispery ripples along their joined mouths.

"*Douce sauvage,*" Adam murmured against her mouth, reveling in the sensual vibrations which passed between them. "You are my own sweet savage," he murmured again, and then dragged his lips from hers. "You know you came for that," he said, shaking her lightly to gain a reply. "Say it!"

Giselle had registered the touch of his lips as a shock of warmth. Never before had any man kissed her, yet the experience jangled inner bells of alarm. The touch of his hot mouth, the unexpected nip of his teeth, had roused something terrible within her.

She felt it now, hammering her heart and tingling the fingers of the hand she raised to her tender lips. The knowledge of that response shamed her more than his action had. This feeling must be the wild sinful thing her mother had warned her against when she spoke of evil men.

Adam saw the naked fear in the depths of her great dark eyes and the sight repulsed him. Hers were the eyes of innocence and that meant he was very close to committing rape. He might be a fool, but he was not that depraved.

With a vicious string of curses, he dropped a hand to her shoulder, spun her around and gave her a little push toward the door. "Get out of here!" he ordered roughly in English. "And don't come back!"

The sudden anger coming upon the heels of an

equally unexpected and appalling emotion moved Giselle to flight. She ran to the door and was halfway through it when her way was blocked.

"Giselle!" Laurent's gaze flew from the flushed face of the girl, who nearly collided with him, to Breedon, who sat on the edge of his desk smiling in derision.

Giselle turned back to Adam, her eyes flared in anger. *"Bête sauvage! Yanqui chevelure d'or!"*

A second later she was gone.

"What'd that little Frenchy call me?" Adam questioned in English as he picked up a clean strip of linen. He ignored his shaking hands. Damn the girl! She was only a child. He needed a woman beneath him—and soon.

"She labels you a wild savage," Laurent translated as he leaned against the bulkhead. "A golden-haired Yankee savage, to be precise."

Adam paused in winding his bandage, cocking his head to one side in consideration. After a moment a wide grin split his features. "I think I like the sound of that."

"What did you do to frighten her?" Laurent questioned.

"Little enough," Adam declared unrepentantly. Whatever his own feelings, they were not Lavasseur's business. "Is it my fault she suspected my less-than-honorable intentions? Didn't even touch her—hardly."

"Don't touch her at all."

"Hey, friend!" Adam protested. "I've done the same thing in Havana often enough. Those little caramel girls are always rearing for a ride. She came in here on her own. I just took her up on her offer."

Laurent met Breedon's blue stare calmly. "Giselle is not a whore. She is a quadroon but she's been as strictly raised as a Creole girl. Indeed, I am inclined to believe that girls like Giselle try harder to master the social graces, for their livelihood depends on a *plaçage*."

"What the hell is that?" Adam asked as he finished his bandage.

"A *plaçage*?" Laurent rubbed his chin with a forefinger. "It is the contract between a white man and a free woman of color. The man provides shelter, protection and care for the girl in exchange for her love and fidelity."

"Sounds like a fancy word for a whore to me," Adam muttered.

"Not at all," Laurent maintained. "It is more a form of marriage. The girls are virtuous and faithful. Often the natural children of these alliances are baptized and their names listed in the cathedral register."

"You Frenchies always have to tie up your dirty linen with a fancy ribbon," Adam sneered. "I find it damn more honorable—and satisfying —to pay out of pocket for my night's pleasure with a woman who knows her business."

"I take that to mean you will not pursue your interest in Giselle," Laurent remarked, "since, of course, that would be against your scruples— and your tastes."

Adam wiped at the sweat from his face with

his shirtsleeve as he considered the subtle request. "Why are you so all-fired determined to keep me from acting like the bastard I am?"

Laurent gave a Gallic shrug. *"Quant à ça*—I like you."

"Don't."

"Don't what?"

"Like me," Adam replied, and reached for the half-empty mug of beer by his plate and downed it in one gulp. Suddenly his thirst was great enough to consume a full bottle of rum. "I don't like people getting too close."

"You didn't seem to mind Giselle—"

Adam looked at Laurent over the rim of his mug, his blue eyes like chips of ice. "Don't push, Lavasseur. It makes me itch to push back."

Not for the first time since they had sailed, Laurent sensed a tension between them. Adam appeared to be an outwardly open man, a good drinking companion and able seaman. But there was a deeper secret man who would allow no one close.

Laurent smiled. Every man was entitled to his privacy. "As long as we are in agreement about preserving Giselle's virtue, I have no interest in your other pursuits."

"You!"

Both men turned to the door at the same moment to confront an enraged young woman carrying a beribboned parasol.

"Mademoiselle Valois," they said simultaneously.

"You are the culprit!" Renée exclaimed, marching across the room to Adam. "You frightened Giselle when all she did was seek to be of aid. Poltroon! Bully! *Coquin!* Preyer on innocents!" she cried, punctuating her mixture of English and French with whacks of her parasol.

Overcome with laughter, Adam halfheartedly shielded his head while the blows fell harmlessly on his arms and shoulders.

When her parasol had been beaten to shreds of silk and bamboo, she turned toward Laurent. "And you! You are no better than he, encouraging such wickedness."

"Mademoiselle Renée," Laurent began placatingly, only to realize the danger of that patronizing tone when she raised her ruined weapon. "I totally agree with you," he injected quickly as his eyes swept over her. It had been days since he had seen her and the sight of her was surprisingly welcome. Anger gleamed in her eyes, making them like brilliant dark jewels, and her flushed cheeks radiated life. Did she realize how absurdly lovely she was? he wondered inconsequentially.

"Though I must deplore your lack of forethought in this regard, mademoiselle," he continued after a moment. "I cannot think why Maman allowed you to bring the girl along as your duenna. Giselle is scarcely old enough to care for herself."

"And me, do you think I am in no position to care for myself?" Renée challenged, angered even more by his self-centered masculine tone.

Laurent schooled his features. "You are safe as long as you are in the company of gentlemen."

"Then I suppose I am doomed," she shot back. "You, monsieur, I would never mistake for a gentleman." She turned back to Adam. "And you, you I don't know. I thought . . . Perhaps I was wrong. You stay away from Giselle or I will find something much bigger and harder to beat you with." She looked down at her parasol, made a noise suspiciously like a snort of disgust, and threw it on the floor before leaving. "Men!"

Renée was still breathing hard from her exertions when she reached her cabin. Despite the suffocating heat, she bolted the door and then closed the portholes, condemning herself and Giselle to stifling semidarkness.

"I took care of everything," she said breathlessly, going to put her arms about Giselle, who sat on her bunk with her face to the bulkhead. "Please, please do not cry so, Giselle. No more harm will come to you, I swear it."

Giselle raised her head, her eyes red and puffy from crying, her mouth blurred and slick. "Mam'zelle, I give you too much trouble. I am too wicked a person. I did a shameful thing in approaching the *Yanqui*. I have no pride left. I should never have come with you, mam'zelle. My mama, she does not want me to come, but I did not know how to say no to you. You have been so kind, from the first. How could I say no?"

The news of Giselle's reluctance to leave New Orleans took Renée aback. "You did not want to come with me? Why didn't you tell me? I would never have forced you."

Giselle shook her head, new tears falling faster and faster as she relived in her mind those moments in the *Yanqui*'s cabin. He had guessed what she could not. She had wanted that kiss! "I . . . I am so wicked—wicked. Mama, she . . . kill me—if she knew."

Renée was young but she knew enough to know there were few things a daughter would fear to tell her mother. She straightened and put a hand on each hip. "There is some man involved in this, *oui?*"

Giselle bent her head, pitiable sobs racking her slender shoulders. Renée gave up her stern attitude to encircle those shoulders with her arms. "Hush, hush, *ma petite*. We will think of something, I promise."

Just what she should have in mind, Renée did not know. She did not even know if there was anything to be done. No doubt Giselle had done nothing more harmful than form an unspoken attachment for one of the gentlemen who frequented Bonne Vie. As for Capitaine Breedon, it was plain to see from his wide male grin that he would take, if unable to charm, anything he wished from an unsuspecting innocent.

"Him I can deal with!" Renée said to no one in particular.

Through the dinner hour Renée puzzled about their predicament. She could barely stand to look upon the meal Ben brought them, and contented herself with the single slice of melon on her plate. Giselle did not even stir from her self-imposed exile on her bunk.

Finally the blessed relief of night came and

Renée relinquished her isolation enough to throw back the shutters and prop open the door. Only then did Giselle move, taking the day's laundry to the deck to do their washing.

Sitting on her narrow bunk in the thinnest nightgown she owned, her chin on her fists, Renée at last gave herself up to her personal reflections. She had purposely refused to put herself in Laurent's path since their meeting aboard the *Pelican*. In spite of her resolution to make the trip as unpleasant as possible for him, she had not been able to think of a single instance where she could gain and maintain the upper hand at his cost. Restless and resigned to her mistake, she had sat for tedious hours staring out the porthole as idea after idea was formed and abandoned. It gave her no pleasure, only infinite self-disgust, to know the mere sound of his voice on deck made her heart pound with excitement. Only pride and the fear that she would be seen kept her from going to peer out at him. But she could not deny it. She wanted to be with him, to be near him, was starved for his nearness. When he was before her, she was never bored, or sad, or restless. He was free but she was as hopelessly caught as ever.

Now that her anger had abated, her mind played back a description of things she had been too busy to give proper notice to that afternoon. The laugh lines framing his face were as she remembered, long and deep and bracketing firm lips. The willful curl of his hair had tried and lost the battle to soften the uncompromising ridge of cheek and brow. Would his skin have tasted salty if she had pressed her lips—?

"The devil!" Renée exclaimed, and reached out to throw her pillow against the teak paneling opposite her. How dare he make her think of kisses! She was furious with him. He had torn her dreams to shreds, helped her to make a fool of herself, had made her all but beg to be his bride. Well, she had gained back her pride in proving that she could sail aboard the same ship as he, and nothing, nothing would make her give up an ounce of the victory, not even a smile that could melt her heart.

At first Renée thought she was mistaken. She had fallen asleep upright with her chin dropped forward onto her drawn-up knees. The lantern light was weak, its oil nearly spent. But then she saw the sharp shadow move again and the shriek of pure terror that erupted from her chest moved her to a standing position on the bed.

Laurent was not the only one to hear the screams, but he was the first to come in aid. He had stripped for the night, the better to encourage the slightest breeze to caress his sweaty skin, and he nearly cracked his skull when he tripped as he fought his way into his breeches. Without a thought for a shirt, he grabbed his sword and a lantern, then raced to the rescue.

He half-expected to find Renée in the clutches of some lust-maddened seaman. What he did not expect as he hurtled through her cabin door brandishing a naked blade was the scene which met his gaze.

Renée stood frozen in the middle of her bunk, her head bent beneath the low beamwork. Clutching the folds of her gown up high on her legs as if to keep it from getting wet, she revealed to the lamp's glow trim ankles, delicately turned calves, and thighs long and softly rounded.

Mesmerized by that tantalizing display of satin-smooth limbs, Laurent paused uncertainly a few feet from her. He had not expected to find her alone, yet the sight that met his eyes stirred in him other wicked thoughts. Suddenly there was motion on the tabletop between the bunk and the door, and Renée screamed.

Acting more out of reflexive instinct to protect her than from rational decision, Laurent lunged at the offending shadow, skewering a sleek gray rat on the tip of his blade.

"A rat! A rat!" Renée continued to cry, her eyes squeezed tight as she danced a frightened jig amid her bedding.

"What the hell!" Adam groused as his bare-chested frame filled the doorway. His eyes went widening with interest on Renée and then, with a thunderstruck look at Laurent, he bellowed, "What in damnation are you doing, Lavasseur, swinging a stuck rat before the little mam'-zelle's nose?"

Laurent looked at the dying rodent in bemusement. "The lady is afraid of rats, *mon ami. Voilà!* I have killed the great fanged dragon for her." He swung the rat around to give Adam a better view of it and the American cursed him roundly when the tail of the beast flicked his face.

"Get that damned thing outta here! Looks to me the mam'zelle's gonna swoon."

Renée stood stock-still once more, her eyes fastened in fathomless horror on the rat, her lips formed in a soundless O of terror. All at once Laurent realized that her fear was more than a simple ladylike aversion to rodents. Hers was a reason-scattering terror.

"Get rid of this," he said brusquely, and thrust both the hilt of his blade and his lantern into Adam's hands. "I'll care for the lady." With a shove he pushed a reluctant Adam toward the entry, now clogged with gaping sailors whose eyes were freely roaming the lovely sight of the half-draped French girl.

"Out of here, the lot of you!" Adam roared, swinging the rodent-tipped blade at those nearest him. "Any man caught ogling the lady again will be the next sea rat to receive the tickle of this blade!"

They scattered before his onslaught, but not as quickly as he would have liked.

Laurent pushed the door closed behind the mob and turned to face Renée. "They've gone," he said gently, moving toward her in the darkness relieved only by the dull glow of the sea beyond her porthole.

"Th-the r-r-rat!" Renée whispered, her voice shaking so she could hardly form the words.

"Dead," Laurent pronounced, and reached out a hand toward her.

He hoped she would accept the gesture of friendship. He did not expect that she would launch herself bodily at him, throwing her arms so tightly about his neck that his breath was cut short. He was filled with blissful wonder as she climbed into his arms, her legs wrapping naturally about his hips as she buried her head in the hollow between his neck and shoulder and wept long, body-racking sobs of fear.

He scooped a hand under her hips to support her weight and found to his utter amazement that he clasped the curve of a bare buttock. The contact of that firm roundness wrought an immediate response in his loins and he hoped fervently that she would not detect the change of that part of him pressed against her naked flesh.

"Hush, hush, *mon coeur!*" he crooned softly in the ear near his lips. Subtly he shifted his hands to enclose both femininely rounded globes, the better to support her. "It's over. The rat is dead—no, no, please do not cry, *chérie*. You will break my heart. The beast cannot harm you."

A new fear made him lean back to try to glimpse her face. "The animal did not bite you, did he? Renée!" he said more sharply. "Answer me!"

Renée lifted her tear-smeared face from his shoulder, her lips white and trembling as she shook her head. "I hate rats!" she whispered fiercely, and gave up a long shuddery sigh. "I hate, hate, hate them! All those days, night after night in darkness, and the sound of their claws everywhere."

She looked past him, her eyes focusing on

some unseen concern of her mind. "The day after the mob took Papa and my brothers Benoit, Adolphe, and Philippe away, Madame Bourgeaux took Gweneth and me into the sewers of Paris. She said we would be safe there. But I hated it, the smell, the filth, and—*mon Dieu!*—the rats! They were everywhere."

"Hush! Don't think of it," Laurent advised as he halted with his lips a fresh tear trailing down her cheek. "Don't remember. All that is past. You are safe now. Never would I let anything harm you, *chérie.*"

Renée was insensible to his words, though the deep resonance of his voice assured her that safety lay in his arms. She whispered again, this time with the faint voice of a child. "I wondered all those days if the walls of the Bastille held such horrors as the rats of the Parisian sewer. They stole our food, they climbed over us if we slept. They even bit a small child whose mother had left it to seek food. Sometimes, when I sat in the dark, afraid to sleep, afraid even to shut my eyes, I longed to be in prison. At least there Papa would have protected me from the rats."

The little girl's voice tore at Laurent's heart. He knew so little of the story of her flight from Paris after the male members of her family were arrested by the French revolutionary committee. He thought of her only as a beautiful, self-centered young lady; not vain or evil, but possessing a simple childish self-absorption. Yet the woman trembling in his arms had suffered things he hoped she would never have to remember again.

"Let me light a lantern, Renée, and I will prove to you that you are no longer in a Paris sewer. You are safely aboard ship."

But when he tried to put her from him, Renée clung to him tighter than ever. "No, no, please don't leave me, not even for a second! Please!" she wailed with pathetic need.

"I promise, I won't leave," Laurent answered. Feeling her relax in his arms, he bent a knee on the bunk with her still in his arms and then ventured to place a quick light kiss at the corner of her mouth as he sat down.

He meant it as a benediction, a sign of comfort to a terrorized soul, but the pleasure of his touch sent Renée blindly seeking a return of that small joy and her lips moved against his cheek until they found his mouth.

Their first kiss was nothing more than the gentle pressure of her cool lips against his. Dissatisfied with that, Renée pulled away, her mind a maze of jumbled feelings. There was something missing, something more to be had from the exciting shape of his mouth. Yet, she could not remember how to find it.

She raised her hands to the rough silk curls of his head, her fingers running over and over his crown as though she were blind and unable to know the pattern of those waves in any other manner. Her fingers swept on, down the bridge of his brow, against the feathery spikes of his lashes, over the high ridge of cheekbones, down the laughter-scored cheeks to the corners of his mouth.

A smile blossomed on her face when, as she

teased the shape of those lips with a finger, he caught the tip of it between his teeth. The flick of his tongue against the sensitive fingertip sent a shiver of delight up her spine and she quickly replaced her finger with her mouth. This time his tongue met hers and a purr of pleasure issued from her parted lips.

Yes, this was better, was what she sought.

Laurent accepted the kisses pressed on him, more than a little afraid that at any moment she would draw back. Excruciatingly aware that her bare backside was pressed to his throbbing loins, which threatened to burst from the unbuttoned placket of his breeches, he could do little more than pray that she would remain blissfully unaware.

Unaware of everything but the slowly receding fear being replaced by the equally numbing joy of his kisses, Renée continued to explore the man before her. Her hands moved over the broad hard muscles beneath the velvet-smooth skin of his back, down over the triangles of his shoulder blades, back past the corded sinews of his neck, where her fingers tangled in the thin gold chain circling his throat. Curious, one hand followed the links to the cross which she remembered hung at the center of his chest

She did not wonder at his nakedness any more than she wondered why she should be seeking pleasure at the hands of the man who had spurned her. Her fear-shaken senses only drove her to blot out the terror, to find a release from the maddening fear.

When she found a flat masculine nipple beneath her questing hand, she rimmed it twice with a finger and heard him gasp in pleasure. Pleased, she repeated the action on its companion.

"Don't, *chérie*, I beg you," Laurent pleaded, his gargantuan hold on himself slipping away as her fingers began tracing the length of each rib.

Renée could not, or would not, hear him. Her fingers dived ever lower, to his waist, just below his navel, which was deep and round and smooth, seeking and finding the first light furring of silk. When the silk thickened and roughened into fine wire, her fingers finally halted.

Laurent held his breath, waiting for her to be repulsed by his blatant desire for her. Her face was a tapestry of shadows, none of them betraying a clue to her expression. He found he could not encourage her, but neither could he ask her again to stop, nor move himself even an inch away from her.

Exhausted and confused, her body humming silently with desire, Renée leaned her head against his chest. "Help me," she whispered.

Laurent's hands rose to frame her face, hidden by the fall of her hair. "I shouldn't, *mon coeur*. Later, you will hate me for it."

His words didn't make sense to her. Renée's head moved to and fro on his chest. "Help me," she whispered again so sweetly that Laurent forgot all else; the world beyond the cabin, the unbreachable barriers which divided them, the consequences that were certain to follow.

"I will help you, *chérie* . . . and myself," he

answered tenderly, and leaned back to stretch out on the bunk.

Renée went with him, luxuriating in the warmth of his flesh against her still-trembling limbs as he pulled her down on top of him. His skin was hot on hers, scalding her breasts as they brushed his chest and her hips as they melted against the bold heat of his arousal. His kisses touched her everywhere: her mouth, her eyes, her cheeks, her throat. And then he lifted her up away from him so that his lips could find the rosy crest of one breast through the sheer fabric of her gown.

She gasped repeatedly as he tugged each peak to sensitive hardness, each breast in seeming connection with the clamoring need centered in her own loins. When the tugging ceased, she collapsed against him in utter surrendering desire.

She lost her night rail to him and then his firm hard hands gently cupped her buttocks to hold her tight. As he arched and rotated his hips under hers, Renée gave up a low groan of pure pleasure born of a knowledge as old as time.

Laurent listened to her love sounds with a tender smile upon his lips. You do love it, he mused in grateful amazement. You love it, and I, only I, shall give you full knowledge of that which you seek!

He moved a hand between them, palm-upward against the infinitely soft skin of her belly. Then he reached lower.

Renée could not catch her breath. She felt no

shame, only a breath-stopping torment that blurred the line separating pleasure from unbearable joy. But then, slowly, she felt herself opening under his tender touch and she knew she would willingly offer whatever he wanted of her.

Laurent, aroused to the point where he could no longer bear to remain separate from her, brought himself up against her and then grasped her firmly by the waist. The first upward motion of his body brought a protest but he silenced it by bringing her mouth down upon his with a hand while the other continued to guide her hips to imitate the motion of his. He felt her tears fall upon his feverish cheeks as he eased deep within her and then he cradled her head in both hands as he paused to catch his breath.

Her sobs came softly from the hollow of his neck as he patiently stroked her from nape to the tantalizing cleft at the base of her spine. After an eternity, he felt the first flutterings of her body about his flesh and he knew that she had surpassed the difficult moment.

Once more his hands moved to her waist, directing with subtle pressure her movements upon him. After a few moments she raised up from him, her hair a wild blue-black tangle that brushed his face.

"Help me," she whispered a third time, and Laurent answered her with an exultant chuckle.

"Yes, yes, *mon coeur!* I will help you and you will help me . . . to paradise!"

It took every ounce of his concentration to

make the moment last until he felt her pleasure, her shuddering, which signaled his own release.

Renée crooned out her joy in wordless articulations.

Laurent held her a long while, long past the time he felt her even breathing on his cheek and knew that she slept. Only then did he wonder if he had done wrong in taking her. She had not known completely what she asked of him, had been so helpless in the aftermath of terror that she might willingly have offered this gift to—

Laurent cut that thought short. He did not believe that she had been indiscriminate in her choice of lover any more than he believed it possible that he might have held out against her. It was not possible to deny her. This hour had been inevitable from the moment he kissed her at Bonne Vie a few short weeks ago. Realizing that, he knew now the source of the reluctance he had felt whenever he was near her. There was an undeniable attraction between them. It was a palpable thing that each of them had instinctively resisted.

But what of the future, of the next hour, when she awakened and realized what they had done? He could not expect her to forgive him unless he offered her a proposal of marriage. It was the only acceptable avenue of conduct for a gentleman after what had occurred between them.

And Renée will have what she wanted!

He told himself he would be less than human and something of a fool if the suspicion had not risen. Yet, it faded quickly. There could have been no deliberate plot on her part. He had seen the terror in her eyes. She had been frightened beyond self-control, and her desire for him—which he had never doubted—had demanded expression. So he would marry after all.

"You are so stubborn, so willful, *mon coeur,*" he whispered into her hair, a resigned smile on his face. "I know I shall pay for what has passed this night. But I may find the coin to my liking, for I have discovered you are more than worth the cost."

Just before he left her, he heard the clanging shut of a prison door in the recesses of his mind. His eyes flew to her figure curled on the bunk, and he sighed. He desired her, wanted even now to rouse her with his lovemaking. But marriage? *Ma foi!* It seemed a great price.

Renée awakened alone to the first gray edge of dawn. Blinking against the light which had sneaked through her open porthole, she saw Giselle asleep on her own bunk. Moving in contented languor, she was brought to abrupt wakefulness by a sudden stinging between her legs.

The quaking began deep within her as her mind refused to accept the sensations swamping her.

"No! No!" she whispered. "I didn't! I couldn't have! Oh no!"

Chapter Seven

MIDMORNING A WEEK LATER, RENÉE AND GIS-
elle stood at the rail of the *Pelican* watching
from beneath the shade of their parasols as the
first small boat drifted landward past the bow of
the ship.

"Bend yer backs to it, lads! Cap'n Breedon
ain't paid yer wages yet!"

The little boat bucked under the pull of four
strong backs at her oars, then shot forward
across the top of the next wave.

"That's the spirit! Pull! Pull!"

Within seconds the small craft was half the
distance between ship and shore.

"What are we to do, mam'zelle?" Giselle
asked.

Renée had been pondering that very question
herself. "I suppose we must go ashore and see

what sort of hospitality awaits us. It doesn't look promising," she added under her breath.

The island of Tortola loomed before them, a mountainous peak covered in the lush green of tropical vegetation. The capital city, Road Town, appeared to be little more than a village.

"I will never be so glad as when I set foot on the land again," Giselle said wistfully. "When do you think the capitaine will allow us to leave the ship?"

Renée glanced toward the stern, where Laurent and Captain Breedon stood in conversation. The sight of the two men fired the consuming anger that had possessed her for the past seven days. "Why do you not ask the capitaine yourself?" she snapped when she turned back to her maid. "You have become most friendly with that *Yanqui*."

Giselle's gaze fell before Renée's censorous look and a rosy tinge blossomed in her cheeks. "Mam'zelle, I never leave you till you let me go. I . . . I . . ."

Immediately contrite, Renée reached out and shook her maid gently by a shoulder. "Silly goose! I was only teasing. My sister often swore my tantrums would be enough to send a saint fleeing in defeat. I think it sensible of you to wish to earn extra money by mending and sewing for the capitaine, though why the *Yanqui* does not simply purchase new clothes from a tailor, I don't know." Her smile straightened. "I hope you do not allow him to take advantage of you."

"No, mam'zelle," Giselle whispered.

"He pays you well?" Renée insisted.

"Five francs a shirt," Giselle answered.

"So much?" Renée shook her finger at the younger girl. "I think you should be very careful until we are far away from that man. He would not be so generous unless he hoped to purchase something besides your fine needlework. Oh, don't look at me like that. Every young girl is warned from an early age against the generosity of a man who is not her relative." Renée bent her head nearer Giselle to whisper angrily, "I do not trust that *Yanqui*. Just look at the company he keeps."

The two glanced once more at the men and then guiltily away. Each had reason for her shyness, but Renée's emotions were stronger. She could keep up her pretense that nothing had changed in Giselle's company, but Laurent's nearness drove splinters of anger and uncertainty beneath the thin skin of her composure.

As she heard his deep voice drift over the deck, the unanswered questions came back stronger than ever. Why had he not come to her in those first anguished, uncertain hours when she had needed his assurance that her surrender to him had meant more than a casual conquest?

Fool! she chided herself. Of course, it meant nothing to him. He wanted her, lusted after her. That was not so strange. And she'd satisfied that lust—had been eager to do it.

Renée closed her eyes as shame washed over her. Upon waking she had thought herself a victim of his lust, but as the day wore on she began to remember things, things she had done and said. And very soon she could no longer call him a rapist. Seducer, perhaps. Certainly she had been seduced by his handsome face, his tender touches, his compassion and his oh-so-sweet kisses. Yet, in the end, she knew that it was she who had boldly wrapped herself about him, had wantonly encouraged his touch, had writhed and quaked in pleasure as he had buried himself inside her.

Oh, but he was unlike anything she had ever expected. He was strong and tender, forceful and gentle, he was what she wanted and could not have. How cruel life could be!

She turned her face toward the sea breeze, her body flaming with guilty knowledge of what she had done—and wanted to do again.

All about him the ship's crew was preparing to disembark for Road Town, but Laurent only half-listened as Breedon regaled him with some bawdy tale of a night spent in the island's best brothel. His attention was centered at that moment in tenderness and admiration upon one of the two women who stood at the midship's railing. Renée wore a white long-sleeved chemise figured with tiny rosebuds. Pink ribbons anchored her straw bonnet, and more trailed from the tip of her parasol. Perhaps he had witnessed a lovelier vision of femininity. If he had, he did not recall it.

A deep feeling of unease stirred Laurent. When he had left her side a week earlier he had had to confront Adam and the avid faces of the *Pelican*'s crew. His half-hour alone with Renée had given them plenty to speculate on, but something in his manner must have warned them not to put into words what their open leers and snickers hinted at. Not even Adam had objected to his explanation that he had merely sat with Renée until she fell asleep.

Since that night he had waited, hoping that she would come to him, speak to him, if only to scream abuse at his head. But Renée had refused to see him since the night she had fallen asleep in his arms, exhausted, bewildered, and —yes, he mused in some pride—contented.

Only late at night, after the night watch took up its post, did she venture forth from her cabin to pace the middle deck. Each time he stood in his dark doorway, a silent witness to her solitary misery.

Laurent wet his lips with a quick swipe of his tongue. He was not comfortable with the thought of playing so great and crucial a part in another person's life. His desire for the freedom to bend to no will but his own had not left him. Yet now she was his responsibility, because he had not been able to deny himself the temptation to bed her.

"Nom de Dieu!" he muttered, and started toward her, completely unaware of the startled look Adam shot him as Laurent left the American in mid-sentence. One of them would have to begin behaving like an adult. Since he was her senior by fourteen years, it was incumbent upon him to act.

"Mademoiselle."

The deep quiet voice coming so unexpectedly close to her jolted Renée unpleasantly. She clutched the rail before she turned to the speaker. "Monsieur Lavasseur, you startled me," she voiced coldly as her gaze wandered to the middle button of his shirt and stayed.

"Giselle," Laurent acknowledged politely. "You will excuse us, but there is a matter of great importance which Mademoiselle Renée and I must discuss."

Giselle looked up at the tall Creole gentleman and then at her mistress, made a helpless gesture with her hands and moved away. She did not know what had occurred in the mademoiselle's cabin the night the monsieur had killed the rat, but she knew enough of the workings of a woman's mind to realize when a woman's feeling for a man had subtly altered.

As have mine, she thought. An emotion forged of delight and sorrow stirred as she approached the *Yanqui*'s cabin. It was madness to love him, a madness that had infected her completely.

"Forgive the intrusion," Laurent said acerbically when they were alone, "but now that we have arrived at our destination, I must know your plans."

Renée felt his searching eyes on her and stubbornly refused to raise her chin. Was it so very obvious? she wondered despairingly. Would every man after this see the guilt in her face and know her for the brazen harlot she could become in his arms?

The thought roused her spirit enough to make her turn to him. "Why do you stare, monsieur? If you were truly any sort of gentleman you would . . ." Frustrated by the sudden tightness in her throat, Renée bit off her words and turned away.

Laurent ignored her outburst. "What are your plans, mademoiselle?" he said softly, and reached out to touch her hand curled on the rail.

Renée snatched her hand from his touch. "I do not know," she said after swallowing back the emotional knot. "I shall contrive something. Road Town is a British government outpost, after all. There will be a ship bound for England sooner or later."

Laurent angled his long body toward her, resting an elbow on the rail as he sought the intimacy of closer contact. "I haven't known what to say to you," he confessed simply.

Renée shook her head. "Then there must be nothing to say. I made a fool of myself. *Mon Dieu!* I no longer understand myself." She sighed and raised overly bright eyes to him. "Still, I am not being well-mannered, am I? I suppose I should thank you for slaying the rat which terrified me. Or were you expecting me to thank you for finishing the lesson you began at Bonne Vie? I'm certain my inexperience must have been a trial . . ." Renée found she could not finish that outrageous thought.

The words stung Laurent into understanding just how much of her self-respect she had lost. He would have to choose his words very carefully if he hoped to repair even a little of the damage he had wrought.

Come, Laurent, he chided himself. You of the glib and facile tongue. Find the words to ease her misery.

"Do not despair of your passionate nature, mademoiselle. No, you will listen," he continued, capturing her hand to keep her from turning away.

"I would be lying if I said I am sorry you found me worthy of your most intimate expression of desire. Never have I . . ." He stopped himself, appalled by the admission that hovered on his lips. *Never have I experienced a deeper, more intense, more satisfying pleasure than in your arms.* No, she would not understand that and he would not explain it to her.

"If things were different . . ." He gave up a little sigh. "You are confused and unhappy now. It will pass, *mon coeur*, it will pass."

Renée said nothing.

"Enough of that," Laurent continued briskly. "What are your plans? Where will you go? Capitaine Breedon has told me he will not take you to England, though I offered to pay your way myself."

"You had no right!" Renée flared, her eyes rising to meet his.

"Gently, *ma mie*," Laurent answered, pleased to see her spirit return. "Answer my question. What are your plans?"

Renée tried to free her hand from his but it was firmly held and nothing short of a tug-of-war would gain it back.

Furious, Renée gave up. "I am going into Road Town to find lodgings until I find a ship."

"I will do that for you," Laurent stated.

"You will not! I do not need your help. You

made it perfectly clear weeks ago that you relish your freedom more than anything. Certainly one mistake has not made you long for responsibility, has it?" she scoffed, and was rewarded by a painful expression crossing Laurent's face. "Do not worry, monsieur, I will not so burden you. I will go to Gweneth, and then, who can say? She will no doubt be horrified to learn that I am not quite the eligible marriage goods I once was, but I've heard the English can be as practical as the French when it comes to finances. I will find a husband who has no penchant for the pristine virgin bride most men profess to want."

Every biting word she spoke struck Laurent like a tiny barb, but he did not interrupt her. He knew her need to strike out at someone and he was the proper target. She was right. He did not want to give up his freedom. But she underestimated his sense of right if she thought he would simply abandon her. "Since you are so determined to hate me, I hesitate to suggest my solution." When her eyes widened he smiled down at her and said, "Marry me."

"Don't you dare!" Renée hissed as she backed away from him. "Don't you dare pity me! I'm not so poor-spirited that I would marry you if you were the only man ever to ask me. Once you did not want me. Now I do not want *you*, monsieur. Not ever!"

Laurent chuckled, proud of her defiance. He had judged her unfairly. She was no broken-hearted rag doll but a fiery-spirited beauty whose anger would sustain her until her pride healed. "I salute you, mademoiselle," he said as he lifted her clenched hand from the railing and brought it to his lips for a tender kiss.

"I hate you!" Renée whispered furiously, her face flaming with emotions not altogether unrelated to the deliciously erotic touch of his lips upon her skin. Then she whispered something very low.

"What, *ma mie*? I cannot hear you."

"I hate you!" Renée said a little louder, but a tiny shock of fear and dread sped through her. That is not what she had said. The words echoing in the deepest recesses of her mind were: *I love you.*

"*Oui.* Of course. I deserve nothing else." There was regret in Laurent's voice, but at the same time he heard beating in his ears the strong, far-soaring wings of freedom. "*Adieu, mademoiselle.* God go with you."

Renée bit her lip and turned first, refusing to watch him walk away from her for the last time. How would she survive this? She did not know.

"You. Monsieur Ben," she hailed, as the ship's steward passed her. "You are going to Road Town?"

"Aye, ma'am, that I am!" His gray head was covered in a stocking cap of red wool despite the heat of the day, and he wore brogans and a faded navy coat. Here was a man ready for the delights of a port town. "What service can I be to ye?"

"Deliver this note for me." Renée tucked a slip of paper and a coin into his callused palm. "Take this to the governor's office at once. And, please,

I beg you, tell no one. Not even your capitaine. Please."

Ben looked at the silver coin winking in his palm and then grinned as he touched his cap to her. "Aye, ma'am. Ben'll see it safe to the gov'ner himself." After another salute, he moved off.

Only then did Renée realize that Giselle had disappeared. When she looked back to the quarterdeck, a frown creased her brow. With one hand Captain Breedon pointed to a portion of the island; the other rode with easy familiarity the curve of her maid's waist.

"Giselle!" she called sharply, causing the girl to move guiltily out of the loose embrace and hurry toward her.

Instantly Renée regretted her angry tone. It was not Giselle's fault that she was miserable.

"But," Renée muttered grimly, "I do not intend for another maiden to lose her virtue on this voyage."

"Ahoy! *Pelican!* Ahoy!"

"What the hell!" Adam heard the hail of an approaching vessel from his bunk, where he was sprawled naked in concession to the late-afternoon heat. Cursing roundly, he staggered to his feet and stumbled toward the stern window. The sight that met his eyes made him bellow, "Good God! It's the island governor himself!"

A military barge with His Majesty's colors flying from the stern had been rowed up alongside the *Pelican* by a half-dozen British seamen. Beneath the red-white-and-blue-striped canopy in the stern stood a round-faced gentleman in formal knee breeches, tailcoat and lace jabot.

"By God! The little bastard's wearing a wig!" Adam expulsed in amazement as he grabbed for his breeches. If they had come to run him out of the bay, he was being set upon in style.

By the time Adam had made himself decent, the governor was being piped aboard his deck.

"Governor Clairborne, at your service," the bewigged gentleman in wrinkled satin informed his unsuspecting host.

"Adam Breedon, captain of the *Pelican*. Welcome aboard," Adam answered, gripping the pudgy man's hand in so fierce a grip the governor winced and his color rose.

"I was delighted, captain, delighted to know of your illustrious passenger." The little man looked about, his watery blue eyes taking in the motley seamen who had come to gape at him. "Well?" he demanded. "Where is your guest?"

"My what?" came Adam's surly grumble. He realized that he had been roused not because he was about to be chased from British waters but because of an error.

"The Earl of Mockton's sister-in-law," Clairborne answered. "I've come to take her into town."

Adam scratched his belly through the opening of his unbuttoned shirt. "You've made a mistake, your Honor, or whatever it is you are. There's no kin of the Earl of Mockton's aboard this ship."

"Oh, but I beg to differ," a feminine voice answered.

The crew parted to allow Renée to approach Clairborne, and the Englishman's beam of pleasure was shared, if more crudely, by the *Pelican*'s crew. Gowned in jonquil yellow and matching satin bonnet, Renée Valois appeared every inch a daughter of the nobility.

"Monsieur Governor," she said in beguilingly accented English, and extended her small soft hand. "But how good of you to come, and so quickly." She lowered her lashes modestly as the Englishman's eyes moved warmly over her. "I did not wish to impose, but I was at a loss to find anyone of—how do you say? . . ." She allowed her gaze to stray to Adam's busy hand inside his shirt. "Oh, *oui,* someone of breeding to aid me in finding suitable lodgings."

"My dear young lady," Clairborne began in a tone that earned him a groan from Adam, "I've already spoken to Harriet, my wife, and she would not hear of your staying anywhere but with us. You will do us that honor."

Renée smiled brightly and clapped her hands together in shameless playacting. "How perfectly wonderful! If your lady wife suggests it, how can I refuse?" She glanced at the alarming pile of luggage set beside her cabin door. "I fear I carry my life on my back, monsieur, since I'm moving from Nouvelle Orleans to Mockton Estate." She gestured reluctantly at the enormous stack. "Perhaps I should leave a few things behind."

Governor Clairborne rapidly calculated the number of trips that would be needed to carry the items to shore, shrugged and said, "I won't hear of a single item being left behind. But perhaps we should have them sent for in the morning, when the light is better."

Renée offered him her best smile and was rewarded by a totally besotted look on the Englishman's face. "Permit me, my dear lady," Clairborne said, and offered her his arm.

Renée paused and turned to Adam, who had been joined by Laurent. "*Au revoir, messieurs,*" she called with a vague wave in their direction. "Giselle?"

Giselle came quickly in her wake, pausing only long enough to hand Adam a stack of neatly folded shirts. "I finished them for you, capitaine." She looked up into the sea-blue eyes beneath a thatch of pale gold hair. "I will miss you," she added so softly only Adam heard her, and then she hurried away.

"If that ain't the damnedest thing!" Adam muttered as he watched Renée being lowered onto the deck of the official barge. "Who'd have thought that little French girl could lie like that?"

"It is no lie," Laurent answered, his gaze steadily on Renée until she disappeared from sight below the ship's rail. "She is the Earl of Mockton's sister-in-law. Raoul Bertrand, the man her sister married, inherited the title not long ago."

"I'll be swabbed!" Adam replied. But he was only half-listening. He was cradling as gently as a child the four shirts in his arms. When Giselle disappeared over the side, the thirst he had been lightly quenching before the governor's arrival suddenly became a vast parching desert of need.

He turned and slapped Laurent on the back. "What say we get damn-your-eyes drunk?"

"My sentiments exactly," Laurent murmured softly, and turned away from the sight of the barge moving toward the shore.

Renée knelt on the window-seat cushions and gazed out the second-floor bedroom window of the Clairbornes' home. Below her the circular drive was filling with carriages and gigs. The Clairbornes were hosting a party in her honor and all of Tortola society had turned out to meet her.

"Just look at that gown!" she declared with a giggle as she pointed out a stout woman ascending the steps of the two-story white-brick mansion. "She's wearing a corset and wide paniers! And her décolletage. If she leans over at dinner to pick up her goblet, she will spill her bosom into her soup!"

"You are feeling better, *non?*" Giselle observed as she laid out the first of three sheer silk petticoats which her mistress would wear under her ball gown.

"Me? Yes, I think so. It's so nice to have a party given in one's honor. But I must practice keeping a straight face. I vow I've seen no fewer than a dozen powdered perukes. I hope not all the young men retain that archaic practice. I prefer a man's own hair."

"You better come away from the window before someone looks up and sees the guest of honor *au naturel*," Giselle advised.

Renée sprang back from the window, a little awed by her own audacity at roaming about her bedroom in the nude. "It's the heat," she confessed. "It makes every fabric feel like the weight of a great woolen cloak is upon me."

"You'd best put on a few tiny little garments," Giselle quipped in amusement.

Renée picked up the first of the tissue-thin garments and slipped it on over her freshly bathed and powdered body. "Will this do?" she asked with a mischievous grin.

Like mosquito netting, the filmy chemise veiled all but hid nothing. It clung to the rounded globes of her breasts, accentuating the dusty-rose peaks beneath, and followed with daring accuracy the full curve of each hip.

Renée looked up to see Giselle frowning gravely and shook her head before both of them dissolved into laughter.

"I think one will be enough," Renée declared when she regained her composure. "One petticoat and silk stockings. No, I will not submit to the suffocating heat of those tights. They are flesh-colored, *non*? So why should I not wear my own skin?"

"Mam'zelle!" Giselle voiced in shock. "You would not! The gown itself is so sheer. Nothing will be hidden. It's too bold."

Renée considered the matter as she rolled a silk stocking up her leg and secured it with a lacy garter trimmed with tiny satin roses. For nearly a week she had been a guest of the Clairbornes, and a more boring week she could not imagine. She was restless, as restless as she had been those months she spent at Bonne Vie waiting for Laurent's return.

"Peste!" Renée muttered, realizing she had torn the silk. That was what thoughts of Laurent did. She would not think of him.

"Mam'zelle had better hurry. I hear the sounds of the orchestra," Giselle advised as she handed Renée a new stocking.

The wistful tone made Renée turn to the younger girl. "You wish to dance too, do you not?" She stood up and hurried over to her armoire. After a quick shifting through her gowns she found a pale pink evening dress and pulled it out. She came forward, offering the gown. "It's for you."

Giselle looked at the lovely pink gown embroidered with silk at the hem but did not take it. "No, mam'zelle. I cannot accept it. It's too nice."

"C'est ridicule! It was made for you. The color of your skin is perfect for it." Renée pressed the gown into Giselle's hands. "I promise you, when we reach England, that I will find a way to make life better for you. I will need a friend more than ever when Gweneth learns . . ." She immediately shook her head to clear away the doubts, and smiled at Giselle. "You will be a mere maid no more. We will go to parties together and you will find yourself a beau and we will both be very happy."

"I think mam'zelle is making very big plans," Giselle answered, keeping her voice carefully neutral.

"Oui! Great, wonderful, glorious plans! You will see."

Giselle set the gown aside after a loving pat. "Thank you. I never thought to own something so beautiful."

Renée ignored the tears sparkling in Giselle's eyes. After all, it was a small enough gift. "Come, I must hurry. I want to make a grand entrance."

The reaction to her appearance was all that Renée could have hoped for. The tissue-silk gown was the color of magnolia blossoms, a blush of cream tempering the too harsh glare of pure white. Below the simple skimpy bodice, boasting short puff sleeves and a depth of just four inches, the gown flared into a long skirt appliquéd in cream silk. A short train fell from a cunningly tucked back which made the bodice firmly hug her breasts.

It was this feature of the gown that gained the approving attention of every male present and drew more than a few none-too-friendly gazes from the female portion of the assembly. Her mane of shimmering blue-black had been caught up high on her crown with a gold comb and fashioned into a simple chignon from which numerous escaped ringlets formed a cascade to skim her bare shoulders.

"Mademoiselle Valois, permit me," her host enthused as he hurried over to meet her at the foot of the stairway.

"Charming," Lady Clairborne declared with a fixed smile. Her eyes lowered and brows rose as she observed the tempting swell of a perfect bosom. "You French are so daring. You quite put us English in the shade."

"Oh, but I think not," Renée returned brightly, reaching up on tiptoe to place a light kiss on the older woman's cheek. "Just look at you, madame."

Renée's gaze swept her hostess's pale green gown. "Only two weeks ago Madame Justin wore a similar gown to a soirée in New Orleans and she boasted that it was straight from a French couturier. Madame Justin should know her fashions, she's the niece of a cousin of our tragically slain King Louis himself."

Lady Clairborne was not certain she followed the logic of that speech but she was pleased nonetheless and her smile softened to genuine warmth. No one could long dislike this exceptionally beautiful French girl.

Within minutes, Renée found herself surrounded by admirers, would-be admirers, and the simply curious.

"Did I hear it said that you are the sister of Gweneth Valois?" an imperious feminine contralto voice called above the general babble.

Turning to the voice which addressed her, Renée found herself facing the baleful glare of a tall, elegantly dressed woman.

"Allow me to present Squire and Lady Nicolson," Lady Clairborne said with a mischievous smile.

"Charmed, mademoiselle," the squire said.

He was a pleasant red-faced man whom Renée dismissed in an instant, but his wife held her attention. Perhaps because her gray eyes bespoke a challenge that Renée did not understand.

"Your sister," Lady Nicolson said in deliberately loud tone. "I've met the gel, have I not?"

"But of course, Evelyn. Lady Gweneth married Raoul Bertrand, now the Earl of Mockton," her husband supplied helpfully.

"Ah, yes." Her tilted eyes narrowed as a smile curved Lady Nicolson's mouth. "I remember her. Your sister created quite a stir in Tortola two summers ago. We are a more relaxed society than on the Continent, but it's not every day we meet a young lady of her pretensions in the sole company of an English privateer." The edges of her smile could have cut glass. "More commonly one finds that sort of man in the company of . . . well, another sort of woman, if you take my meaning."

Anger rushed color into Renée's complexion as she realized that all conversation about them had died. But her voice was full of innocent confusion as she said. *"Non,* madame, I do not know that sort of woman. But since you say you are so familiar with them, I will take your word for it."

She started to turn away, then seemed to think better of it. *"D'ailleurs,* madame. Gweneth was hardly alone. I myself was aboard Capitaine Bertrand's ship, as well as our personal maids."

Lady Nicolson prevented Renée from turning away by putting a restraining hand on her arm.

"Forgive me, dear, but I am so curious. How did you and your sister come to be aboard Raoul's ship?" Her sly smile deepened. "You will forgive me if I refer to your brother-in-law by his Christian name? Knowing him as well as I do, it's impossible to think of him by some formal title."

Renée shrugged off the woman's touch under the pretense of adjusting her gown at the shoulder. "I'm certain Gweneth would overlook any breach of manners on your part," she said as she stretched out a hand to tug at one cuff of her elbow-length gloves.

She looked up suddenly, thunderous black eyes meeting cold gray. "But then, Gweneth is too much of a lady to ever deliberately discomfort someone." She flexed her fingers under the woman's nose. "But I—I am likely to say almost anything that comes into my head. It makes for many embarrassing moments—but few dull ones," she threatened before dropping her arm to her side.

Anger now rose in two high spots of color on the Englishwoman's cheeks, but she was too sure of her position to back off. "Has your sister recovered from her confinement? Ah, yes," she continued, feeling firm ground under her feet once more. "You see, some news does travel quickly. The twins were born . . . ?"

"Nine months after the marriage," Renée tossed back.

"How fortunate!"

Before Renée could swing her fist more than a quarter of the way from her side, her hand was caught up in an iron grip.

"Mademoiselle Renée! How delightful. This is our dance, I believe."

Laurent's mouth stretched into a wicked grin of laughter as his obsidian gaze met the black tempest in hers above the gloved hand he held in a steely grasp.

"Pardon me, ladies, gentlemen," he said as he extracted her from the gawking group of onlookers who had gathered in anticipation of mayhem.

"Ah, yes, now we have room," he continued as he swept her up in an embrace that made no allowance for the fact that she was glaring at him with deadly intent. He did not flinch when her sandaled foot deliberately trod on his foot, nor did he move back a step when she shoved him in the chest.

"Gently, mademoiselle, or they shall have fresh gossip to occupy them."

Renée's gaze followed his down to the front of her gown, where her breasts were strained to the bursting point at the brink of her scandalously low neckline. With a whispered epithet, she allowed him to sweep her out into the center of the circle of dancers.

"Feeling better?" Laurent ventured when the figure brought them back together and his thumb felt the slowed pulse in her wrist.

"I could have scratched her eyes out!" Renée whispered furiously.

Laurent chuckled. "I'm well aware. That's why you are dancing with me."

Renée looked up at him as the full surprise of

finding herself doing exactly that sank in. She had not noticed him among the guests before he materialized at her side. She backed up a step, rejecting the spur of happiness at the thought of being in his company. Then she caught sight of Lady Nicolson dancing with her husband, and even thoughts of Laurent disappeared. "The nerve of that . . . that nasty-minded bitch!" she muttered in French.

"Renée!" Laurent said disapprovingly.

"I apologize," Renée answered with a shrug. "But when I think of what she implied, to say such horrid things about my sister! I could—"

"Madame Nicolson is simply jealous," Laurent inserted into her speech. "There were rumors that she and Raoul were once lovers."

"Lovers?" The news shocked Renée. "She and Capitaine Bertrand? Does Gweneth know?"

Laurent shrugged. "I doubt it. It was over long ago."

"Well," Renée murmured as understanding dawned and a spiteful smile curved her mouth. "All I can say is that my brother-in-law's taste certainly improved."

"I couldn't agree more."

When she glanced up, clearly displeased by this open praise of Gweneth, Laurent smiled down at Renée and gave her hand a little squeeze. "You Valois women make a man forget that he ever experienced temptation before you entered his life."

Renée blushed, ashamed of her jealous thoughts. "I think that is a compliment."

"As you wish," Laurent returned blandly.

"Oo . . . oh! You!" Renée snatched her hand from his. "You make me so angry!"

"I know."

Renée caught her breath in fury at his self-satisfied tone. She stopped dancing. "Go away! Leave me!"

Laurent paused. "Here? Now?"

"*Oui!*" Renée stamped her foot. "*Tout de suite!*"

Laurent bowed gallantly. "As mademoiselle wishes." Still smiling, he turned on his heel and left the floor.

"Have you lost your partner?"

Renée took a deep breath and turned to Evelyn Nicolson, who was smiling maliciously at her. "Sometimes we all lose our favorite partners. I'm told it's good for character-building, *n'est-ce pas?*"

Before the woman could answer, Renée moved away.

"What is that man doing here?" Renée demanded of her host when, a little later, she saw Laurent dancing with Lady Nicolson.

"Captain Lavasseur? He's an old friend. His ship carried cargo for me, took over Lord Mockton's trade here on the island. Frankly, I'm glad to see him," Clairborne declared. "We thought he'd met a watery death."

Renée's brows rose. "What do you mean?"

"Have you not heard? I thought you knew him well, since you traveled together."

"He's known to me," Renée answered.

"Then perhaps he did not tell you his tale

because he is embarrassed by his plight. Could have happened to any man. The black-hearted devils who make our waters their hunting grounds are—"

"Monsieur Clairborne," Renée entreated, easing her rude intrusion by placing her hand lightly on his coat sleeve. She was not interested in island problems and the man seemed to be puffing up for one of his long-winded expositions. "Monsieur Lavasseur's loss?" she prompted.

"Of course, of course. The best account to come to my ear is that Lavasseur took on a vicious crew in Jamaica a few months back and the devils mutinied, casting him out to sea along with his most trusted men. Then they took to piracy. When the British Navy swept out a nest of the vipers last month, they recovered Lavasseur's ship."

"You mean someone stole the *Christobel?*" she asked incredulously.

"That's it exactly, my dear. You can imagine the gentleman's consternation, and his relief, to learn that his vessel has been recovered. Still and all, it's going to cost him a pretty penny to retrieve it. Usually the Navy torches the scum boats they capture. Most of the lot are so filled with rats and vermin . . . Oh, my dear, I *am* sorry."

Renée suppressed a second shudder. "Do go on, monsieur. The British Navy is giving Capitaine Lavasseur back his ship?"

"Not quite. You see, there's the salvage cost of towing the vessel back to Tortola. The ship's being put up for auction. I don't imagine that anyone will outbid him, but we must have the government's expenses returned."

"I see," Renée murmured as her eyes narrowed on the couple across the room. She did not miss Evelyn Nicolson's provocative glance at Laurent, nor his outrageously bold smile as he bent to whisper something into her ear.

"So, Capitaine Brother-in-law is not the only one with a weakness for taloned matrons," she muttered.

Clairborne bent his portly figure nearer her. "What did you say, my dear?"

"Nothing, monsieur, nothing at all," Renée declared, but there was a mutinous look on her face that would have better suited a ten-year-old ruffian.

Chapter Eight

THE AUCTION WAS HELD IN THE EARLY MORNING light on the wharf at Road Town. The number of gentlemen present numbered sixteen, the number of ladies just four.

"All interested parties being present, we're ready to begin." The naval purser, a young fair-haired man, reset his tricorner on his head and tugged his blue coat straight. "For auction this morning, the salvage prize claimed by His Majesty's Navy, the brig *Christobel*. Salvage fee two hundred pounds. The bidding opens at two hundred pounds."

The first few bids came quickly, pushing the price to five hundred within minutes.

"Five hundred, do I hear five and twenty?"

"Five hundred and forty pounds!" came a cry from the rear.

"Five hundred and forty it is. Do I hear five and sixty?"

Laurent turned at the front to smile at the British merchant who had raised the bid. "Monsieur Nicolson, do you intend to become your own shipping merchant?"

Squire Nicolson chuckled. "Just keeping you honest, Lavasseur. "'Twouldn't do for you to have her back for so little when you stood to lose her entirely."

Polite chuckles accompanied the shifting of feet in reply to the man's sally.

Laurent smiled and inclined his head before saying to the purser, "Six hundred and fifty pounds." He looked back over his shoulder. "I hope that will satisfy the squire's sense of exacted retribution."

Squire Nicolson roared his approval while Lady Nicolson favored the Frenchman with a warm smile from beneath her red-lacquer parasol.

"One thousand pounds!" came a woman's cry. The startling pronouncement turned all heads in her direction.

"One thou-thousand?" the purser stammered. "Ma'am, are you certain that's your bid?"

Renée greeted the gawking throng with a bright smile. Gowned in jade-green muslin, she carried a red silk scarf draped over the crooks of her arms and wore matching red kid slippers. A fetching bit of color among the stiff uniforms and morning clothes, Renée made her way to the front of the crowd.

"Monsieur Purser, am I not correct in believing that the bidding is open to any person of means and desire?"

The young officer looked down at the lady before him and fell instantly in love with that perfect oval face framed in short silky ringlets. "Ma'am, I don't . . ." He paused as embarrassment darkened his face to a choleric hue.

"Of course she cannot bid!" Squire Nicolson objected. He turned to Renée. "My dear young lady, this is not a game. I know it may seem to you a delightful distraction to divert us, but the matter is serious, nonetheless. Captain Lavasseur makes his livelihood on the sea. It is unfair of you to force him beyond reasonable means in order to buy back what, in essence, he already owns."

Renée tilted her head thoughtfully. "Am I to understand that this is not an open auction after all, that it has been rigged in favor of someone?"

Under the storm of protest this question evoked, Laurent moved to her side.

"*Chérie,* how charming you look," he began with a brief salute of her hand, which she had reluctantly surrendered to him. The slyest hint of mockery touched his smile. "If you are so anxious to do me harm, may I suggest that you reserve your personal vendetta until the conclusion of this matter? I will then be more than willing to subject myself to any amount of ill-use your vivid little imagination may conjure." His smile deepened into gentle laughter at her outraged expression. "You never cease to be a source of fresh surprise, mademoiselle. For that I thank you."

Renée was aware of the pressure his lean fingers exerted on hers. The strength of that grip threatened but did not offer any pain. It was as if her hand were trapped in the jaws of a hunting dog; the teeth did not bite the flesh of their prey but were tantalizingly poised to halt any struggle.

Renée shrugged noncommittally.

Laurent frowned in annoyance, which brought his black brows briefly together over his aquiline nose. Then, like magic, the frown disappeared. "*Merci*, mademoiselle. You will now rescind your bid?"

"No."

So certain of her answer was he that Laurent had begun to turn away. "What?" he barked, his head swerving back to her.

"No," Renée repeated softly. "My bid stands," she continued loud enough for the purser to hear.

"*Ma mie*," Laurent said low, his voice slipping naturally into French. "You will rescind your bid. Now. Later we will discuss whatever it is that has stirred you to spiteful fury."

Renée met the black stare accosting her in great trepidation. Never before had she seen Laurent so angry. No, no, it was not anger. It was the righteous fury of a captain facing a recalcitrant seaman. It was the look that preceded the order that the man be lashed to the mast and flogged.

Renée shivered, feeling as if the bloody lick of the cat stood just out of reach at her own back. No! No! Laurent would have no need of that kind of torture to call his women into account. It would be done with a persuasive caress of those strong fingers, with the warm satin of those lips that still smiled down at her, with licks of the moist heat of his own tongue.

Memory of that tongue rimming her mouth, open and helpless under his assault, brought back to her the thoughts and feelings she had repeatedly shoved from her mind. With so little effort, if she leaned up on tiptoe, she could lay her mouth on his and . . .

She saw the softening of his expression and knew that he was reading her mind. And more, he was laughing at her!

Beneath her skirts her legs trembled, but her voice was curiously calm. "One thousand pounds sterling. It stands."

For one wild second she thought he would kill her. She saw him stiffen, saw a brutal swift look of rage harden his features beyond recognition . . . and then it was gone.

"Mademoiselle has made her bid," she heard Laurent say, and then she was looking at his back. "One thousand and twenty pounds," he added as though it was a pronouncement from the blue heavens vaulted above them.

She did not hear her own voice. She did not realize she had answered his every bid until the amount rang out in high astonishment from the purser.

"Three thousand pounds! Do I hear another . . . ?" The young man's voice faltered in the stunned silence of those about him. "Going once, twice . . ." The final words were announced like separate edicts. "Sold for three thousand pounds to . . . to the mademoiselle in green."

Laurent turned to her, but Renée saw only the hard ridge of his chin, for she dared not to look any higher.

"Mademoiselle has bought herself a fine ship. I hope mademoiselle can afford the price of her revenge." His laughter was self-mocking as he strolled away.

"What will you do with the *Christobel*, that's what I'd like to know?" Squire Nicolson stood at Renée's elbow as she signed the appropriate papers. "A fetching piece the likes of you should be buying baubles and setting her cap for a man who has the heart in him to appreciate a fine figure and the depth of pocket to appreciate your inheritance. Ow! There's no need to poke a man, Evelyn. The gel knows as well as I that she's a damn fine catch. Three thousand pounds thrown away. Damn, if she couldn't snare a man with half her looks."

Renée accepted this dubious assessment of her charms with a quick smile. "Monsieur Clairborne? Would you be so kind as to see to the transfer of funds?"

Clairborne, still reeling from the shock of unexpected events, said, "My dear child . . . er, lady. What possessed you? That is, a ship—what will you do with it?"

Renée tapped a gloved forefinger against her lips. "I will take her to England *Oui!* That's what I shall do. I've been waiting for transportation. Now I have it. After that? Perhaps my brother-in-law can be persuaded to purchase her from me."

She looked out across the placid expanse of the bay at the *Christobel*, its deck littered with cable and the debris of a fallen foremast. Even to her inexperienced eyes the vessel was not seaworthy as things stood. "My ship appears to be in need of repairs," she mused aloud.

"That she is, ma'am," the purser agreed, unable to take his eyes off the lovely face before him. "I'd be willing to direct the work myself, with your permission. I think the cost of purchase should include a few reasonable repairs."

"Merci, monsieur." Renée gave him a brilliant smile that immediately set the young man to thinking of ways to retrieve the ship's confiscated furnishings, carpets, silver and porcelain without incurring the wrath of his superiors.

"That doesn't solve your most immediate need," Squire Nicolson observed. When all eyes had turned to him, he said, "You need a captain and a crew."

Renée nodded absently, her mind a thousand miles away. "You must hire someone for me," she murmured in Clairborne's direction. "I trust your judgment completely."

As she walked away from the wharf, she pondered what she had done. She had bested Laurent Lavasseur. She had won from him the thing he held most dear, his ship. He had lost his most precious prize. She had her revenge.

Why was there no joy in the victory? Why did

she feel within her the same pain of loss she had heard so briefly in his last words? Why did she care?

"You hurt, monsieur? Well, so have I!" she whispered fiercely to herself. "We are even, I think."

"What do you mean by that?"

"Just what I said. I kept my part of the bargain, I expect to be paid. No fault of mine that the ship was lost to a higher bid." The man's voice was a sneer. "Told me you had it rigged. Said Lavasseur would get his ship back. Well, things didn't turn out the way you planned. No skin off my nose."

"You won't be paid, sir. You were paid in New Orleans twice the worth of your services to us and you failed to bring us the expected results."

The man folded his arms across his chest, as unconcerned in the room of three masked strangers as if he had been aboard his ship. "You won't pay me the other half? All right. It doesn't much matter. I've other business to tend to. My ship isn't out for hire for smuggling purposes. You want to trap Lavasseur, you find other bait."

"Wait!" The call stopped the man in his tracks. "We haven't concluded our business."

The man turned back and shrugged. "I see the matter differently. I won't do any more spying. I don't much like what I was paid to do. It leaves a man feeling like he's swallowed in slime." He smiled at the three hastily indrawn breaths of his audience.

But the spokesman of the group was not nonplussed. He pulled a sack from beneath the table and the distinct clink of many coins was heard as he placed it before the seaman. "I don't suppose this will drown your sudden attack of . . . conscience."

The man eyed the sack a long while, then slowly shook his head with a smile. "I been a long time learning a lesson that every schoolboy knows: 'The love of money is the root of all evil.'"

"Have you not heard the words, 'By right means, if you can, but by any means make money'?" the spokesman rejoined.

The answering laughter was hoarse. "I'm a determined blackguard, I freely admit it. And the power of 'saint-seducing' gold I won't deny. Only, I am a simple man, and simple pleasures and vices suit me."

"Then I must regretfully inform you that you will service us . . . for free," the spokesman replied as he reached for the coins and tucked them into his waistcoat. He then unrolled a sheet of parchment on the tabletop. "Ah, yes, here we are. The information that has come into my hands concerns the bounty placed upon the head of one Adam Stephen Southey of Charleston, South Carolina."

"Hell!"

"Having a change of heart? By all means, do have a seat. It makes for quite entertaining reading. I've never before met a man who had murdered his own kin. A sister and her child, I believe?"

* * *

Giselle wrapped her cloak more tightly about herself as she sped along the waterfront of Road Town. It was well past dark, at an hour when the only women roaming the streets were those who sought to relieve gold from sailors' pockets with lascivious favors.

Sweat trickled down her brow but she did not throw back her hood for fear of attracting attention. From the governor's home above the city the waterfront had appeared like a sliver of sky fallen to earth, its many lights twinkling like a splash of the Milky Way along the water's edge. Up close, the rows of unpainted wooden wharves and taverns had the appearance of bleached bones, and the laughter and music streaming from the unscreened windows were as rough, boozy, and passionate as the clientele.

Giselle kept to shadows until she found the place she sought. It was identified only by a primitive sketch of a mermaid on the lintel. With a deep breath of apprehension, she put her hand to the latch and opened the door.

The first thing to assail her senses was the tangible heat of the taproom. A rum-sodden breath of humanity enveloped her and then the golden haze of tobacco and cheap, smoking tapers. A moment later a hand gripped her arm just above the elbow.

"'Ere, then, girlie! Lookin' for a bloke for the evenin'? Ye found 'im."

Giselle shrank from the boisterous voice but she was caught. "Capitaine Breedon!" she called loudly. "Capitaine Breedon!"

"What's that?" a man questioned from the

144

dim recesses of the room. "Did someone say Cap'n Breedon?"

"This 'ere little tart's a-bawlin' fo' 'im," her captor answered. "Ye know the bloke?"

"Aye, that I do."

Ben, the *Pelican*'s steward, made his way past the throng of disinterested seamen until he stood before Giselle. "Ye're Mam'zelle Valois's maid!" he voiced in amazement. "Leave go the lass or ye'll be havin' Gov'ner Clairborne to deal with," he warned the sailor, and Giselle was reluctantly released.

"Come here, girlie." Ben took her by the arm. "Ye got business with me cap'n?"

"I must see your capitaine. He is here, *non*?"

Ben dipped his head. "Aye, he's here. Only he ain't in no mood for business. Come back on the morrow, that's what ye do."

Giselle shook her head. "I cannot. I must see him tonight."

Ben seemed to ponder her statement. "Must be important, yer mistress sendin' ye here this time of night."

Giselle nodded, keeping her gaze from the man's face lest he read the lie in her eyes.

Ben jerked a thumb toward the set of steps at the back of the taproom. "Last door on the left. Best knock afore you go in. The cap'n is most particular 'bout being disturbed."

Giselle found the door easily. When she knocked she heard a crash from within followed by a muffled oath. A moment later a voice bellowed, "Come in, damn your eyes!"

A heartbeat of indecision kept her on the out-

145

side of the door and then she raised the latch and stepped inside.

The room was only a little brighter than the gloomy hall, a single rushlight holding sway against the night. Again the smell of rum met her, along with the sickly-sweet odor of an opium pipe.

"Well, damn you, what do you want?"

Frightened by the unfamiliar thickening of his voice, Giselle did not move from the door, but her eyes searched until they found him.

Adam was seated on the edge of the bed, his head held in his hands. The candle's glow revealed his bare chest and shoulders in a dusty golden softness, while his hair shone like polished gold. Even as she took in his nudity, noting small inconsequential things like the fact his shirt was neatly folded and placed on the bedside table and his boots were perfectly aligned beside his bare feet, horror and revulsion began churning within her.

He was not alone.

She was a thin dark-skinned girl with a wild tangle of black hair that was only partially hidden by a yellow silk *tignon*.

Giselle gasped. She recognized that length of silk. It was the scarf she had lost aboard the *Pelican*.

The girl was nude, her elbows and knees showing through in hard counterpoints beneath the sleek satin-smooth luster of her caramel skin. There was nothing pretty about her; her dark eyes were cunning and her painted mouth was stung to a permanent pout.

146

Roused by the opening of the door, the girl smiled a slow lopsided grin when her gaze met Giselle's. "You no say you want more company, capitaine," she said in a husky lilting voice of the islands.

Giselle watched in fascinated horror as the girl rose up on her knees and snaked her arms about Adam from behind, one hand walking spidery fingers down his chest to disappear in the shadow of his lap. "Is Io not enough woman for you?"

The action seemed to rouse Adam, for his head shot up, his eyes suddenly focusing on the figure by the door. "Who are you?" he demanded gruffly.

Giselle clutched the front of her cloak, her knees melting under the weight of her own body. "I . . . I come to say . . ." The sound of her own voice horrified her. It was weak and tear-filled. But more, she saw the dawning of recognition of her voice in his face, the look of surly indifference changing into stunned disbelief. It was too much, to know that he did not even want to see her. Turning back to the door, she groped blindly for the exit.

"Wait!"

A prayer for salvation from this place on her lips, Giselle gave a moan of defeat when strong hands closed over her arms, dragging her back from her goal.

"No! No! Please!" she cried. It had been a mistake to come. From the moment she had overheard the governor discussing with Mademoiselle Renée his visit with Captain Breedon at the Mermaid Inn, she knew she must go to the *Yanqui* one last time. She knew her plan was dangerous, knew that she would suffer if caught, but she had not thought that there would be pain in finding him.

Adam would not let go of the girl he held. If it were only a pipe dream, then he did not care. It only mattered that he held the most dear image in the world, a figment more real than the harlot he had purchased a scant half-hour ago, and one he would not easily give up. As he lurched away from the doorway, he stumbled, a foot caught in the hem of her gown. He reached for Giselle, but she went sprawling before him across the dirty floor.

"Ah, don't cry, darlin'," he drawled, reaching down to lift Giselle from the floor. "I meant you no harm, my *petite vierge*. There, there," he comforted as he drunkenly tried to maintain his footing and brush back from her face a strand of hair that had fallen loose from under her crooked *tignon*.

The gesture was strangely gentle, but still Giselle shuddered. She tried to hold him away, but his strength easily outmatched hers as he lifted her against him and enfolded her in an embrace so tight it hurt.

"Capitaine, she gon' join us?"

Adam raised his gaze to the girl kneeling on his bed and blinked, willing away the unwanted intrusion. "Get the hell outta here!" he roared. "Get out! Now!"

The anger in his voice forestalled any protest the girl might have made, and she began reaching for her clothes at once, a soft muttering of island curses issuing from her pouty lips.

"Out, slut!" Adam ordered as he half-carried, half-dragged Giselle to the bed. As easily as he might have swung a baby, he lifted her off her feet and deposited her on the bed. A moment later, he caught his paid companion by the arm and ushered her to the door, overriding her screams of invective with a sharp silencing slap.

"There," Adam said in satisfaction when the door was closed and bolted behind the girl and he leaned against it.

With self-conscious hands she tried to rearrange her scarf. All the while, Giselle's eyes never left him. She had never before seen a nude man, and he stood before her round-eyed gaze as casually as he might in full dress. He seemed bigger, broader, without his clothes. The thick golden fleece marching down his chest narrowed into a trickle that flared again just above his manhood. His thighs were heavy and corded with muscle, but his calves tapered to slim ankles and his feet were long and narrow and almost daintily arched.

"Don't do that," Adam said easily in French as he watched her trying to rewrap her scarf. "You should never cover your hair. Once, aboard the *Pelican*, I dared to put my hand in that thick black hair and I knew the time would come again." He smiled slowly, tenderly. "I knew that you would come again. I willed it. Here. Tonight."

"M'sieu', I come—"

"I know why you've come," Adam cut in quietly. "I know." He leaned away from the door and started toward her. "I nearly came for you, but I don't have that right. I should not want you, should not keep you here against your will, should not even dare to touch you. But I will, I will dare that and more before the morning's light."

He paused at the edge of the bed and reached out to pull her scarf away. He brought the material to his face and rubbed the silk lightly against the golden stubble on his cheek as a small smile blossomed on his face.

His smile grew infinitely more tender as his eyes roamed her face. "Foolish, a grown man stealing a bit of cloth because it belongs to a woman he desires. I bought a slut tonight because I could not sleep for thoughts of you. I gave her that wisp of silk. I needed to pretend that it was you I held, your lips I kissed, your body I felt beneath me. But I no longer need rum or opiates or sluts, do I?" He dropped the scarf and lowered himself onto the bed.

"I couldn't come for you, but now that you've come to me, I have no scruples about taking what I want." He reached for the opening of her cloak just below her throat, the action slow and easy as if he were moving in water. The fastening gave way easily under his hand and it fell open upon a gown of dusty rose.

Giselle lowered her gaze. "I wore it for you," she whispered.

"I know," he repeated with a hint of laughter in his voice. "Poor *petite vierge*, my little virgin, how frightened you are. I should be shot for what I am about to do, and perhaps I shall be. But I will not be denied, not even by you," he added when she grabbed his wrists in protest as he began sliding her gown from her shoulders.

"Sweet savage," he admonished softly as he took her by the shoulders and pulled her across his lap. "Pretty sweet little girl," he murmured against the tender velvet of her bare throat. "Come and abandon your innocence to one who's never known innocent love, never dreamed innocent dreams."

Fear flickered in Giselle, becoming a raging blaze of alarm as his hands found the lacing at the back of her gown and began unworking it. He was drunk, the fumes of rum were strong on his breath. And there was something more, a cloying sweetness that overlay the natural taste of his kiss when his cool lips settled on her mouth. This was not the man she had come to see; there was a glazed, unseeing look in his usually sharp blue eyes, a smoky diffusion of mind that had nothing to do with lust.

She saw the door beyond him as he bent his head to place a kiss at the lowest point of her bodice. She counted the number of steps, gauged the distance and waited.

The moment soon came, an instant when his hands released her. Her swift shove sent him toppling backward against the bedding and she leaped up and dashed for the door. She didn't make it. A braided rug slid under the tread of her foot, unbalancing her, and she stumbled heavily against the table, upsetting the candle. In horror she heard his footsteps behind her, and then the weight of his foot snagged the hem of her skirt.

She screamed her fright until fingers closed over her throat, cutting off sound and breath. The stupor within which he had operated seemed to vanish as he forced her back against the hard wall of his chest.

"You have no choice, Giselle," he whispered into the curve of her ear as his fingers eased at her throat to permit a breath, nothing more. "You must yield to a superior force. I know of such yielding. I have done my share of it this day. For your suffering I accept the blame. But tonight we will make a pretty romance, I think."

Giselle fought him as best she could, but there was no resistance to be made before his strength. When he followed her body down into the mattress, she thought she would suffocate. But, miraculously, she found that she could bear his weight. Yet there was little tenderness in his touch. His kisses seared her skin, the caresses of his callused hands offered as much pain as pleasure. When he tore to shreds her gown in seeking the woman beneath, she gave in to the tears that she had held.

But he was not nearly finished with her. No sooner did she adjust to one experience at his hands than a newer, more shameless, more intimate one took its place. She was borne away on a surge of pain and pleasure, the two blending into a sensuous sea of sensation. When the weight of his body shifted over her and his knee drove hers apart, she cried out, but the sound was trapped in her mouth by his lips, hot, wet, and scoring the intensity of his desire upon her flesh.

And then her fear drowned in the white-hot pain that seemed to tear her apart. He was unaware of her torment, his fitful plumbing of her body a hard, heartless, endless series of thrusts that forced gasp after gasp of wordless cries from her.

Yet even in the midst of her fear, in her hurt and confusion, there throbbed an innate harmony that went deeper than the abrasion of mere flesh. Giselle heard a reflection of her misery in his deep moans that changed into unintelligible murmurings of love against her lips and hair. It was a union forged in the furnace of trial by fire, an alloy of souls that could only be blended by the annihilation of their separate natures.

And when the assault ended and the torment receded, it was Giselle's arms that embraced heaving shoulders, her passion-swollen lips that cooed comfort, her body that offered the ancient succor of her breasts as a cradle for the head buried there in lamenting misery.

Chapter Nine

Neither of the two women riding in the Clairbornes' carriage on the road to Road Town were in the mood for conversation. Neither of them enjoyed the luxury of satin-and-lace interior in which they sat. Neither of them gave any attention to the world going by outside the windows. Each was lost to thoughts centered on the inexplicable, unpredictable and thoroughly exasperating male in her life.

Every day for a fortnight Renée had wondered whether she had made a grave mistake in purchasing the *Christobel*. The extravagant purchase had severely depleted the remainder of her yearly stipend. Worse, it had made her the center of attention of Tortola society, and not all the onlookers were in sympathy with her.

"She should be ashamed, flaunting her advantage of wealth, and in public no less. Captain Lavasseur must be furious!" was Evelyn Nicolson's opinion, which Renée had overheard the afternoon following the auction.

"The gel's headstrong, and remember, she's French. High-spirited, those froggies, and above all, arrogant. 'Tis a telling trait which goes a long way toward explaining why a great number of aristocratic heads rolled a few years back." That pronouncement had been made by Governor Clairborne to his wife when he thought Renée could not hear him.

Renée snapped her fan open and began fanning at a feverish rate. She had not been able to avoid accepting invitations that had thrown her into the same company as Laurent, though neither of them had acknowledged the presence of the other. Not that she had wanted him to speak to her. She never wanted to hear his name spoken in her presence again.

Her delicate brows drew together over the fine arch of her nose. Laurent was an outrageous flirt, something she was forced to witness in fuming silence on those evenings. His black eyes scoured every gathering until he found a bit of female pulchritude; then his engaging smile would expand to really ridiculous proportions as he neared his choice. Indeed, his actions bordered on caricature.

If that is so, then why am I so jealous of those smiles? she wondered, and then answered with wry self-knowledge: Because I wish they were all mine.

Renée's gaze wandered to the seat opposite her and to Giselle's unhappy face. She had given little thought to her companion in days. She had been nearly impossible to live with since her ill-advised actions at the auction. Nothing could please her. She had often given Giselle the evening off just so that she could be alone. Perhaps that explained the sorrow she now noticed pulling at the corners of Giselle's mouth and the purplish smudges beneath her eyes.

Renée shifted uncomfortably on the seat. For days she had wanted to scream and throw things, to rage and thunder, to kiss and hold Laurent in her arms . . . and there was nothing she could do about it. She had lost him forever.

Forever.

The word tolled in her head, over and over, until she clapped her hands to her ears as though it would blot out the hollow, empty despairing sound echoing in her thoughts.

"Mam'zelle has the aching head?" Giselle inquired when she saw her mistress holding her head between her hands.

Renée shook her head. "No, I . . . it's just this heat. I hate it. Thank goodness we'll be leaving this island soon."

Giselle said nothing, but she turned to stare out the carriage window. When her mistress left the island, she too would leave, and she did not know how she would bear the separation that would bring.

Giselle closed her eyes, willing away the daylight hours. They were her enemy. It was the nights she longed for, prayed for, and despaired of. There was no future in her present happiness.

It was wrong, this love she bore the *Yanqui* captain. But she was helpless to alter in a single degree the feelings that had swamped her from the moment of their first meeting. She had marveled at the unique color of his hair, likening it at once to cornsilk, and his strangely light eyes, so deep a blue she had seldom glimpsed its match in the sky. Only after a storm, when the wind and rain had swept away all traces of dust and humidity, was the sky that blue.

The *Yanqui* was like a storm and she feared the devastation that he wrought. Everything about him was grand. He towered over her, his brilliant gaze seeming to seek her very soul. He had known why she came to the Mermaid Inn even before she could face the reason herself. He had not been kind or gallant or even shown a little pity for her helpless need of him. He had taken her . . . and given her what she could not have asked for. But even as he had done violence to her innocence, she had sensed in him a desperate need for her, too. She had had proof of that in the theft of her scarf. She had been afraid, was afraid still, but in that fear was a love for him that would not be denied.

"You are a quadroon, never forget," her mother often warned her. "You are attached forever to the shadow world, neither white nor black. You may love only where you may find the safety of a *plaçage*. To love where there is not protection offered, that way lies destruction."

Giselle bit her lip, refusing to acknowledge

those wise words, and sought instead memories too private to speak aloud.

The grass of the Clairborne estate had been coolly moist beneath her feet, rimming the hem of her skirt with beads of early-morning dew. Past the kitchen she had sped, on past the smokehouse and the privy, until at last she came to the gate and the road beyond. He had been waiting just as he promised, a lone figure on a horse, and she had gone to him, raising her arms and encircling his neck as he bent down to lift her up before him.

"You came!" he rasped against her ear. "I was beginning to think you would not!"

"Capitaine, I—"

"No! No, my foolish innocent. You must call me, your lover, Adam."

They had not gone far before Adam found a place of safety and seclusion and there they had lain beneath the canopy of a banyon tree and joined their bodies in an exuberant dance of love. The fierce need of a week earlier was in him still, the barbaric pleasure of his lovemaking bordering on assault, but there was a difference. It was as if a silken sheath had been slipped over his rough passion—there still, but gloved in a rapture that sought and elicited from her a return of his delight that she had never known existed.

Did other women experience with their lovers what she experienced in the *Yanqui*'s arms? She did not know. But it was that joy which made her hold him fiercely to her, which drove her to emulate his movements, to grasp handfuls of golden silk to pull his mouth down hard against hers. And when she heard his triumphant chuckle, she knew that this is what he wanted—no, demanded—of her.

"Giselle! Is that a bruise on your neck?"

Giselle started guiltily at the sound of her mistress's voice, and a hand crept up to the place above her collar. "Too much starch in the fabric, mam'zelle, it chafed my skin," she said, her eyes downcast with the enormity of that lie.

A love bite, that's what Adam had called it. There were other such badges of his love, on her thighs, her shoulders, her breasts. They tingled at the thought of him, they throbbed with a return of the passion that had set them on her skin. They were the physical reminders of the all-too-brief moments they would know.

Giselle bit her lip. It was better that she not remember, not hope, not dare to think of the ecstasy of the stolen moments which were already past. She and her Golden Barbarian had no future, no future at all.

Laurent sat behind the captain's desk aboard the *Christobel* and wondered at the enormity of his foolishness.

"You're an imbecile!" he murmured, but the slightest curve of a smile edged up the grim set of his mouth.

When approached, Clairborne had spent several seconds sputtering his dismay until Laurent had smoothed over the bad moment by pointing out that he, above any other man who might apply, knew the workings of the ship and could be trusted to see the lady safely to England.

"So, here I sit, like a jackass, shaking in my boots because the hour of retribution is at hand. Laurent, *mon ami, c'est incroyable!*"

In reality he was appalled by the fractured reasoning which had persuaded him to apply for the post of captain of the *Christobel*. He had told himself, as he walked away from the wharf after the auction, that he would never again permit himself to become embroiled in any manner with Renée Valois.

She was anathema to his good sense. One kiss from her lips and he almost ravished her within hailing distance of his family. He did not want to see her again after the very unfortunate circumstances surrounding the dissolution of their engagement. Yet his heart leaped in joy at finding her in New Orleans and he could not bring himself to remain behind when she booked passage aboard Adam's ship. She had sneered at him and snubbed him until the night he rescued her from a rat. He had not meant to take advantage of her hysteria. Yet he was not able to resist the wild and passionate woman who flung herself into his arms.

Laurent's lids shuttered down as memory stirred. It was a memory of small cool hands, of inquisitive fingers tenderly stroking, of a sweet-scented breath caressing his cheek, of the nearly unbearable joy of her cool satin flesh gliding over his skin. Those small hands roused him to a need unlike any he had ever experienced. He became a man afire, an incandescent being all light and kinetic heat.

And she, Renée, had been utterly unashamed of her own passion. Untutored and innocent, she had been borne upon the wings of primal instinct, offering her innocence upon the pyre of their desire. She had become a part of that flame and fury, of the turbulence that raged within the boundary of their joined bodies. Neither had been consumed when the raging inferno exploded into blistering shards of crystal flame. The afterglow had bathed them in the cooling mist of completion as ribbons of incredulous wonder lowered them gently back to earth.

"Mon chaud papillon!" Laurent opened his eyes to the uncomfortable knowledge of his manhood stirring. So much for thoughts such as those, he mused ruefully. He could not sail out of Road Town's harbor and then lock Renée in his cabin until one or the other of them succumbed to satiated exhaustion.

But it has crossed your mind, you rogue, he admitted. He wanted her, wanted her now more than ever.

The one taste, the one moment, had been too fraught with emotion and newness to be enjoyed in the fullest knowledge of what they had done. The emotional intensity that blurred the final moments had left him hungry for fuller knowledge and the luxury of time to learn what pleased her most, what pleased him most, what gave them the power to recreate their first union.

Why did he feel this way? Certainly there had been other women. Laurent's mouth softened at last into a smile. Many women. They were women of various skills and of much experience, women who had made him believe that paradise was, for short moments, attainable on earth. Why should his one night with Renée be different?

You love her.

The idea made Laurent burst into laughter. Mercy's grace! Since reaching the age of sixteen, he had often thought himself in love. In fact, he knew himself to be a romantic of the most sentimental sort. The woman of the moment who held his heartstrings could always count on his generosity, which included gowns, expensive perfumes, jewelry, and as courteous a courtship as any lady might know.

He sobered on an instant. If it were simply a matter of being in love, then why had he never showered on Renée the kind of gifts any woman of his fancy would receive?

There had been ample opportunity for him to show his appreciation of her passion since their arrival in Tortola. What matter that she was not the usual sort of woman a man took as his mistress? That did not stop him from compromising her, he reminded himself grimly.

He knew the answer. If he so much as laid a daisy upon her doorstep, he knew she would crush it beneath her slipper or throw it back at him. She would not allow him to salve his conscience with simple gifts. He had betrayed her; she wanted a more exacting revenge—and she had gotten it.

At the "crack" of the quill in his hand, Laurent looked down at his fist to see ink running like blue blood from between his fingers.

"*Merde!*" he exclaimed, and threw the useless instrument through the porthole.

All this speculation was ridiculous. He must deal with the present. He had gotten the captaincy of the ship, and before the matter was finished he meant to regain ownership of the *Christobel*.

If she thought him too much of a gentleman to use any means necessary to gain back the *Christobel*, "Then you are deceived, mademoiselle," he finished the thought aloud.

Love her? Perhaps. Succumb to her? Never!

Renée thought she had bested him, but she was wrong. He knew a dozen ploys and tricks with which to bend her to his wishes, things she had not yet begun to experience at his hands. She was ripe for passion, had succumbed to it once. By the voyage's end, he would teach her to so value the lesson he would teach her that she would forget her anger and return to him his ship—for a fair price.

That clarified in his mind, Laurent was almost happy to spy the skiff headed toward him from the shore. Mademoiselle Renée was about to begin the first of many lessons. She might own the *Christobel*, but it was he who captained her!

* * *

Clairborne had always considered himself to have a way with the ladies, but he stood in the *Christobel*'s captain's cabin, his mouth opening and closing like a suffocating fish's as he endured the tiny Frenchwoman's wrath.

Renée's dark eyes flashed bright bolts of anger. "No! I will not stand for this! You, monsieur, you are to blame! How am I to believe that you were not bribed by this . . . this libertine!"

"You abuse the man unfairly," Laurent objected, but he could not resist an amused glance at the suffering Englishman.

"Do not speak to me, I forbid it!" Renée snapped at him. "You," she continued, pointing a finger at Clairborne. "I have heard of such as you, monsieur. Greedy, grabby, you will be lucky to escape this island with your hide once my brother-in-law hears of this duplicity."

"Dear lady!" Clairborne croaked, his face an alarming shade of red.

"Oh, I think I shall go mad!" Renée swung away from the choleric man and stood staring out at the blue-green water of the Caribbean as she fought to control her temper. How could the magistrate have been so gullible as to agree to give Laurent the captaincy of her vessel?

"Mistress Valois, you did give me full authority," Clairborne wheezed behind her.

Renée bristled at this truth, but she did not turn around.

"You were most specific about not wanting to have any part in the refurbishing of the ship or in the selection of its crew," Clairborne continued. "You would not allow me to discuss the

164

matter of my selection with you. I distinctly recall beginning such a discussion."

Renée crossed her arms resolutely, as if to ward off these words. So what if he were right? She had not expected him to choose anyone of whom she would not approve. She had not cared who captained the *Christobel* . . . because it would not be Laurent.

But now it would be—if she allowed it.

The thought made Renée angrier than ever. Of course she would not allow it!

She swung back to the two men. "You, I do not wish to talk with," she said, pointing at Laurent. "Go away!"

Laurent accepted this ungracious dismissal by leaning his long frame against the edge of the desk and calmly folding his arms across his chest. "Someone must stay to see that you do not badger Monsieur Clairborne to death. How would it look if it were published abroad that you soundly trounced a man twice your size? Your reputation as a fragile blossom would be gone forever."

This ridiculous statement seemed to revive Clairborne, as he ceased tugging his waistcoat down over the stubborn bulge of his waistline. "Mademoiselle, I have done only what you requested of me, and done it admirably, if I do say so." He pretended to miss the thunderous bolt the lady shot him from beneath her drawn brows. After all, he was the governor of Tortola, appointed by His Majesty, King of England. No French upstart would beleaguer him.

"I stand by my choice!" the Englishman

vowed, as though defending England against foreign invasion. "Captain Lavasseur has completely overhauled the ship, repainted her, retarred the hull, done all and more than was necessary to see to the complete refitting. The *Christobel* has never been more sound or fit."

"What dedication," Laurent murmured in amusement.

"You, *coquin*, silence," Renée admonished her unwanted captain. "Monsieur Clairborne," she continued, fixing the Englishman with a smile meant to dazzle him as she moved closer to him. "Monsieur, you must understand a matter of which I had hoped to spare myself the telling."

"Mademoiselle," Laurent murmured ominously as he realized what was coming.

Renée tossed her head, the high brim of her bonnet nearly raking the Englishman's nose. "You are a man of discretion, I know," she continued fearlessly, taking Clairborne by the arm and leading him away from Laurent.

Laurent considered himself to be above the sort of tactics that led some to press an ear to a keyhole or an eye to a crack. But the sight of those two with heads bent together, one Renée Valois and the other a choleric Englishman in the throes of a middle-aged passion, made Laurent itch to commit some act of eavesdropping.

He watched, chagrin beginning to redden the tips of his ears. What he would not give to know the lie the girl was spinning for the old lecher.

Surely she had more sense than to repeat his seduction of her or even the fact that they were once engaged. There would be no telling what interpretation the old goat would put to that revelation.

His lips twitched in amusement. Strange, he had never thought of Renée being in any danger from the Englishman while she resided under his roof. Renée had a way of making every man her slave without encouraging any of them across the barrier of discretion. Any but himself, he amended.

"So, now you know it all, monsieur," Renée finished in a loud voice as she turned to face Laurent with a cat-in-the-cream smile.

If possible, Clairborne's color had deepened, making his heavy-jowled face positively beet-like. "See here, Captain Lavasseur," he began in a somber tone. "I will not be taken advantage of because the lady's natural modesty prohibited her from fully confiding in me. Do you have an explanation for your rascally behavior?"

Laurent shot Renée a thoughtful glance but did not straighten up from his perch on the desk. "Perhaps I would, if I knew the sort of 'rascally' behavior of which I've been accused."

"Do you deny that you pressed your attentions upon this young woman?"

Laurent's black-eyed gaze became as serene as glass. "I beg your pardon?"

Clairborne had seen that look before, and for the first time wondered if he would have to swim back to shore, after having been tossed over the side by this man. Then a more chivalrous thought replaced the first. If he feared the man, how much more daunting Lavasseur would appear to the tiny lady by his side. He owed the young lady his assistance, whatever the personal cost to himself.

"I will state the bald facts once, captain. Mademoiselle Valois has related a most distressing story to me. She says that you, captain, once pressed upon her a suit of marriage. When she refused you—which is a lady's prerogative—you refused to quit the field and have continued to pester her. Do you deny it?"

Laurent's gaze moved back to Renée, who smiled at him with the mischievous spite of a naughty child. Twice now she had managed to turn that lie to her advantage, and then, as now, his honor would not allow him to contradict her. He owed her that much. "I deny nothing."

Before Clairborne could answer this, Laurent went on, "But I will challenge the man who impugns my honor by repeating anything that has passed in these quarters." His eyes remained on Renée. "My sole concern is for my ship, *my* ship," he repeated softly. "One would begin to think the mademoiselle protests too much, buying my ship when she freely admits her dislike of me."

Renée stiffened under the impact of his words. He implied that she, not he, sought to keep them bound. She saw that thought reflected in the doubtful gaze Clairborne bestowed upon her.

"Capitaine, you, as always, seek to twist matters to your advantage. I bought the *Christobel* for no more devious purpose than to provide a means to travel to England. If the means are extravagant, I stand corrected. But to imply that I—"

"I implied nothing, mademoiselle," Laurent cut in neatly. "But allow me to point out that you will find no safer or more skilled captain than I in these islands. If your wish to be rid of me supersedes your desire to see England, then by all means search for a new captain. It should take no more than three or four months of interview to accomplish your goal."

Without knowing exactly how it happened, Renée knew she had been outmaneuvered. How could she defend her purchase of the *Christobel* as an immediate need and then balk at the quick execution of her desires? To protest that Laurent had the power to so unsettle her that she did not trust herself to be in his company was tantamount to giving him the satisfaction of knowing that she felt emotions for him too strong to be endured. What matter that the emotions were ones of hate, bitterness and resentment? Their volatile nature was bound up by the short fuse of desire—something he must never know.

"How soon can you weigh anchor, capitaine?" she challenged.

"As the mademoiselle wishes, two days, three?"

"Tomorrow," Renée stated. "I will come aboard this evening, to help facilitate matters.

My baggage will be waiting on the docks an hour before sunset. Monsieur Clairborne, you will see to it, of course."

When she had disappeared onto the middeck, both men stood staring after her.

"I wonder at the upbringing of that young lady," the Englishman murmured indiscreetly.

"I, myself, wonder at my own naiveté," Laurent muttered to himself. He had an uneasy feeling, and was no longer certain who had bested whom in that struggle. Had Renée known all along that he would be unable to resist an opportunity to captain the *Christobel*? Had she plotted to have him offer freely to spend two months in close confinement with her? To what end?

It is a case of the spider and the fly, surely, he thought. It remains only to be seen who is the victor and who the victim.

"Giselle, I promise you it won't be so bad. Only, you must cease crying. You will make yourself sick."

Renée reached out to stroke the younger girl's hair, remembering her own fears the first time she had sailed the Atlantic. *Mal de mer* was a sad reality for most sea travelers, but even she had gotten over it.

Of course the girl was distraught; she felt like crying herself, but it would not do.

When the little boat they sat in pulled up alongside the *Christobel*, Renée heaved a sigh of relief. Once they were settled aboard, they would both feel better.

Minutes after being ushered on board, Renée was not so certain of her prediction.

"But I don't understand. Why do I have this small cabin?"

The boatswain's mate looked at the small space, one end of which was crowded with bags and trunks, and shrugged. "Cap'n's orders, ma'am. This room is for passengers."

A very determined look came upon Renée's face as she stated in clear English, "I am no passenger. I am the owner of the *Christobel*. Surely this is not the best accommodation my ship affords."

The young man scratched his head. "Yes'm, it is, exceptin', o' course, the captain's cabin."

"The captain's cabin," Renée repeated softly. "Then the captain's cabin it must be."

"What?" The man gawked.

"Take my things at once to the captain's cabin. No, you may leave my maid's things here." She turned to Giselle with the look of one offering a sweet to a tearful child. "I promised you things would be different once we left New Orleans. Beginning today, you shall have your own quarters."

"Ma'am, I can't move the cap'n's things without his orders. I'd lose the skin o' me back."

Renée looked down the length of her slim nose at the seaman. "If you do not move my things at once to the captain's quarters, I will fire you. "I can . . ." Renée paused. "I can have any accommodations I wish. I am the owner."

She had nearly bragged that she could dismiss the captain himself, but she was not so ignorant as to undermine the crew's faith in the captain's authority. On the other hand, this change of cabins was a domestic matter which she was certain Laurent could handle. The owner was exerting her prerogative. Little matter if he must bunk in the forward cabin. However, she did owe Laurent the courtesy of apprising him of her decision.

"You will tell the capitaine that I wish to speak with him."

"Ain't here," the man answered. "'E's havin' supper aboard the *Pelican*. Said to give you his regards and to say he'd be callin' on you first thing in the mornin'."

"*Alors!* The capitaine shall find some changes when he returns." Renée picked up a small valise and started toward the door. "I am exhausted. I'll have a tray in my cabin before I retire."

The boatswain's mate stood mouth agape, his arms dangling by his sides. What was a man to do? If he did not follow the owner's orders he would be fired before he had a chance to be flogged when the captain returned and learned what he had done.

"God almighty!" This voyage was already fraught with more dangers than any he had known.

Just as she expected, Renée found the captain's cabin to be all that she desired. Though she had sailed aboard the *Christobel* before, she had never had more than a glimpse of Laurent's spacious personal quarters. What she saw greatly impressed her. The bulkheads were paneled in mahogany and there were cupboards neatly fitted into them. Highly polished floors and painted shutters folded back from real windows at the stern made it seem like a drawing room. A large desk was bolted to the floor in one corner of the room and a dining table with four chairs occupied another. Fit into one bulkhead was a large bunk, its mosquito netting draped and caught back to reveal clean bedding.

Renée ran her fingers lightly across the well-worn sun-freshened sheets, thinking: Laurent sleeps here.

Moving away, she walked past the desk, looking over the rolls of parchment, quills and ink. There was a small stove nearby and even a looking glass mounted over the cupboard holding a Sèvres porcelain basin-and-pitcher set.

She touched the leather strop hanging beside the mirror and then reached for the straight razor which lay beside the basin. It was folded closed into a handle of carved ivory. Constant use had darkened the ivory to the golden sheen of cherrywood.

Laurent's hand has done this, she thought as her fingers traced the detailed work. Closing her eyes, she imagined him standing here and shaving each morning, stripped to the waist, his lean torso bathed in the morning light.

A rill of desire raced through her veins, and Renée quickly replaced the razor.

As she opened a cupboard the faint odor of Laurent's tobacco tickled her nostrils. Impulsively she lifted a shirt from its peg and gathered it to her cheek. His body's fragrance lingered in the folds, reminding her of the moments when he had held her.

Since the morning she had realized that fate was once more throwing them together, she had been unable to still the excitement racing like blood through her body. How she had convincingly managed to portray the offended party for Clairborne's sake, she did not know. Perhaps because she had been truly angry at first, believing that Laurent was plotting against her. But soon that reasoning was overlaid by an undeniable fact: she and Laurent would be sharing the close confines of the *Christobel* for months.

Renée gave up a shuddery sigh of misery. She was as much in love with Laurent as she had ever been. No, she was more in love, more ensnared—and helpless to wish herself free of that emotion. He had never displayed more than the most general of human emotions for her: pity, lust, and compassion for a frightened soul. He did not throb with remembered desire as she did. He did not ache for the sight of her as she did him. He did not so forget himself as she did, stealing the dregs of pleasure by touching things that belonged to the man she loved.

Dear Lord! She loved him so! How could he not return a little of that love?

Tears began to stream down her cheeks and she buried her face in his shirt to keep back the sounds of her sobs.

"At least I will have you all to myself," she whispered into the folds of the fabric. "I will have two months to prove to you that you cannot live without me, *mon cher*. If you think I will be a docile, ladylike creature, you are mistaken. There is no pride left me where you are concerned. I will be a wanton if necessary, using every means in my power to entice you to share my love. By the voyage's end, it will not be only the *Christobel* you cannot bear to leave behind!"

Chapter Ten

LAURENT WAS IN NO MOOD FOR TROUBLE WHEN
he set foot on the deck of the *Christobel*, a cloth
sack in one hand, a cigar in the other. A quick
sharp-eyed look about his decks convinced him
that the night watch was in place. The only light
on deck came from the fore and aft lanterns.
Judging by the dull glow flooding from beneath
his door, the lantern in his cabin had been
turned low. Once more his eyes raked the scaf-
folding, noting even in the dark, with precision
born of experience, that every inch of sailcloth
and rope was in exactly the correct position.
Once at sea, a man never knew which particular
piece of equipment might mean the difference
between safety and disaster. All was well.

Laurent cast a speculative glance at the dark
middeck cabins where, he assumed, his passengers were fast asleep. As Renée had ordered,

they would set sail on the tide at dawn. There had been the usual scramble for a crew. The ship was severely but not dangerously under-manned. He would have to pick up more crewmen before crossing the Atlantic, but he meant to give Renée no cause to have him replaced as captain before he could guide the *Christobel* out of Road Bay. Thanks to foresight, and an acute awareness of his tenuous position, he had laded and provisioned the ship before-hand.

He waved off the first mate, who came striding toward him. He did not want any man's chatter disturbing him until he had digested the bit of news that had ruined his appetite for Breedon's lavish dinner.

When he reached the quarterdeck, he set a booted foot upon a raised beam, dropped his bundle and leaned on his knee as he inhaled a breath of his cigar. The news that the ship's owner wanted to set sail with the morning tide was only the first of a series of unpleasant jolts he had had this day. The knowledge that he sailed with an entirely new crew did little to comfort him either. His reputation went before him, making the commissioning easier than it might have been for another captain, but that did not allay his natural concern about the reliability of men who had never worked togeth-er before. Also there was the problem of women on board. He would speak to Renée first thing in the morning. She must keep to her cabin as much as possible and speak to no jack-tar among them.

He exhaled a thin cloud of smoke that wafted away from him like a retreating ghost. Those problems and a hundred others were no more than the usual concerns of a new voyage. But Adam's information, imparted over the dinner table, had been an unexpected complication.

There were six crewmen from the *Christobel*'s last voyage imprisoned in Kingston, Jamaica, being held on the charge of smuggling. No one needed to tell him that they faced the hangman's knot or that it was his fault that they had been caught.

Breedon had appeared surprised by his concern. He said the information had come to his ear only that morning but that he thought Laurent must be aware of it.

Laurent gazed long and hard at the dark water of the harbor, his thoughts roaming back over four months.

The thunderous shot from British frigates had caught the inhabitants of Juan's Cove totally unprepared. The attack had begun just after midnight, the sky glowing blood red under the flare of cannon blasts which turned many of the vessels under attack into fiery infernos. Hours earlier he had gone ashore, offering his crew a special treat after the successful completion of their delivery of smuggled cargo. A careful man, he had seen more than one smuggler's haul turned into a prison sentence when the crew came ashore at a regular port of call a little too flush with money and high spirits to miss catching the authorities' eyes.

Juan's Cove held a half-dozen hulks which

had been turned into floating pubs and bordellos where a seaman could find all the rum, women and games of chance he could afford. This night, the party had spilled onto the shore and he had been persuaded to leave only a skeletal crew behind. That was his first mistake.

The second mistake had been not to fight for his ship, Laurent decided grimly as he touched the healed wound on the inside top of his right thigh. If he had not been struck by a scrap of metal when the British turned their fire on the beach, he would have swam out to his ship.

As the deck of the *Christobel* rolled smoothly beneath his feet, he smiled. No, perhaps it was just as well he had been wounded. All but the *Christobel* had suffered serious damage because all but his ship had returned the British fire. At the time he had thought his crew had abandoned ship. Now he knew that they had not. They were too few to stand against the British, but they had stayed—and now rotted in a British jail.

With an angry gesture Laurent flicked his half-smoked cigar into the water. It arced from his hand, its glowing ash winking like a firefly as it somersaulted through the air and then disappeared below the rail into the water.

Breedon had called him a fool to consider going after the men. They had taken their chances, the same as he, the *Yanqui* reminded him. Breedon had not seemed surprised by his vow that he owed those men his loyalty, but there had been a hint of broad derision in the American's smile, he remembered in irritation.

The crew of the *Christobel* had not betrayed him when they might easily have done so in return for their freedom. No, he could not turn his back on his men now that he knew their fate.

Even though Breedon had called him a principled fool, he had agreed to help find a way to have the crewmen released. They would meet in the Leeward Cays off the coast of Jamaica within the week.

It was the American's smile that bothered Laurent. Something in it that hinted at amusement at his expense.

With that disturbing thought to keep him company, Laurent turned back toward his cabin. It was the fitful stirring of the canvas bag by his foot that reminded him of its presence. The string that held it closed was loosely tied and slipped off easily. No sooner did he release it than the top of the sack burst open and a ball of fluff catapulted itself onto his shoulder to the accompaniment of an indignant "Mee-oow!"

The first smile of the evening wreathed his face as he reached up to capture his prize. The setting free of his crew was only one of the challenges before him. Thank the gods, a few of the others were more pleasant.

"You should be one gift Mademoiselle Renée will not fling back in my face," he said. Almost immediately he began to have second thoughts as he held up the cat to the lantern light and felt needle-sharp claws rake his palms.

The scrap of kitten was so thin its frail birdlike bones were easily discernible beneath its orange-white-and-brown calico coat. One eye was green but the other had already been irrevocably damaged in some brawl, leaving him with a permanent squint.

"*Alors*. We must hope the mademoiselle has a small space in her heart for rogues and strays," Laurent murmured to himself, and tucked the kitten into his coat as he started toward her cabin.

A second glance at the dark cabin altered his course. Perhaps the mademoiselle might do well to have a complete night's rest before being given her gift, he decided, and turned toward his own quarters.

Laurent swore his astonishment under his breath as he entered. Masses of boxes and trunks shrank the space of his cabin by more than a quarter. Some imbecile had undoubtedly lost his last grasp on sanity. How could he be expected to sail with loose baggage tumbling about his ears?

He turned toward the door to bellow for the boatswain, when a movement behind the mosquito netting of his bunk arrested him. On a silent tread he moved to the bedside and lifted the veiling.

Dressed in a sheer muslin gown, Renée lay on her back with her knees drawn up together on her right side. Her left hand lay palm-up beside a river of inky curls streaming out across the pillow. Her right hand protectively rode the slight concavity just below her breasts. Laurent's eyes strayed to the lovely silhouette of breasts rising and falling in the pattern of sleep. His eyes traced the rosy shadows of areolae beneath the thin fabric of her gown; then his gaze wandered down to the dark cleft shaped by the stretch of fabric caught between her thighs, and he found himself holding his breath.

Renée was here, in his bed, waiting for . . . ?

Laurent expelled his breath. He was not so arrogant as to believe she had simply decided to give herself to him. So why was she here?

His gaze roamed the beautiful oval of her face with its sweep of soot-black lashes, wild-roses-and-honey complexion and tenderly shaped lips deliciously parted in sleep. Without conscious thought, he reached out and touched her lower lip with a finger.

She stirred as his callused skin lightly abraded the sensitive area, arching her neck just before her tongue swept out to remove the annoyance.

The flick of her velvet tongue against his fingertip made Laurent jerk his hand away. But he could not tear his eyes away from her. Fascinated by the innocent eroticism of her actions, he watched the faint tremor of her lips as her breath escaped and another quick flick of her tongue again touched the pink flesh.

He knew it to be a foolish, irrational thing to do, but he could not resist. Bending low, he brought his mouth down to within a hair breadth of hers and then touched his tongue lightly to her full lower lip.

To his astonishment, she did not awaken but sighed in pleasure, her breath carrying the warm moist aroma of her taste. Once more he applied his tongue to her, this time completely rimming the edges of her perfect bow. She moved fitfully under the application of his flesh, arching her spine as if to touch the body she expected to be connected to this lover's caress. But Laurent refrained from touching her in any other manner, though his body throbbed now in longing. Instead he traced the inner circle of her lips, stealing her breath as his senses filled with the fragrance of her gardenia perfume.

It was madness. It had to end. And so it did.

Renée blinked and then opened sleepy eyes fully upon the man standing over her. For an instant she thought she was dreaming again, dreaming the same dream that had haunted her for weeks. Laurent had come to her. Already her lips tingled in anticipation of the kisses to come, and she raised slender arms, a smile of welcome on her mouth.

Reality intruded abruptly as a fuzzy weight pounced upon her chest. With a cry of fright, Renée sat upright on the bunk. "You!" she cried in an accusatory fashion as the reality of Laurent made itself known by his amused laughter.

"A thousand apologies, mademoiselle," Laurent said in good humor as he scooped the scrawny bit of kitten from her bedding. "I did not expect my present to announce itself so precipitately."

Renée grabbed for the sheet which she had thrown off against the heat and held it up under her chin, gazing resentfully at the handsome man regarding her. "What do you want? Why are you here?"

Laurent smiled. So she was not aware of what he had done. Good. He did not want to explain his actions even to himself. "Since you are to be at sea again, I thought you might appreciate a protector." With a slight bow he presented the kitten in his hand.

Before she could reach for him, the kitten leaped once more into Renée's lap and then bounced up onto her shoulder, where it brushed its fuzzy face against her ear as the most amazingly loud purr rumbled up from its tiny body.

"Oh, a kitten . . . but how wonderful!" Renée exclaimed, her anger at the intrusion evaporating. She reached up to hold the kitten, cradling it under her chin with both hands. "But why should I need a kitten as a protector?" Her dark eyes smiled warmly up at Laurent.

Laurent returned that smile, wondering if she would be so sweet if she knew the taste of her lips was on his tongue. "May I suggest that you name him Pied Piper? With luck, he will be as successful as the fairy-tale character."

Renée frowned momentarily and then her eyes grew round. "There are rats aboard the *Christobel*?" she squeaked.

Laurent shrugged. "One or two."

"Two?" The whites were now showing all around her irises.

"Perhaps only one," Laurent conceded, hoping that the lie would not come back to haunt him.

Renée gazed down doubtfully at the scrawny feline, which didn't look an inch bigger than the rat she had encountered on the *Pelican*. "He's rather small and weak."

"Then you must feed him well," Laurent suggested, and reached out to retrieve the bedding she had lost in her interest in the kitten. "Sleep well, mademoiselle," he intoned as he began tucking the covers under the mattress.

"*Merci*, Laurent," Renée whispered, and as he bent across her to tuck in the far side of the sheet, she placed a quick kiss on his neck behind his ear.

Laurent stilled, hardly able to believe her touch or that she had called him by name, and then turned his face to hers. "Do I not deserve a better reward?" he asked, his voice low and rich with meaning.

Renée did not let herself think of the promise, or threat, in those fathomless dark eyes only inches from hers. She had said she would do anything to gain his interest and keep it. The gift was thoughtful and sweet; why should she refuse? Shutting her eyes, she leaned forward and placed her mouth on his.

It was a gentle kiss, hardly more than the meeting of lips, but Renée found she could not open her eyes to meet his gaze again.

Laurent found that he was more than pleased with himself when he raised up away from her. "Sweet dreams, *mon coeur*."

Renée leaned back against the pillows, her eyes still closed. Why does he call me "my heart" when we both know he doesn't mean it? she pondered forlornly as she heard his retreating footsteps.

"But he cares a little, he must," she said at last. Opening her eyes to the kitten perched in her middle, she saw him knead the covers to his satisfaction before he curled himself into a ball and shut his one good eye.

Laurent did not realize that he had given up his cabin until he was once more on deck breathing in the cool breeze lifting off the water.

"*Eh, bien!* There will always be tomorrow to fight for what is mine."

Renée awakened to the disconcerting premonition that she was being watched. The feeling was confirmed when her lids popped open. The single eye studying her, only inches from her own dark gaze, was bright green, slanting up toward the edge and surrounded by orange-and-white fur. Before she could move, a sand-rough tongue reached out and raked the tip of her nose.

"Piper!" she squealed in delight, and sat up, scooping the kitten against her bosom. The great purring that trembled its delicate frame began again as the kitten rubbed itself against her.

"I'm glad to see that you two have so quickly become friends."

Renée shot a startled glance at Laurent, who was seated at his desk, a pleasant smile on his face. "What are you doing here? How long have you . . . ?" A blush suddenly stained her cheeks as she broke off the speech with a grab for the sheet.

"Long enough," Laurent answered in a tone that was anything but reassuring.

"You've been spying on me!" she accused as she pulled the covers higher.

Laurent's brows rose. "You're quite enchanting to watch in your sleep, mademoiselle, but I must admit to a more pressing need." He tapped the desk before him, where a chart had been unfurled. "A captain must have his course plotted when he sets out to sea."

For the first time Renée became conscious of the gentle rise and fall of the *Christobel*. This was not a ship at anchor, this was the motion of a ship at sea. "We're under way? So soon?"

Laurent began rolling his chart. "Precisely. That was your wish, was it not, mademoiselle?"

"Of course. We're bound for England, *n'est-ce pas?*"

Laurent slipped the chart back into its place on the shelf behind him. "No, mademoiselle. We must have a larger crew before we undertake so difficult a voyage."

Renée's expression became one of annoyance. "Then where, precisely, are we going?"

Laurent shrugged. "That is for you to say, mademoiselle, but I do have a suggestion or two. It would be a foolish waste not to carry cargo across the Atlantic. The profits would go a long way toward paying the crew. Then, too, we need the additional weight as ballast. Third, you are bound to make a better impression on your brother-in-law if you show an aptitude for the merchant trade by bringing a profit with you."

This all made perfect sense to Renée, but she was not so much interested in good sense as she was in the discomforting knowledge that he was in her cabin, and had been for who knew how long. "Do you always barge in on your passengers when they are asleep?" she questioned tartly.

Laurent accepted this change of topic with ease. "Mademoiselle must realize that I had no choice when she makes the mistake of sleeping in the captain's quarters."

"These are now my quarters," Renée replied. "I have decided that I prefer them to that tiny cabin you would provide for me."

Laurent said nothing for a moment. He had spoken with his boatswain's mate and knew exactly what had occurred while he was aboard the *Pelican* the night before. Yet he had no intention of sharing the first mate's quarters, as he had the night before, for the rest of the voyage. The hammock was not uncomfortable, but it was a matter of principle. "Mademoiselle is welcome to share my quarters," he said at last.

It took a full second for Renée to take in the meaning of his words. "Share? I have no intention of sharing anything with you, capitaine, but the confines of this ship, and that is only temporary."

Laurent did not rise to the challenge. He looked about the cabin, his eyes moving with significant languor over the books, charts and maps, his logbook, the cupboards containing his personal belongings, his chest, and then back to her. "Then I suggest that you allow me to have your things moved back to the forward cabin."

"I will not," Renée maintained. "As the owner of this ship, I have the right to choose any quarters I wish—and I wish to occupy this cabin."

Laurent sat back from his desk and propped one booted foot over the other on the top. "It would appear that we have a problem. You are entitled to your wishes—that I concede."

Renée's smile of triumph was cut short. "I, too, as captain, have certain rights. I have the right—no, I have the responsibility—to retain free access to my charts and maps and to keep my navigational equipment and records in the soundest and safest circumstances. While I will not quibble over where I lay my head"—his gaze swept warmly over the length of the lovely form in his bunk—"I must insist that my belongings remain where they will not be broken or damaged. Further, I must insist on total access to these things."

Renée opened her mouth to protest and then thought better of it. She could not fault his logic at a single point. Besides, what could be better than that they should share access to the same cabin?

Still, she must not seem so eager to put into operation her plan that she could forgo a thought for propriety. She could hardly admit to herself what her hopes were for this contact. Did she hope he would make love to her, given the opportunity? Perhaps. Renée looked down at the kitten in her lap, a present from the man she loved. No, more than that. She wanted Laurent to fall irrevocably in love with her. The loving itself—that would be the bonus.

She looked up, her chin a fraction higher than in a friendly greeting. "Capitaine, I will consider this sharing of space, if you can provide me with irrevocable proof that your crew will not misconstrue the situation."

"You want me to make certain that there are no reasons for whispers to circulate? *Bien.* I can provide against that." Laurent rose, a satisfied gleam in his black eyes. "With your permission, I will see to it immediately."

Renée watched him go with faint stirrings of misgiving. She knew that he was never more dangerous or devious than when he was smiling. She scratched the fragile chin of the half-starved kitten. "You know what I think, Piper? I think our capitaine has bested me again. The devil of it is, I don't know how."

Less than an hour later, Renée began to discover just what Laurent had in mind. No sooner had she dressed with Giselle's help and the two girls shared a breakfast, then six stout seamen appeared at her cabin door.

"Cap'n's orders, mam'zelle," the first one said. "We're to move this cargo belowdecks."

Renée turned to her luggage. "All of it? But I will need some of it."

"One chest and a small case, that's what the cap'n said you should keep. The rest must be lashed below. Won't do for a gale to catch us with all this weight free to be tossed around. Might stave in a bulkhead."

Reluctantly Renée conceded the truth of this and watched as her clothes and personal items were carried on deck and lowered through the main hatch into the hold.

When the last item was hauled through the door, two new men appeared with a length of rolled sail canvas. "Cap'n's orders," one of them assured her. "Said you might care to join him on deck while we work, mam'zelle."

Renée shot the canvas a dubious look beneath raised brows and then decided she would join her captain—if only to discover exactly what he had ordered.

Laurent was seated beneath the shade of a canvas shelter which had been hoisted up behind the ship's wheel.

She paused a moment on the ladderway to gaze at him, head bent over the chart on the small table before him. The line of his straight nose was visible, but hidden from her gaze were his fine mobile lips and the level stare from his black eyes, which always seemed to find unerringly the vital, vulnerable places within her.

Sunlight, reflected off the sea, splashed gold medallions about the deck of the ship. A few of them glinted in the silky blue-black of his hair, while others danced over the white expanse of his shirt. Still another found its way inside the open shirt and sparked a golden arrow of light off the cross resting against the smoothly muscled walls of his tan chest. Shamelessly her eyes followed his hand as he reached inside his open shirt to stop the path of a perspiration bead as it skied down his sternum.

It was an inconsequential act but it made her

tremble with the desire to reach out her own hand and touch that moisture-laden flesh. She was aware only of his body and hers, of the power of his simplest gesture to elicit a response within her. It was as though he had taken control of her senses. His breath seemed to have been soldered to hers, his every action evoking a sympathetic resonance in her nervous system. She shivered, remembering the old saying of falling under the shadow of another. His shadow was on her now and she could not, had no desire to, escape.

Laurent looked up and for an instant his onyx-black gaze fused with her coffee-dark eyes. There was a dreamlike quality in her beautiful face, contrasting with the startling clarity of desire in her luminous dark eyes, a desire that she was helpless to deal with. And he knew the reason why. He had made her a woman. She was no longer able to dismiss his disquieting presence as feelings of dislike or resentment of his mockery, or even maidenly unrest in the presence of a virile man. She knew clearly and exactly what the responses of her body were preparing her for—and there was nothing she could do about it.

That knowledge struck a chord of sympathy within him. He was sorry for what he had done to her. She deserved better than she had gotten from him, she deserved to be courted and wooed and gently won to her husband's bed.

That thought brought Laurent to his feet with a whispered curse. It always came back to marriage.

"Mademoiselle, do join me," he intoned with a warmth just lacking in conviction. It was not her fault that he felt responsibility for her, he reminded himself, and forced a friendlier note in his voice as he said, "The Caribbean sun is full upon us, so I offer you shade."

Renée allowed him to take her hand, reveling in the firm strength of his fingers on hers. "What is this, a tea party?" she exclaimed.

A brunch had been laid out on a table on the other side of the canvas, complete with slices of cured ham, cheeses, biscuits, dried fruits, nut meats and East Indian chutney.

"I want to make certain that our owner realizes that the *Christobel* has the very best to offer in every way," Laurent answered as he held her chair.

Renée sat but ignored the open invitation to praise the *Christobel*'s captain. Instead she reached for a dried date and chewed it thoughtfully as the static current of desire slowly faded from her. After a moment she said, "You will explain to me, capitaine, what you have in mind for my ship."

Laurent did not miss the possessive note in her voice, but did not respond. Instead, he spent the next half-hour quietly and patiently explaining the workings of a merchant ship.

"Where do we find this crew we need?" Renée asked when she had drained her third cup of lemonade.

"Jamaica is a good bet," Laurent answered, satisfied that she would bend to his wishes and that, when the time came, he would be able to handle her curiosity over his change of plans. For now, all he needed was her consent for easy sailing to his appointed rendezvous with the *Pelican*.

Renée nodded. "How long will it be before we can set sail for England?"

"A week at Jamaica, where we'll pick up molasses, and then a brief stop in the American port of Charleston for a Leewards cargo of lumber and tar. After that, we will be ready. Though I should point out that the north Atlantic in late fall is fairly treacherous."

Renée turned rounded eyes on him. "You are not afraid, capitaine?"

"Of very little, mademoiselle."

Renée rose from her chair, wishing she could say the same. The quiet interlude with Laurent had calmed her suspicions that he was out to deceive her in some manner which she could not fathom. But the other, the longing, had not abated. It was all she could do to turn away from his handsome smiling face without touching her lips to his as she had the night before.

She had completely forgotten about the work going on in her cabin until she arrived in the doorway. The hammering and general carpentry work she had heard came from many sources throughout the ship. Now she realized that a part of that din came from here. The room had been neatly divided by a canvas wall, which, attached to the overhead beams by pegs, ran the length of the cabin. On one side were the bunk and cupboards and half of the stern windows. On the other side were the captain's desk and charts and chest and navigation equipment and the other half of the windows.

Renée studied the arrangement in disgust. She now had even less room than she would have had in the smaller cabin. But if the captain thought to run her out with this ploy, he was sadly mistaken.

She turned to the two men anxiously awaiting her reaction. "Tell the capitaine his solution couldn't be more to my liking," she said with a broad smile. "Of course, as a gentleman, he will knock before entering." That said, she walked inside and closed the door behind her.

Chapter Eleven

THE BLUE-GREEN WATERS OF THE CARIBBEAN turned indigo at night, capped by lacy white roiling only in the wake of the *Christobel* slicing through the gentle swells. But tonight the usually smooth sea crests were beginning to rear white heads in the distance. The night watchmen began hauling down sail even as the ever-present winds began to die. Then there was nothing to do but wait. After midnight, nothing stirred on deck as the men waited to learn what fate the sea held in store. There were only the faint familiar sounds of creaking wood and the muted sigh of wind through shortened sails.

Giselle, who had been prothetic in her dislike of the sea, emerged from her cabin just after one A.M. to hang her head over the starboard side in the shadow of the forecastle and spill her supper into the dark waves below.

After what seemed an eternity, the heaving of spasmed stomach muscles ceased and she dabbed her mouth with the cloth she had brought with her. It was not the first time she had been ill in the last four days; it was a part of the constant nagging queasiness she had experienced since her first day at sea. This illness had risen quickly and suddenly with the detached knowledge of impending nausea.

The suspicion that had been circling in her mind for days now soared again into her mind. The conclusion was compounded by other details: swollen sensitive breasts, loss of appetite, and an innate intelligence common to most women. Only time would bear out what she knew in her heart: the *Yanqui* had planted his seed in fertile ground.

Wiping the cold beads of perspiration from her brow, she clung to a ratline of the shrouds with her free hand. *"Mon Dieu!* I am finished," she whispered brokenly.

She had gone to meet Adam Breedon a total of five times in the month she spent in Tortola. And after each visit she vowed it would be the last. But she had not been able to stay away. In him she had found the only true moments of happiness she had ever known. She was like a wanderer who had come at last upon an oasis in an unfriendly land, a source that both slaked her thirst and yet fed her need for more.

He never spoke the word "love," it was not needed between them, but she sensed his very real need for her that went far beyond the mere lust of flesh for flesh. Each time after they satisfied the clamoring of their bodies, he held her hard against him, as if by pressure alone he could absorb her into himself. And she wanted to be absorbed, to become so much a part of him that her own identity was lost.

When she was with him she felt no longer a part of her body, but part of a greater will, freer than at any time in her life. In his arms anything seemed possible. Her love for the *Yanqui* made her bold.

He teased her about her tears when last they were together, and told her not to spare a thought for him in the future—he was already on his way to face his judgment.

She had wanted to beg him to take her with him, but he had given her no sign that he wanted her. The man who set her down on the path to the Clairborne estate for the last time had not been the same man who had made fierce and gentle love to her. The lover in him had both frightened and beguiled her, the rough magic they created overwhelming every other thought. But passion had been strangely absent as he bent in his saddle to kiss her the last time.

He was already forgetting her, she could see it in the faraway look in his eyes, so pale they seemed silver in the starlight. She knew then that she would never utter that plea to be taken with him. And she did not.

Now, alone, she had to face the consequence of her love for the *Yanqui*. She would never see him again. He would have forgotten her completely by now. Perhaps he had already sought solace in the arms of the slut she had found him with at the Mermaid Inn.

A sob escaped Giselle as her fingers worked fitfully in the ratlines. What would happen to her when Mademoiselle Renée realized that her maid carried a baby in her belly? She would be turned out, perhaps abandoned to the streets of some strange island town. How would she survive? Even were she to be sent home, she could not go to her mother. Her shame must not be her family's. Where, then, could she go? How would she live without Adam Breedon?

The dark water caught her eyes, its glossy surface like a dark portal opening into another world. Mesmerized by dancing water which seemed to beckon to her, Giselle felt her anguish subsiding. To slide down into the darkness, to cease to be—was that the answer?

"Giselle!"

She tried to wrench free of the strong hands that had grasped her shoulders, her head swinging wildly back and forth. "No! No! Let me go!" Kicking and squirming, she clawed the ropes with frantic hands, trying desperately to launch herself into the warm flood that waited below. But even as she saw the means of her escape, it receded from her and she was hauled back from the railing she had climbed.

Unable to sleep, Laurent had been pacing behind the wheel, watching the black southeast horizon for the telltale sketchings of lightning by which he would gauge the distance of the bad weather closing in on them. At first he thought his eyes played tricks on him. Every man jack of his crew was in place and knew the need to husband his strength against the blow which would find them fighting wind and sail and sea.

But then he saw the shape of a woman's skirts and thought Renée must be as restless as he. That is what had drawn him to the forecastle companionway in time to keep a tragedy from happening before his very eyes.

"Giselle—please!" Laurent commanded as he roughly shook her.

All at once she stopped struggling and Laurent turned her to face him, a tight grasp on her shoulders. "Nothing, *ma fille*, is so bad that death is preferable."

Her face was unreadable in the dark companionway, but suddenly she collapsed against him as great sobs shook her small body. "Oh, m'sieu, I am ruined!"

Thunderstruck, Laurent nonetheless enfolded the crying girl in a protective embrace and allowed her to weep her heart out against his shirtfront.

Emboldened by unreasoned certainty that this man who shared her unique precepts of society would not spurn her, Giselle found herself confessing her sins.

"I know that it was wrong, m'sieu, when he did not mention the matter of the *plaçage*. 'He is not our kind,' I say to myself. 'He is a *Yanqui*, no gentleman that Maman will approve.' I know I should not go to him. But I couldn't keep away, m'sieu. I love him so!"

Laurent cradled her kerchiefed head with a gentle hand, but his thoughts were racing. "You speak of Captain Breedon," he said to himself, confirming his own appalling suspicions. *"Pardieu!"* Anger surged through him. So Breedon had dared to seduce the girl after being warned off.

He remembered now that Adam had often asked about Renée, and then her maid, during the weeks they were in Road Town. At the time, he had thought it surprising that the American would extend polite inquiry to a servant's health. But then, Laurent realized grimly, Giselle was no longer simply a servant in Adam's eyes.

"Hush, hush, *ma petite,*" he murmured, and produced a handkerchief. As he mopped her tears he said, "I do not approve of your behavior, but the remorse you're suffering should suffice as punishment for your foolhardy mistake. Captain Breedon's actions were not those of a Creole, but perhaps you should not have expected this." He lifted her chin with a forefinger. "I promise I will keep your secret."

The words were hardly out of his mouth before he realized how priggish and utterly useless they sounded. A flash of self-knowledge, so strong it made him light-headed, flared within him. *He would keep her secret of seduction—as he did Renée's.*

He was a fine one to stand in condemnation of what Adam had done. If society were to rule on both men's transgressions, they would find

Adam's actions less contemptible than his own. After all, society deemed Giselle to be little more than corrupt by the nature of her birth, while Renée was seen as inviolate for the same reason.

Laurent gazed down at the head bowed in abject misery before him and wondered again at the self-satisfied nature of a society so certain that it held the rules to differentiate the good from the bad. He himself held no such assuredness. If anyone were to ask him to pronounce judgment on both women, he would be bound to hold them innocent. Yet here was one of them willing—no, eager—to condemn herself into the merciless torment of a watery death.

With gentle pity he framed Giselle's face in his hands and arched her chin with his thumbs until she was forced to look up at him. She was quiet now, so still that he knew at once that she was not finished with her tale. And with a flash of insight, he knew the rest. "There is to be a baby, *non?*"

Giselle did not answer him, but it was unnecessary. She trembled under his hands like a body with the ague, and the faint whiff of her recent bout of nausea still clinging to her now took on new meaning. "Ah, Giselle," he sighed, drawing her against him once more. As he looked out over her head at the dark sea, he admitted, *"Pauvre enfant,* I do not have a glib answer for that."

He could not tell her that he would find Breedon and make him own up to his responsibilities where she was concerned. What little he

knew about Breedon convinced him that the
American did very little that was not to his
liking. But perhaps if he knew that the girl
carried his child . . .

"Come." He turned her toward her cabin. "I
want you to lie down. I will send the steward
with a drink for your stomach. It contains brandy and I want you to drink every drop. It will
help you rest. In the morning I will tell Mademoiselle Renée that the *mal de mer* plagues you.
You are to stay in bed until we reach Jamaica,
understood?"

Giselle nodded, too weak even to give words to
her tremendous thanks that he had saved her
from the sea.

Once she had shut the door behind her,
Laurent leaned against it, his arms folded
across his chest. He dreaded that Renée must
learn of Giselle's plight. Yet he knew that she
would be all sympathy for the girl. More than
likely she would say nothing, but he knew she
would wonder what his own reaction would
have been had he found himself in Adam's
situation.

"Peste!" As he stared at the cabin door just
opposite him across the middeck, his eyes darkened and his mouth tightened. Even now, after
just consoling a brokenhearted girl with a bastard growing in her belly, he could feel his
manhood swell at just the thought of Renée. She
would be asleep now, her head pressed into his
pillow, her slender flushed body veiled in the
lightest muslin. . . .

Laurent jerked his thoughts away and started across the deck, purposely cutting a wide berth around the captain's cabin. He was no better than a cur who had sniffed the scent of a bitch in heat. He wanted Renée, had wanted her for so long a time that the wanting had become a constant ache. And he could not, must not, ever touch her again.

The promise of bad weather came to fruition just before dawn. A gale blew up out of the south, pushing a dirty blue-gray curtain of wind-churned clouds before it. The first blast came suddenly, the wind a stunning blow out of a becalmed sea that knocked the *Christobel* nearly abeam, though all her sails were shortened and securely lashed.

After that, the daylight came weakly into mist-laden skies beneath sheets of rain so heavy the forecastle was obscured from the quarterdeck. Time after time the ship dipped, plunged, and reared like a leaf in a rain gutter, completely at the mercy of forces beyond the control of captain and crew.

About nine A.M. Renée managed to lurch across the cabin to unbar her door to insistent pounding.

"Compliments o' the cap'n," the cook announced as he waved a pot of coffee in one hand. Under a waterproof wrapping of sealskin he carried bread and cheese and pickled meat.

"Too dangerous to build more'n a wee fire," he announced as he set down this cold repast. "Coffee's warm enough. Cap'n says you're to drink it all. It'll be the last till the gale's blown over." With that he was gone.

After two unsuccessful tries, Renée managed to pour a half-cup, which she immediately brought back to her bunk. She had tied hand-holds made from linen strips around the over-head beam to keep from being tossed out when the ship abruptly fell into a wave's deep trough.

What seemed like days was, in reality, only a matter of hours. The gale quickly spent itself. By midmorning a hot tropical sun baked damp decks and sail. But both women kept to their own cabins because the deck was a mess of tangled ropes and torn sails.

Finally dinner arrived, a thick porridge of beans and smoked pork. "Sorry, mam'zelle," the cook said when he saw her face. "'Tis all I could manage, what with all the work and such."

Renée shrugged and helped herself to a por-tion. But though she left plenty, Laurent did not come to join her for dinner as he usually did. In fact, she had not seen him all day.

Finally, long after dark, the sounds of carpen-try and bilge pumps ceased and Renée discov-ered that she was more tired than she had been in weeks. After undressing, she turned out the lamp on her side of the canvas curtain and curled up on the bunk with Piper. She left the latch off the door as an afterthought, remember-ing that Laurent would want access to his maps when he finally gave up work for the night. No doubt they had been blown off course and he would need to chart a new course.

* * *

"In here. Yes, I said, in here. I've very little patience with having to repeat my order. *Morbleu!* I stink, horribly!"

Half-sleep, Renée rolled onto her side at the sound of Laurent's voice. Immediately the curtained-off half of the room was lit up by lantern light. Shadows of men moving in and out of the cabin were thrown against the heavy canvas, their outlines so perfectly sharp she recognized each of them. She saw two men carrying half a barrel, or was it a tub? Yawning, Renée shut her eyes. She did not care. But her nose twitched. What was that terrible smell?

Laurent did not wait for the first bucket of heated water to begin stripping off his clothes. He had spent most of the evening belowdecks making certain the water they had taken on in the bilge was pumped out. It was an unlucky misstep that had landed him headfirst in the filthy water.

Cursing in low methodical gutter French, he gathered up his discarded garments and tossed them out a stern window. Even when clean, he knew the odor would never completely leave them. After a minute's hesitation, he sent his favorite pair of boots into the same watery oblivion.

"Ah, that's fine," he said when the first steaming kettles of fresh water splashed into the tub. "Now, the other cask," he directed, and two seamen opened one of the ship's drinking-water casks and poured it in after the boiling water.

When he was satisfied with the level of water,

Laurent ordered them out and then lowered himself into the tub with a sigh of contentment.

Renée was not quite certain what awakened her the second time. The wall of canvas was lit up like a candle's globe and she noted anew that the profile of a man was projected there. Like the perfect focus of a silhouette, his every movement was clearly delineated.

Seated with his knees drawn up in the narrow confines of the wooden tub, utterly unaware that he could be seen, Laurent was washing himself.

She knew she should turn away from the sight, but she could not. The full glory of a naked man, of Laurent, was not to be denied. Dry-mouthed and trembling slightly, she rose up on an elbow and stared in helpless fascination as he lathered himself.

He ran the soap over the strong arch of his neck before he bent forward to splash water into his hair. Then with both hands he scrubbed briskly until the lather made a frothy cap on his silhouette.

As she watched the perfect lines of his masculine body rippling in the sensual grace that was his by nature, Renée became aware of a curious heat suffusing her body. In slow, leisurely circles, his hand moved the cake of soap down over the flat contours of his chest, so different from a woman's, to the sleek concave of his belly, and then back up under one arm.

Following the trail of that hand up, down, and around, the heat finally came to settle in her loins. When his hand disappeared below the rim of the tub, it was as if every stroke of that hand lathered her own body. When she heard his soft sigh of contentment, her eyes widened and her breath came in harsh quick gasps between parted lips as flickering licks of desire stroked delicately between her legs. Embarrassed, she sat up, pressing her knees together to stop the insistent throbbing.

Suddenly he stood up, and the whole of his physique was revealed in profile. The symmetrical planes of his broad chest tapered from wide shoulders to exquisitely narrow male hips above strongly formed long thighs and calves.

When he bent forward to lather a leg, she eagerly traced with her eyes the graceful arch of his spine to the tight curve of his buttocks, vividly aware of her ignited flesh and of a slow, steady melting of moist secret places within her body that clamored for the touch of his flesh.

As if his hand followed the dictates of her eyes, it slipped up the slope of his thigh to pause momentarily on the curve of a buttock. With gentle, economical strokes his hand moved forward and down to lather the wiry tangle at the base of his belly and then the masculine *pendentif* below.

She caught her lower lip between her teeth, her ragged breath coming to a full halt as the honey flowed within her. She felt faint, as if all the air had been sucked from the room. Her pulse was hammering in her ears, her lungs aching inside the captivity of her chest, and she knew she must escape, break free of the aching darkness that enveloped her.

Sound carries on the sea, better still on a night so still. The ripple of the canvas was but a whisper of sound, like the rustle of a leaf as it falls, but it was enough to make Laurent look up over his shoulder.

Renée stood before the canvas divider, the fabric puckered where her fingers clutched the curtain. The silhouette had whetted her appetite but it had not prepared her for the reality of the man before her.

Dripping wet, he glistened in the lamplight, his gypsy-dark skin like melted gold. Stretched to his full height, he could have been a Greek casting in bronze.

Oh, but he was alive, so very alive!

In breathless adoration her eyes wandered from the pulse beating strongly in the hollow of his throat, down over sculptured muscle and ridge to a tautened belly trembling lightly beneath the pressure of his breath. She felt that breath move her own chest. Then her gaze fell lower and the sight snatched an uncontrollable gasp from her.

The triumphant arc of his erection proclaimed that he sensed the source of the vibrant fire in her blood and that it was answered within his own body. He made no move to cover himself, yet he did not move to close the gap between them.

It was Renée who moved toward him, her feet scarcely treading the boards beneath her. The aching became acute as she gazed up into his black eyes edged with spiky wet lashes. Reverently she touched his face, tracing the rough stubble and dark hollows of his cheeks. Her fingers strayed to his firm lips, which parted in surprise, trembled over the softness, and after a moment drew away from his mouth to touch her own.

He did not want her, had spurned her offer of love. Why did she stand before him now, in brazen need, grateful for the fleeting moment to look upon him?

But of course she knew the answer. Now, in this place, she faced her feelings. Love, fierce, protective and finite, surged exultantly through her. It glowed from the core of her being, burning as sweetly as the fever in her body. It was not mere physical triumph that broke through her defenses. The love she bore Laurent, and could not defend against, came from a knowledge more certain than sexual affinity. An emotion more primitive and basic than those given names proclaimed him hers and she his. They were destined, whatever the future, to share that bonding.

When he first saw her standing there, Laurent did not move for fear of frightening her. He merely stared at her across the small separation between them, feeling the temptation for conquest and the contrary desire to protect her from his body's demand. But he could not stop his body's reaction to the sight of her delicate beauty thinly clothed in the sheerest of muslin. His manhood rose against his will, proud and strong and ready.

When she came to him and touched his face, he knew that she no longer feared him. In her dark melting eyes was a brilliant reflection of the desire spreading outward from his own loins. She wanted him, simply, directly, and beyond all reason. It was there, written in every line of wonder on her face. Once more she was offering him the sweetest, tenderest, most precious gift of her heart and body.

Tormented by the turbulence of his emotions, he could only stare at her. He did not deserve her, and he knew it. Because of him she had experienced shame, despair and hate. But he could not turn her away. He ached to hold her, but he knew she must make the decision. If she came to him, it would be her choice.

With infinite tenderness he raised a hand to stroke the beautiful face before him, caressing the petal softness of her cheek. "Renée?"

All at once Renée realized the enormity of her boldness and her eyes swept down before his too-hot gaze. "I . . . I . . ." She could find no words. How could she ask for, explain her need, without incurring his disdain? Humiliation swept up through her, sweeping a sting of blood into her face, and she looked away, defeated.

"Renée?" When she did not look up, Laurent cupped her face in his lean fingers and raised her chin. "Renée, *mon coeur*, do not be afraid," he whispered, and bent to catch with his lips a single tear sliding from beneath the sweep of her black lashes. "Shh. *Doucement, m'amoureuse.*"

It was the encouragement she needed. Rising on tiptoe, she grasped his shoulders and pulled him to her. The feel of water-cooled skin that soaked through her gown was welcome as she angled her head back to receive the sweet shock of his lips on hers. The kiss was so much more than the mere touch of lips; their mouths sought the mating with all the ferocity of their natures, the melding of warm wet surfaces sliding and mingling in perfect harmony.

She stroked the heavy cords of his back muscles over and over as she had seen his hands do. And then her fingers curled into the indentation of his spine, sliding down the slope to his waist. Her eager hands slid around to grasp that slim waist, the smooth satin of his damp skin sending waves of pleasure trembling up her fingers to her arms.

Emboldened beyond any confidence she had possessed before this moment, she submitted to the primitive, possessive, sexual being that lived within. She held in her small hands the strong, virile, beautifully naked body of the man she loved. She would know all of it, grasping, touching, and caressing at will, until she had learned through her fingertips all that her eyes had viewed.

Softly, tenderly, she traced the outline of each hard, forward-thrusting hip bone. And still he held her face between his hands, his mouth devouring hers in voluptuous delight. She dug her nails into the flesh above each rounded point of his pelvis while her thumbs circled repeatedly and then, together, delved into the depth of his navel. She heard his groan of pleasure and joy. The power to so move him made her reckless.

Greatly daring, she allowed her hands to follow the slope of his hips to his buttocks. The satin-smooth hillocks covered by rough-silk hair contracted at her touch, but she did not alter the path of her hands until she held each globe fully in the palm of a hand.

Finally Laurent dragged his mouth from hers. He threw back his head, and like a man too long underwater, inhaled a long deep breath, his shivering delight transmitting itself to Renée's breasts thrust gently against his chest.

"Enough, *mon coeur*, you torture me," he whispered raggedly.

But Renée, beyond control or caution, had only begun her exploration. Dissatisfied with the separation of their bodies, she stepped into the tub and once more pulled him to her with hands still grasping his buttocks.

His dark head moved down, eclipsing the light from her sight, while his hands drew her face up to guide her mouth the short distance to his parted lips. And they were lost completely to thought, feeling only the anguish of weeks shrivel under the intense heat of the fires of desire.

The meeting of their hips sent a savage heat flashing through Renée's body as, through the barrier of her sodden gown, his manhood sought the natural canal of her femininity. A fog of desire descended over her as she sought the source of that eager rampaging flesh, enclosing it in her hands. It trembled there, like a captured animal, hot and firm and pulsing with the very life of the man she loved.

Laurent lifted his lips from hers once more, but now he knew that nothing mattered any longer. All he understood was the subtle fragrance of her body's perfume, the glorious reality of her hands on his flesh. As he gazed down at her, his hunger fed on the golden pools of flame that caught and reflected his image in the depths of her eyes.

He lifted her easily, one hand going under her hips while his other hand clasped her about the shoulders as he stepped out of the tub. Wet footprints marked his passage across the floor to the bunk hidden behind the canvas curtain. With infinite tenderness he laid Renée on her back as his body followed hers into the confines of the mattress.

Slowly his hand traveled the length of tiny pearl buttons which fastened her gown. A shuddery breath made her quiver beneath him when he slid the tip of his warm tongue into the shell of her ear.

Renée felt his hand reach inside her gown, and then the gown was slipped from her shoulders and the hot moist cave of his mouth found her breast. Over and over his velvet-rough tongue laved the sensitive crest until it stood hard and high. Satisfied, he pulled it between his lips, the soft suckling sounds feeding her nearly unbearable pleasure.

When the barrier of her clothing no longer separated them, Laurent moved over her. With light quick strokes of his tongue he sought first her breasts, then her navel, circling higher and then moving lower until he heard her lose her breath in tiny gasps of surprise. The taste of her was sweet potency in his mouth, and Laurent drank of her with a thirsty urgency.

No words were spoken. Both of them were beyond the effort. Their bodies, touching, seeking, receiving, answered all needs.

The dark longing, the wild hunger that was both pain and delectation, made them arch against one another time and time again until they were both nearly weeping with need.

When Laurent positioned himself for the final caress, Renée arched her body upward to meet the muscular embrace enfolded in her flesh. His heat and scent consumed her until she belonged to him completely, the boundaries of their own existences melting into a single being. The strange wild soaring bore her into the realm of rapturous defiance where body fought body in a near-silent struggle of sensuous delight.

They were one rhythm, holding back from the final measure in mutual understanding that to play it would defeat the mounting temperature of the blood and cease that tormenting pleasure.

In the moment when desire triumphed, Laurent felt with never-before-experienced intensity the slow shooting forth in which he gave of life's force into the quivering acceptance of the woman beneath him who was life itself.

Ecstasy jagged through Renée, an explosion of sweetness too great to sustain. Her world tilted, darkened, brightened with the splintering of a thousand shards of light, and then dissolved.

The rhythm of the ship was still directed by the wake of the morning's gale, the dip and rise of the waves, deeper and shorter than normal. But Laurent noted the difference only in the far recesses of rational thought. His mind was focused no farther away than the circle of his right arm, in which Renée slept.

So this is real love, he thought in amused wonder. Dear Lord! He had nearly allowed Renée to leave the circle of his life, had deliberately tried to drive her away. Perhaps that was why. Perhaps some warning instinct had cautioned him against submitting to her, because he knew that the ties to this woman would be far deeper and more dangerous than any game of love he had ever known before.

Chapter Twelve

WHEN RENÉE HAD LICKED THE LAST OF THE honey-spread biscuit from her fingers, she leaned forward, propping her elbows on the table, and let her chin drop into her cupped hands. Her ebony hair had been braided and pinned up to prevent tangling, but inky wisps of curls had escaped, forming natural ringlets at her nape, ears and brow.

To the casual observer she appeared the model of youthful innocence. Not one of the *Christobel*'s crew suspected the thoughts stirring inside her lovely head. None of those rough crude men thought her capable of lusty thoughts. Yet at this very moment she was contemplating the exact shape and color of the birthmark on the cheek above their captain's left thigh. No one suspected that the calm, courteous lady who chatted briefly with the captain during her daily stroll about the ship's deck was the same lady who entertained their captain in her bunk in the dead of night.

It had become a game between them, their pretense at politeness before the eyes of the crew, when each longed for nothing so much as nightfall, when, for a few short hours, they lay entwined in one another's arms. It was wicked and wanton . . . and totally wonderful.

Perhaps, Renée thought with her new insight gleaned from the last few days, that was the reason people objected so to lovers. It was jealousy that made people proclaim such bliss was wicked.

Renée stirred, her gaze coming to focus on the tabletop before her. Taking advantage of his mistress's wandering thoughts, Piper had climbed up and was availing himself of the last drops of sweet black coffee in her cup. With infinite delicacy he dipped a paw into the cup to capture a drop and then raised it to his mouth, where he licked it dry with quick swipes of his rough pink tongue.

Smiling, Renée nudged a pared rind from her breakfast cheese toward the cat. Piper touched it with his damp paw, sniffed it and then dragged it from her plate.

"You've a curious appetite," his mistress mused as she watched him masticate the tough rubbery substance. "Cheese and coffee for breakfast." She tickled him under the chin and Piper purred in appropriate appreciation.

"Appreciation." Renée rolled the word off her tongue as she turned to look out her open cabin door. Across the middeck Giselle's cabin door was visible. "Some are certainly more appreciative than others, Piper."

Of course she knew that Giselle was unhappy. It was to be expected. The poor girl had never been any farther from home in New Orleans than Bonne Vie. Traveling to England must seem like traveling to one of the cold bright stars in the night sky. But to think that Giselle would go behind her back to plead her case to Laurent, that she would plead so convincingly that Laurent would side with the girl over her own wishes . . . Giselle wished to return to New Orleans, and Laurent was in complete agreement.

"Ma foi! I won't have it." Renée stood up abruptly.

When Laurent had broached the subject to her the night before, she had been too stunned to think of any objections besides the most obvious and, unhappily, selfish ones. How would she manage the voyage without a maid? Laurent had laughed out loud before reminding her that she had managed one Atlantic voyage without a maid, she would survive another.

Renée cringed, remembering how silly and small that laughter had made her feel. But Laurent did not understand. She and Giselle were much more than mistress and maid, they were friends.

Renée glanced once more at the opposite doorway. Giselle suffered so severely from the *mal de mer,* they had seen little of each other since leaving Tortola.

Guilt pricked her. In part she was glad Giselle

was ill and confined to bed. It meant that she did not have to explain her own bemused state or wonder if some small forgotten detail would give away her own guilty secret as Laurent's lover. But perhaps Giselle felt unwanted and neglected and that was why she wanted to go home.

"*Oui!* That must be it," Renée exclaimed as she scooped Piper up from the table. "I have been a very neglectful friend. But we will amend that slight right this moment. Come, Piper, we are going visiting!"

The first thing Renée noticed when she entered the cabin after receiving Giselle's weak greeting was that it was very dark. Giselle lay on her bunk, her head propped up by a single pillow. With her *tignon* removed, her hair rippled out over the bedding in long thick waves. Soft dark eyes the color of plums dominated her face, pinched with illness. She looked thinner than Renée remembered, and when she reached for the younger girl's hand, she became truly alarmed.

"Giselle, you're so thin! Have you eaten nothing?" Renée asked as she bent over the girl.

"The steward . . . he brings me soup," Giselle murmured, her voice hushed with the effort of speech.

"But you have not been eating it," Renée finished, her brows gathering in a frown. "Silly girl, how do you expect to get well? I will have more soup brought immediately, and I insist that you eat a little of it."

"No." Giselle's hand clutched Renée's with

surprising strength. "Later," she added with a weak smile. "I am sorry . . . so much trouble for you. I am sorry."

The apology strengthened Renée's sense of guilt. "Oh, why didn't you say something, send word that you were so ill? I would have come to you, sat with you. I did not realize . . . Oh! I feel so thoughtless and selfish!"

Giselle's brows rose in amusement and immediately Renée blushed. "You're right, I'm still thinking about myself. You must get well so that we can plan what we shall do first when we get to England."

Giselle's smile disappeared. "No, mademoiselle. I cannot go to England."

Renée decided not to answer that statement directly. After all, Giselle was ill from sailing, and the thought of weeks more at sea must seem overwhelming. She looked around, spied the basin, and went to fetch a damp cloth.

As she mopped Giselle's brow she said, "You're just afraid because you don't feel well. You will become accustomed to the roll of the ship very soon, and then all will be well."

There was only one way to deal with a sick person, and that was firmly. "You don't think so now, but you will see, London will be a place of wonder and delight for you. We will find a young man for you, a handsome suitor—wouldn't you like that?"

To Renée's utter surprise, Giselle began to cry. It was not loud sobbing, just a trickle of silent tears from the corners of her eyes.

Appalled that she had made her feel worse,

Renée asked, "What did I say? I'm truly sorry, Giselle. Please, please don't cry. What can I do to help?"

"Nothing. You can do nothing," Giselle answered in a miserable voice. "I have been so wicked, and now I must be punished."

"Of course you're not wicked," Renée maintained. "You have the *mal de mer*. That's not a punishment." Trying for a more cheerful tone, she added, "You should have seen me on my first voyage. I was positively green for three days."

Giselle turned her face toward the wall and said nothing.

"Are you angry with me because I haven't been to see you?" Renée asked. "Please try to understand. . . ." She leaned closer to the girl, her voice dropping in volume. "I have something to tell you. Giselle? It's a secret only you will share with me. You have known that I have been in love with Monsieur Lavasseur for months. Well, I lied to you and Madame Lavasseur and everyone at Bonne Vie when I said that I refused Laurent's proposal of marriage. It was he who refused to marry me, Giselle."

Giselle's head swiveled back toward her and Renée smiled. "It's true. He said he did not wish to marry me or anyone. He made up the lie to save my pride. At first I hated him, I wanted only revenge for having been spurned, but I lied to myself. I knew that the moment we met again in New Orleans. I love him so, Giselle, I could not bear to lose him."

Renée glanced down at her hands, her boldness finally making her shy. "I would do anything to win him, Giselle. Anything! And I have." Her voice fell to a breathless whisper. "I let him make love to me."

"No! No!" Giselle bolted upright. "You mustn't do that, it's wicked! Wicked! God will punish you, like me! He will!" Giselle shook her head, her hair flying about her shoulders like a dark nimbus. "You don't know what you do, mademoiselle. You'll win no man that way. A man will take whatever a woman offers him and then he will go away, like that!" She snapped her fingers, her dark eyes wide with pain and sorrow. "If the man does not want you, you've got nothing left when he's gone. Nothing but trouble!"

Giselle lay back panting against her pillows and began to cry again. "I must go home, I must! And you . . ." Her eyes opened, fixing Renée with a stare. "You stay away from the man who won't marry you. Fine ladies make babies just like bad women. Then what will you do?"

Her words struck Renée with a force that silenced any reply. With both hands she hesitantly touched her flat stomach beneath her gown. No one had ever explained to her exactly how and when a woman came to be with child. Certainly she knew it came from lying with a man, but did that happen each time? Surely not. She remembered tantalizing glimpses of women of the streets who traded their favors for cash. They did not all have round bellies.

Renée turned troubled eyes on Giselle. How

did she know what happened between a man and a woman? Had Giselle fallen in love with someone?

Renée moved back to the bedside and touched Giselle's hand with a finger. "Is there someone you love?" she asked gently. "Did you think I would stand in your way? Oh, Giselle, I would not. I know what it is to love."

Giselle turned eyes full of pity on the lady standing over her. "Nothing you do can make a man love you, mademoiselle. Love comes not for the asking. It comes when you would tear your eyes out not to see it. If it is not returned, you better run away, mademoiselle. He will leave you, even when your heart is bleeding with love for him."

Renée did not answer this. She could not. Instead she emptied the basin and then began cleaning Giselle's cabin. She hardly noticed the time, and the work was welcome. The physical toil of washing sheets and gowns was not unknown to her. While hiding from the French revolutionary committee in a country village before they were smuggled out of France, she and her sister had washed clothes for a living.

Only once, when Laurent paused beside her as she bent over a wooden tub of soapy suds in the gangway of the forecastle, did she feel tears sting her eyes. Yet she did not even look up. For suddenly she was very much afraid that their idyll was over. After a moment, without so much as a word, he passed on.

It had taken Giselle's bitter regretful words to raise the blinders of love which she had worn.

Never once had Laurent spoken of his love for her. It had not seemed necessary. But now she wondered if she had been wrong. If it were really love, freely given, would it be afraid to speak its name?

"Bull Bay, off the starboard bow, cap'n," the first mate called. "One ship sighted."

Laurent picked up his telescope and after a quick look collapsed the instrument and returned it to his pocket. It was the *Pelican*. Breedon was waiting for him, just as he had promised, though the *Christobel* was three days late for the rendezvous.

The island of Jamaica had been in view most of the day, its lush tropical green peaks staying off the starboard as they coasted down the eastern point of the island and swung under the southern edge, to come to port just fifteen miles east of the entry to Kingston harbor. Now the scent of jasmine and warmed earth, of verdant forest and honeysuckle rising from the land, eclipsed the sea smells on the breeze.

Laurent inhaled the sweet perfume of the flora. It reminded him of the faint odor of gardenias that clung to Renée when she lay in his arms, the thin sheen of her perspiration her only cover.

Laurent cast a speculative eye at the forward cabin, where Renée was helping Giselle pack for her transfer to Kingston.

"Shorten sail!" he cried as he turned an eye toward his canvas. There would be time enough for personal reflections. Now he had much more

immediate business before him—and not all of it
to his liking.

"Breedon, *mon ami,* you are about to have a
little of your private affairs given a public air-
ing."

It was still stiflingly hot when the *Christobel*
lowered a boat into the late-evening turquoise-
and-purple-marbled waters of the bay. Under
sea anchor the ship quietly rode the swells, her
masts bare of sail.

As he sat in the stern of the boat being rowed
across the short distance to the *Pelican*'s gangway, Laurent ran a hand through the crop of
damp curls at his brow. He was not surprised
that he was sweating—and it had nothing to do
with the heat pervading the evening.

Laurent's reluctance was not abated one jot by
the sight of Breedon. The only sign of life in the
American's ashen face was the brilliant blaze of
blue within the bruised sockets.

"If it ain't my favorite froggie. Welcome
aboard!" Adam greeted broadly as he stepped
forward and clasped Laurent in a brief bearlike
hug. When he moved back, a slack smile distorted his agreeable features to the point of ugli-
ness.

Laurent's mouth tightened. No detective work
was required to discern the reason for this deter-
ioration. When he glanced at the ship steward,
the older man's gaze fell in embarrassed confir-
mation before his black stare.

Adam saw the look pass between the two men
and his amiability faded. "Hell take you both!"
He swung around, the movement more forceful

than necessary, and just in time Laurent reached out to grasp him by the shoulder. An instant later, that steadying grip changed into a familiar embrace as he patted the American on the back.

"Mon ami, I believe you are more eager than I to make mischief for the British," Laurent said when Adam turned an irritated look on him. "After you, *capitaine,*" he added as he gently urged the man toward his cabin.

The cabin was littered with the squalor of a man who had been senseless for most of the voyage from Tortola. Adam paused just inside the doorway, as if seeing the scattering of clothing, empty wine bottles, and putrefying remains of several uneaten meals for the first time.

Adam seemed to consider the contents of the room, and then, swearing under his breath, he lurched across the space to collapse in the chair behind his desk. He grinned at his companion. "I was all right till you didn't come. Three days is a long time for a man. Long enough for him to—"

"To commit suicide?" Laurent suggested. "I ask myself why, and I can find no reason, Breedon."

Adam made a disparaging gesture. "Leave it. It's of no moment."

"You look horrible," Laurent continued conversationally.

"Thanks," Adam said sourly. "Didn't know I had to gussy up for you, Lavasscur. Now, were you to bring that little mam'zelle of yours over, I'd see to myself." He leered obscenely. "Don't suppose you've crawled under that gal's petti-coats yet? No, I suppose you haven't. Too bad. She's all sweetness and light on the surface, but there's something about those eyes of hers. Do you know, she looks at a man like she's seeing him mother-naked, and liking the sight."

"You stink, too," Laurent offered quietly.

"That's your trouble," Adam replied without anger.

"My trouble?"

"You keep making the same mistake. You think me basically a decent man, a man like yourself." Adam threw back his head and roared with laughter. "By God! You let that little girl get away with turning you down. First thing I'd have done was tip her on her pert behind and give her happy acquaintance of what my breeches cover.

"That's your trouble: you've a soft heart. Well, I won't soothe your pride by apologizing. Bad luck to you!" Adam laughed again. After a moment he mastered himself, but a stream of vile curses poured from him and he sat forward and dropped his head into his hands.

Laurent accepted his taunts without so much as the twitch of a finger. "You're killing yourself, Breedon. I don't know the cause, but I doubt it would convince me of the necessity." He swept a hand toward the empty glasses on the desk, distaste in his expression as he eyed the telltale reddish-white residue of laudanum mixed with wine. "You must put this behind you."

A ghost of Adam's eager grin curved his pale

lips. "You, mighty Creole gentleman, what do you know of opium-eaters?"

Laurent did not return the smile. "Few men deserve so wretched an end."

Adam snorted. "Mistake, Lavasseur."

Laurent smiled. "I have my share of guilty secrets."

"There's a price on my head," Adam challenged.

Laurent nodded. "There would be on mine if the British learned that I'm one of the smugglers they seek."

Adam turned his head to look at Laurent, a strange expression in his hot blue eyes. "Sometimes we get our wishes," he said softly. Then, louder: "I'm wanted for murder."

"I, too, know what it is to kill a man," Laurent replied in a more sober tone.

Adam began to grin in earnest, as if he were the hoarder of secret amusement. "The charge is for the death of a woman."

Laurent's answer came more slowly this time. "You are innocent?"

Fresh laughter burst from Adam, so high as to be near hysteria. When his gaze came back to rest on Laurent, it was white-hot with defiance. "She was my sister. I'd bedded her."

This time Laurent offered no encouragement. Like a boil that had been squeezed too hard, the first green bilious pus was erupting with Adam's confession, and he longed to close the breach but knew it was now too late.

"What?" No more companionable comparisons, *mon ami?*" Adam sneered. "But now that you've forced that much of the story from me, surely you must long to know the rest."

He leaned forward, his elbows braced on the desktop. "The facts are these: Aurelia and her bastard son were found drowned off the docks of Charleston, South Carolina, back in eighty-seven. Yes, I see that you are able to read between the lines. Her husband was quick to do the same."

Adam shut his eyes, a spasm distorting his features. His eyes flew open. "I was to marry and didn't want Aurelia's obsessive jealousy to ruin things for me."

Laurent rose to his feet. "Forgive me for doubting you, Breedon."

Adam cackled in delight. "So you're a squeamish man, for all you fancy yourself a devil. Take your fancy airs, and you know what you can do with them!"

Laurent turned and with quick strides reached the doorway before Adam's call arrested him.

"Wait, Creole! What of your need of me? What of your seamen in Kingston?" When Laurent turned, Adam rose, grinning like a fiend from hell. "You still have need of me, revolting though I am. Are you so revolted that you will let six good men—men who trusted you—hang?"

"You swine!" Laurent spat softly.

"Aye. Maybe. But you've a use for a swine, a greased pig with a ship as fast as lightning, don't you, Frenchy? Will you lie down with swine that you may realize your goal?"

"I'll find another way," Laurent answered.

"And risk the neck of that sweet lily-white purity you're aching to soil?" Adam taunted. "I don't think you will, Lavasseur. She owes title to the *Christobel*. If you're caught or followed back to that ship, she'll hang beside you, and you know it."

Laurent leveled a look of disgust at Breedon. "When this matter in Kingston is done, we will finish this discussion—that I promise you."

"I wait upon your convenience," Adam returned formally.

"I will return at daybreak with those few men I trust. You will sober up before then," Laurent demanded coldly.

Adam nodded. "Knew you'd get over your like of me, Lavasseur. Most men do."

Laurent paused, considering. "Why did you tell me?"

Adam grimaced. "Giving the devil his due. Infamy is a powerful weapon, Frenchy. Most men dare not what they fear. Because your friendship has given me more unease than any I've known these last ten years, I'll tell you another secret."

His gaze locked with Laurent's. "I have no desire for death. I can and will do anything necessary to save my miserable hide. It is only when events make me wish for something else other than my lot that I seek the oblivion of opium dreams."

"This wishing, does it have a name? Is it Giselle?"

For the first time Adam seemed incapable of

sustaining his reckless swagger. He sat down heavily. "Dammit! You go too far even for me!"

Laurent crushed a spark of pity for the miserable wretch before him. "I came to plead a cause, but now I think not. You'll never lay your hands on the girl again. She's under my protection now."

"Protection." Adam repeated the word dully. "So you have found a scratch for your itch after all." He looked away. "I should kill you for that admission, but there are other ways, other ways."

Laurent rode back to the *Christobel* in silence. After a few brusque orders, he went into his cabin and poured himself three inches of brandy, which he finished in a single gulp. The second serving disappeared more slowly but as completely.

The rending of canvas startled Renée from sleep, but her scream of fright broke off in mid-cry as Laurent's tall form revealed itself behind the fallen curtain. He grasped the last of the fabric wall and tore it free, sending the wooden pegs holding it flying in all directions.

"Now, then, mademoiselle," he roared at the top of his voice. "We will have no more of this pretense. You are my mistress. When I return from Kingston I will take you as my wife. Until then, you will inhabit your bed alone!"

With that he was gone, leaving Renée to stare slack-jawed after him.

The bay waters lapped softly against the *Pelican*'s hull just after midnight. The soughing of the breeze in the lines, the rhythmic creak of stressed wood, the strum of a battered guitar in the distant forecastle—none of this brought Adam peace.

"Sleeping rough." The term applied to his present state between consciousness and convulsion in the aftermath of his most recent binge. He lay sprawled on his bunk while the icy sweat squeezed in fat droplets from the pores of his skin. The gentle roll of the sea echoed as great heavings within him, and his stomach, perched once too often upon the crest, emptied itself involuntarily. Weakly he turned his head to one side to keep from choking on his sickness.

"Dear God, help me!"

It was a whimper so like a child's that he was certain it had come from some other source than his own throat. But the words repeated over and over in his ears like the mournful sighing of the wind.

He had thought he could forget. He thought that opium would dim the memory of loving her. He had hoped the rough mating that was meant to exorcise his demons would leave him lighter, freer than at any time in the past ten years. But he was wrong.

Giselle loved him. That was what he could not understand. What was it she thought she saw in him?

The search for the answer had drawn him back to her time and time again. And still he was in ignorance of the reason for her love. In the end, it had driven him away from her. He could not bear to watch that love wither and die and he knew it would. He would have cut out his heart and offered it to her if he thought that would prevent her from ever learning of his past.

And so, in a way, he had done that. He had walked away. She would have come with him, but she could not ask him to take her. She had been raised to serve and not question, just as she had served first his lust and then his love for her. Selfishness was beyond her. And so it had been easy to leave her.

Light and shadow danced off the surface of the water, throwing writhing shadows upon the bulkheads of the cabin. In those shadows he thought he saw Lavasseur's shape. Giselle was under the Frenchman's protection now. She would serve his carnal needs. The perfect Creole gentleman—that would be Lavasseur's fascination for the girl. She was a product of Louisiana, taught to prize the attentions of a man of Lavasseur's caliber above all else.

Shadows danced and melted until two figures, dredged up from his feverish jealousy, seemed to embrace. It was too much. Adam levered himself into a sitting position, vile oaths spewing from his lips as imagination fed obscene designs into guileless shadow play.

Tears dimmed the shadows and blurred the wild gaze of a man caught in a living nightmare.

"Damn you, Lavasseur! She's mine! Mine! For that I'll see you fed to the sharks! You were a fool to trust me! They're circling in Kingston bay and you don't even know it. But I know their shape and place. I'll point out the bait! You!"

Ben came running at the sound of his captain's bellow. When he left the cabin a few minutes later, he was the bearer of a note to be delivered to the British military in Kingston.

"Just our luck," he groused to his companion as they rowed ashore. "The cap'n sleeps like a baby while we pay a midnight visit to the limeys."

Giselle sat in the middle of the little boat, afraid that at any minute a hail from Capitaine Lavasseur would call them back.

The sight of the *Pelican* off the starboard bow at sunset had seemed a mirage. But it was real, and she knew that she must see Captain Breedon once more. Miraculously, Capitaine Lavasseur had paved the way, saying that together with him and a few of his crew she would be transferred to the *Yanqui*'s ship for the trip back to New Orleans. There was a smile in his voice that did not reach his eyes as he warned her not to hope for too much.

It was useless advice. She hoped for everything.

That hope had been shattered when Lavasseur returned from the *Pelican*, the anger in his voice sending his men scurrying in all directions. He had come to her and said that she would not be going with the *Pelican* after all, that he would find another ship for her.

Only when Lavasseur succumbed to sleep did she dare to put into action her plan to disobey him. To her relief and delight she discovered that, unlike his new orders to her, Capitaine

Lavasseur had not bothered to countermand his orders to his boatswain. That is why she was now headed across the glassy surface that separated the ships, her one small bag tucked safely at her feet.

"Your capitaine?" Giselle questioned of the seaman who helped her board the *Pelican*.

The man shot an unhappy glance over his shoulder. "He be sleepin', mam'zelle. Best not wake him afore mornin'."

Had the man said his captain was entertaining two dozen harem girls, she would have gone ahead, so great was her desire to see and touch the man she loved.

The stench that invaded her senses made her momentarily pause at the doorway. And then she realized that the illness must be Adam's, and she raced across the small space of boards to his bunk.

He lay in the dark. She heard him groan, and heedless of her gown, she knelt beside the bunk and gathered him close, pressing his sweaty cheek to her breast as she crooned soothing words of comfort.

The feel of arms about him was so unexpected that Adam did not at first credit it with reality. The iridescent bubble of his opium dreams had long since deserted him, but perhaps some tranquilizing vestige had reached back to claim him. Of course it was his favorite dream: Giselle's arms, her soft dulcet tones, her sweet yielding body easing the burden of his tormented mind.

"*Merci, ma chère,*" he murmured, afraid his voice would frighten away his exquisite dream.

And then he began to cry.

Giselle clutched him tighter, his pain racking her small form. How could this be? What could so move her Golden Barbarian that he sobbed like a baby?

"Shhh, my capitaine. The others will hear you," she whispered, and pressed her cheek to his damp hair. "Giselle will hold you until you are well, I swear it."

Through the blur of her own tears she looked down into the shadowed face cupped in her small hand and smiled. "See? I am here, *mon capitaine*. You are sick, but I can make you well. I *will* make you well."

"Don't leave me," he begged in a rough voice. "Don't leave me. Please!"

Only when he was asleep did she slide him carefully back onto his bed.

For more than an hour she worked, gently bathing him as he lay inert under her ministrations. She felt no shame at stripping him. She offered him small sips of water mixed with brandy when once he stirred to wakefulness, supporting his naked body against her while he gulped thirstily. It was as if she had crossed a bridge of no return in boarding the *Pelican*. She was the captain's woman now—for a night, for a week, or forever: that would be determined by him when he was well again.

Adam awakened to the unwelcome state of consciousness reluctantly. His limbs were weighed by fatigue, his head grown twice its normal size. Slowly he tested the limits of his ability and found that turning his head from side to side was sufficient effort for the moment. Finally he became aware that his eyes had opened, that he stared at the paneling above his head. He heard the first bell of the first . . . No, that must be the *second* watch. It was still night.

The shadow that passed over him did not surprise him. There were no surprises left in him after the journey he had undertaken this night. Yet there was a persistent memory of comfort, of a blessed ease he had never before experienced. It came back to him not as pictures or words but as all-pervading sensation.

"Monsieur, you are awake?"

That voice! Adam shut his eyes briefly, as if by cutting off all evidence of reality he could hold the ecstasy of the voice within him longer. But reality was claiming him, dragging him back by the pressure of a hand on his arm.

"Capitaine, please, are you better?"

Adam's lids flew open. "Giselle?"

He did not know how she came to be standing over him, her lovely face etched in worry and a compassion too beautiful for him to endure. All he knew was that he must blot out that raw tenderness in her dark eyes, assure her and himself that the miracle of her presence was what he needed. With greater effort than he had thought himself capable of, he lifted a hand and reached out for her.

With a cry of thankfulness, Giselle grasped his hand in both of hers and brought it to her lips for a kiss as she knelt beside him.

The feel of her warm tears upon his hand

surprised and shamed him. "Don't cry," he said with a tiny shake of his head. "I warned you once that I was not worth your tears."

With belated embarrassment Adam remembered his own foul state. But even as he turned away from her, he realized that his breath was not displeasing, that he was naked under the sheet, that his bed was dry, the sheets harboring only the aromas of sunshine and sea. Someone had bathed him.

His gaze came back to Giselle with such a shock of gratefulness that her hands flew up to frame his face. "Monsieur, are you going to be ill again?"

Adam smiled. "You are so beautiful, too beautiful and too good. You don't see the irony of our situation, do you? We are the damned and the damnable. This time I won't let you go. I'm not capable of a second act of generosity. No, you'll stay, and be damned with me. Forever!"

Giselle melted against him without hesitation, her fingers working the buttons of her gown, which were too difficult for his trembling hands to master. When she shrugged free of the last of her garments, his head moved down to the natural valley of her soft breasts.

Slowly Adam stroked the woman beside him, enchanted by the feel of smooth feminine skin beneath his fingertips. She was softer than anything he had ever known. The knowledge scored the agony of desire through him, but his body did not respond.

He trembled slightly as his full consciousness came to center on that unresponsive part of him.

He wanted her. Dear God! He had never been so glad that he was a man as when he held her lovely body to his. But now, suddenly, loomed the frightening possibility that he could not perform.

Adam's mouth tightened. Dammit! He had learned long before most boys his age the uses of his eager flesh in lusty coupling. He had suffered worse repercussions from opium and still found himself eager for the woman who shared his bed when he awakened from the stupor. What was wrong?

With a groan, he rolled away from her and onto his back.

"What is wrong, capitaine?"

Adam felt Giselle's hand on his chest, and his muscles flexed when that hand slid down the indentation of his abdomen and then below. In shame coupled with a strange sense of amusement he acknowledged that in his few meetings with her, he had stripped her of any pretense at maidenly modesty. Now her small warm hand gently explored him, testing and weighing, lifting and encompassing him in an attempt to assess his desire.

He stirred in her hand, the trembling moving lower to settle there as her hand remained, but after a moment the response failed and her tentative caresses ceased.

Giselle removed her hand, her head lowering so that she could no longer see his face. "You are angry with me?" she asked. "You do not want me any longer?"

Adam shut his eyes, his whole body tensing.

"You should not have come," he managed through tight lips. "I can do nothing for you."

"Why?"

The effort at laughter hurt his ribs. "Why? Why?" he mimicked. "Because, sweet silly mongrel child, I am a base, bastard-born defiler of women. There! Do you cringe? Well you should. Ask your precious Capitaine Lavasseur to tell you of my ways with women. It will give him great satisfaction to turn you against me."

"Je t'aime, mon capitaine," she whispered before burying her face in the juncture of his neck and shoulder.

"Don't talk of love!" he said coldly, but he did not move away from her. "You know nothing of love. You only know a little of the habits of lusting men and women. That is my legacy to you. Nothing else! God's death! I should loathe you for wanting me. You do not know the man you profess to love. But I can cure you of what ails you, Giselle. That I can."

He took a deep breath, uncertain of where to begin after ten years of steady attempts to put the matter from his mind. Where did it begin? Was it when he first saw Aurelia?

"Yes, that's when," he mused aloud. "My father was a great man, or so I've been told. My mother must have thought so, she gave herself to him often enough, in the cellar, on the back stairs, in the pantry. My father never tired of telling me how eager she was for his lustful embraces."

Adam turned to smile tenderly into Giselle's bewildered eyes. "Not all slaves are African, *ma chère*. Some of them come from the streets of London Town. Such a one was my mother. A convict, she was transported to the Carolinas to serve as a bondswoman. My father bought her contract, and all her services. The news of my imminent birth greatly inconvenienced him. He sent my mother away. He was married, of course—all great lechers are. There was his child, a daughter, to be considered, but I cannot fault him. He did not completely turn his back on my mother. She came to bed with a boy child—the one thing my father could not get from his legally wed wife.

"Not to draw out a maudlin tale, he kept us twelve years on charity. A year after Mother died in her third failed attempt to bear him another child, he came for me. His wife, too, had died. He said we'd be a family—he, myself, and dear sweet half-sister Aurelia."

Adam closed his eyes to better frame the memory. "She was the most beautiful thing I had ever seen, hair the color of summer sunshine and periwinkle eyes. She was sixteen to my fourteen years—but she was old beyond the reckoning of time. Brought up a bondswoman's bastard, I had no manners or education, but I had a broad back and a workman's physique. How she must have lusted after me even then."

Giselle gave a sharp intake of breath and Adam realized that he had been speaking in French. "What, are you afraid of my tale? You've not heard the half of it. For the next two years my father cajoled, threatened, and beat a little

242

learning into me. You have him to thank for my French. Aurelia, too, took a part in my lessons.

"I won't excuse myself by saying that I did not understand the implications of her hugs and pats and kisses," he went on. "Yet I was the rudest of lads, untried in the ways a minx has to inflame a man. She offered me incentives for my lessons, a kiss for every correct verb, a hug for every new mastered page. The sweet sisterly pecks quickly became the press of full lips on lips as we studied Latin and French behind closed library doors. But, I must confess, I was not prepared for her forays into my bedchamber."

"No, monsieur, I don't—!"

Adam took Giselle's hands from her ears and ruthlessly forced them to her sides. "Oh, but you must hear it all. Then you may tell me if you still love the thing I am.

"She came to me first in the spring, and I, green fool, huddled under the covers like the frightened virgin I was. You will be amused to know that she came twice more before I could be induced to cast away my nightshirt," he continued in a flat, emotionless voice.

"After that we studied the human form all through the summer. Her knowledge far surpassed that of most ladies I've known since. It did not occur to me to wonder at her boldness or whence came her knowledge. It was enough that I was a walking torture chamber of guilt and randiness those months. The mere sight of her on the lawn below me, the curve of her chin, the gentle swish of her hips—Lord!—I'll burn in hell for that summer.

"I died a thousand deaths when Father sent her to the English court—the Breedons were royalists. Twenty-two long months she was gone. When she returned there was a pale male specimen attached to her arm, her husband-to-be.

She came to me only once after that, and it ended in near-disaster. Perhaps if we'd been caught dead to rights, she might be alive now. Father found us embracing, no more than a lascivious kiss behind the library door. He sent Aurelia to her room in tears. Me, he beat nearly senseless. I let him. To raise my hand against him would have been to admit I felt no guilt. I was sent west while Aurelia was safely married to her English gentleman.

"I did not come back for three years. When I returned, I brought Amy. Aurelia detested my poor Amy on sight. Amy was a little brown wren, as unlike the shining Aurelia as I to King George. Aurelia and her husband constantly baited the poor girl, who had no learning and little sense. But I was determined to have her as my wife. That's why Aurelia came once more to my bed. To show me what I could not live without, she said.

"To my everlasting sorrow, I did not let marriage vows or blood ties deter me, nor even the little love I bore Amy."

"Your sister had bewitched you!" Giselle whispered, her voice coarse with horror.

Adam smiled and stroked the dark head near

his. "Would you defend me even now? You're as simple a soul as Amy, I fear. But let me finish. I did not let love for Amy or moral grounds halt me. Something quite basic and human and self-ish stopped me.

"I had been in the wilds of Tennessee those years away and found that there were many women willing to cuddle with a man of my form and feature. I had no knowledge of virgins when I left, but I came back a learned man. It was that experience which taught me that I had sinned with my sweet angelic Aurelia, but I had not robbed her of her virtue. Aurelia, bless her for the whore she was, had seduced me! That's what stopped me that night, the overwhelming jealous realization that I had not been Aurelia's first lover."

"You loved her."

Adam choked on mirthless laughter. "You must promise to die with me, so as to plead my case with Saint Peter, *ma chère*."

"You loved her so much and she betrayed you," Giselle said softly.

Adam did not listen. His thoughts were trail-ing back over ten years' time to that fateful confrontation. "I remember Aurelia's laughter. She called me a fool. She said she had wanted me as she had wanted no other, before or since.

"Before or since: how calmly she said it. There had been others, before and after me—she ad-mitted it freely. I tried to throw her out. She was like a wild thing, scratching and ripping my face with her long nails. She said that I belonged to her, that she would see to it Amy would not have me, that she had a hold on me that even I did not know of."

Adam fell silent a moment, his breathing deepening. "I've thought about it often. Was it only jealousy that stopped me? I don't know. I wanted her. I could feel the wanting. But I left her hurling curses after me. I dressed and climbed out the window, never looking back. There was a desperation about her that I could not fathom, but I knew I must get away.

"As I look back on it, I believe leaving was my mistake. Aurelia's husband must have come looking for her, or heard her cries. They told me she was ranting when he found her still naked in my bed. They fought, and Aurelia revealed to him our secret lives that summer long ago. She told him of the time, three years earlier, when our father found us. She lied and told him that her three-year-old son, Jason, was my bastard."

"Noooo!"

Adam continued without pause. "After I left Aurelia, I went to the docks, a local pub where I often drank. No one mentioned my clawed face. And then Aurelia arrived, her fair hair streaming down her back, her eyes wide with the madness that drove her, and Jason in her arms. It's a wonder she found me, but then, she knew me. We left together, it's said. I only remember the streaming hair, the once-soft mouth now hard at the edges, the wail of a frightened child.

"She broke her neck in a fall. I don't remember how it was accomplished. Some say I pushed her, babe in arms, from the dock. I don't remember whether I ran to her, or away from her. I was caught and found guilty. But even after the trial there were those who had their doubts. They aided my escape. I've wondered how many of them were her lovers. I made it to freedom. But poor Aurelia never made it. I killed her."

"No! No . . . you did not! She was evil! A witch! She wanted your soul!" Giselle cried.

Adam gathered the trembling girl to him and rocked her body slowly from side to side. "Ah, Giselle, you cannot be broken of this fascination you have for me. I think I knew that—it's why I told you my tale when I've never before admitted the whole to another living soul. Will you stay, after everything?"

Giselle snuggled against him. "Where would I go?" she questioned, mostly to herself.

"You may go to hell with me." When she raised her head to look down into his face, she saw that he was smiling. "You've heard my confession and absolved my guilt. Will you still love me, Giselle?"

A smile wreathed Giselle's face, even though her lower lip trembled. "Yes, yes, oh, yes!" she cried as she flung herself against him.

Chapter Thirteen

THE MORNING AFTER A SLEEPLESS NIGHT IS UN-welcome at any time. The manner in which it came to Renée was more the unwelcome for its abruptness.

"*Nom de Dieu!* Do your wits go wanting? *Merde!* There'll be skin off your back to pay for this!"

Renée sat up in bed as Laurent's voice thundered from the quarterdeck above. It was barely dawn. The pink haze of daybreak filtered thin light through the stern windows. She threw a sacque over her gown as the shuffle of footsteps sounded on the ladderway and flung open her door just as Laurent stalked past.

"Capitaine Lavas..." She stopped as his angry gaze swung around at her first syllable. His gaze swept over her, noting in disapproval the cascading of her hair over her shoulders. Finally his look zeroed in on the hand clutching her dressing gown. Blushing, she asked, "What is the matter, capitaine?"

"It is none of your business, mademoiselle," Laurent said coldly. "Kindly close and bolt your door. Better yet, go to your bed and cover your ears with your pillow. There is unpleasant business afoot."

"But I'm telling you, cap'n, you didn't rescind your order. How was I to know the girl lied?"

Renée looked from Laurent to the boatswain, who stood pinioned between two seamen. "Something has happened to Giselle? Tell me! What's wrong?" She glanced at the cabin Giselle had occupied and started across the deck.

Laurent halted her with the words "She's not there."

Renée turned to him with a questioning look and he answered, "She boarded the *Pelican* during the night. Against my orders," he added with a damning glance at his boatswain.

"But why should she . . . ?" All at once the answer came, complete in every detail. The realization was so strong that she would only wonder that she had not realized it before. Giselle's lover was the *Yanqui* captain.

The realization must have shown in her face, because Laurent nodded grimly. "I myself came late to the news. But that is no excuse for your poor discipline of the girl."

"My poor . . . ?" Renée's mouth opened and closed in utter amazement at his words. His accusation was patently unfair. "You dare question my behavior? You . . . you . . . Why didn't you tell me if you knew? Where was I to learn such news?"

Laurent regarded her dispassionately. "Perhaps if you had been a little more charitable in your concerns for others, mademoiselle, you might have been privy to the girl's pathetic confessions rather than I." He turned to the boatswain. "You, I will deal with when I've returned from the *Pelican*. Secure him below," he ordered.

Renée clutched Laurent's arm. "Wait! I will go with you."

The expression in his black eyes was unreadable but the tone of his voice was not. "You . . . will . . . not!" He pronounced each word distinctly, as if they might be misunderstood.

Renée jerked her hand away, stung by his high-handed manner. "You seem to forget, capitaine, that this is *my* ship. You work for me. If I say you will wait upon my pleasure, then you will."

For the space of several heartbeats they stood facing one another. Renée remembered her trepidations the day she had dared to outbid him for the *Christobel*. He had been in a fine rage that day, too. Yet she had sensed a respect for her audacity in that anger. She saw nothing of tribute in the gaze now accosting her. Finally he smiled, and the sight of that wicked smile made her heart plummet.

"When I have returned you to Tortola, you may have full and complete charge of this vessel,

Mademoiselle Owner. Until then, consider your-self the victim of a mutiny."

He took a step toward her and then another, his smile widening as she began retreating be-fore him. "Make no mistake, mademoiselle. If you make the tiniest protest, I'll have you clapped in irons next to the good boatswain."

"You wouldn't!" Renée voiced defiantly, but her feet were carrying her backward all the same.

"Mais oui, mademoiselle," he answered sweetly. "Do not put me to the test."

Renée did not quite believe him. After all, had there not been a proposal of marriage in that thunderous speech of the night before? Why, then, was he looking at her as if he would like to turn her over his knee?

Finally the unyielding barrier of the cabin bulkhead touched her back and she was forced to a halt. Laurent did not stop until he was within inches of her, his hot breath warming her already flushed face.

"For once, think of someone else, *mon papil-lon,"* he voiced for her ears alone. She stiffened as his hand moved behind her back as though he was about to embrace her. A second later she felt cool air at her back as the door yawned open behind her.

"Don't make me more sorry than I already am," he continued in the same undertone. "I cannot erase what has happened but I may be able to salvage your maid. *Mon Dieu!* What is this power you women have over us mere mortal men?"

The last was said with such bitterness that Renée turned away from him. It was a rejection of his desire for her. She made no protest when the door slammed behind her. His words were ringing still in her ears.

What had he said of her neglect of Giselle? He had implied that she thought only of herself.

"That's not true!" she cried, the noise rousing Piper to wakefulness as he lay on the window seat. "I am not selfish! I was preoccupied."

No, that was a half-truth. Only yesterday she had scolded herself about neglecting Giselle. Yet, even after their conversation, she had not suspected the extent of the girl's troubles. She had been too eager to smooth over the rough spot, too quick to reassure Giselle that every-thing could be put to rights, too certain that she had the answers to all Giselle's problems. No wonder Giselle had turned instead to confide in Laurent.

"*Mère de Dieu!* I have been such a fool!"

How vain and self-satisfied she must have sounded, confessing girlish confidences in hopes of winning a smile from Giselle. Giselle must have wanted to shake her until her teeth rattled.

"Oh, Gweneth, *soeur!* Where are you when I need you?" Renée sighed as she slumped down in the bunk.

Gweneth always knew what to do and say, how to keep the confidence of everyone about her. No wonder Laurent had admired Gweneth from the first. Gweneth had a calm self-possession that came from wisdom.

"And I, I have the unthinking, unfeeling impetuosity of a . . ." What had Laurent whispered just before he closed the door?

Mon papillon.

Is that how he thought of her, as a butterfly? Somehow she could find nothing romantic in that. The title conjured up images of a flighty, thoughtless, insubstantial being of no real significance. Beautiful but useless.

She did not object as Piper traded the window seat for the comfort of her lap. "Are you not angry with me too?" She scratched him under the chin. "If not, you are a minority of one this day. Why do I never think before I act? I might have saved Giselle much anguish had I known she had formed a tendre for that yellow-haired *Yanqui.*"

She had thought the American handsome but too . . . brutal? No. Too uncivilized? No. Too desperate. Yes, that was it. He seemed to be a man who held a grudge against life. What had drawn Giselle to him? Was it the same thing that had drawn *her* to Laurent?

"There, I'm doing it again, thinking only of myself!" she declared in disgust, and pushed Piper from her lap as she rose to dress. "If only I would think of some way to prove my worth to all of them. A chance to prove myself, Piper, I need the opportunity desperately!"

Laurent's expression came back to her, the bleak, sad and bewildered look that he had worn just before he slammed the cabin door. He looked like a man caught in a trap. Was she that trap? He had asked what power she had over him. Did he feel powerless to resist her?

The thought of Laurent, caught and tangled in a web of her design, did not please her. Once she had hoped to make him sorry that she was not his. Yet, now he seemed miserable that she was.

The moth and the flame, attracted yet bringing ultimate destruction with their union. Was that the legacy of her fortune? Had she been so anxious to reap the fruition of the voodoo woman's prophecy that she had refused to even acknowledge the possibility that it was not the way to happiness?

"Oh, Mama Theo, what have I done?" she whispered forlornly.

The first explosive volley sounded so much like thunder that Renée scarcely heeded the noise, but the violent eruptions of the water near the *Christobel* a few seconds later sent her to the boards with a cry of fright.

"British frigate off starboard beam!" she heard a seaman cry. "They're firing rounds!"

The cry was followed by a tumult of water and sound that lifted and tossed the *Christobel* to the accompanying cries of its crew.

Renée grasped for and missed the edge of her bunk and was sent sliding across the floor as the ship heaved under her. She saw the captain's desk looming before her and tried desperately for a handhold to break her fall. Nothing came within reach of her spread fingers. She could not stop the inevitable collision. For an instant she felt nothing, just the stunning surprise of stout oak against her more fragile cranium. The next instant bright white stars shot across her field of vision, leaving a trail of blood red that faded into welcome darkness.

Laurent kept remembering Renée's face—white as linen, a smear of scarlet blood trickling from the purple gash over her right temple as she was dragged from the captain's cabin. *Mon Dieu!* He had wanted to slaughter the entire British Navy for having touched her, but he had not even been able to take her in his arms, secured as he had been between two red-coated soldiers, his wrists tied behind his back. When the young ensign declared the ship impounded and all of the ship's crew under arrest, she had turned and stared at him as if seeing a ghost, a stranger whom she feared.

The volley of shot from the approaching Navy frigate had ended quickly enough with the hoisting of the white flag, but not before damage had been done to both the *Christobel* and the *Pelican*. Caught off-guard by the British Navy for the second time, in a dinghy at sea between both vessels, he had screamed in impotent rage for his first mate to raise that flag. All the time they rowed back toward his ship, sickening heartbeats marked his fear that Renée would be killed before they could surrender.

Laurent stirred, unaware of his surroundings until the pull of the length of chain connecting his wrists together stopped his movement. Seated with his back to a wall and his legs drawn up, he gazed about the small cell in disgust. For three weeks he had sat here in the Spanish Town jail, chained arm and leg in a sweltering cell which reeked of uncollected refuse. Where was Renée, sharing a companion cell with God-knew-what-sort of creatures?

Laurent leaned his forehead against his bent knees. No one would speak to him, answer any question. Only once, the first night, the cries of an enraged man had stirred him to curiosity and he had risen and gone to the door to see three jailers rushing toward a cell down the hall. They had gone in with shouts and oaths and, by the sound of muffled blows, beaten the ranting man to silence. With a heavy heart, Laurent had retraced his six paces and slid down into a sitting position. He had recognized the man's voice. It had been Breedon.

"The bastard deserved it!" Laurent's face set in angry lines as he rejected the natural swelling of sympathy for the pain of another human being. That had been the greatest blow of all, to discover that Breedon was a spy in the pay of the British. To have been caught by a spy was humiliation enough. But to know he had been betrayed by a man he had considered a friend, that gnawed at his belly until he seethed with the desire to find himself alone with Breedon. He would beat the man senseless with his bare hands!

He had been successfully involved in smuggling too long not to realize that the British would be seeking him. The capture of the *Christobel* would have intensified their interest in him. He knew that, too. Laurent smiled grimly. The danger, the exhilaration of sailing close to the winds of disaster—that was the reason he had taken up the smuggling trade. Nothing could compare with the thrill of that adventure . . . not until a tiny raven-haired beauty had come into his life.

His mind had been so much on Renée these last weeks that he could think of nothing else until Breedon whispered the irresistible rumor of the imprisonment of former members of his crew here in Jamaica. Because of his uncharacteristic neglect of secrecy and precaution, Renée had nearly been killed. That thought remained uppermost in his mind. Where was she? Had her wound been treated? Did she lie ill on a cell floor of rotting hay with no one to comfort her?

Hot rage rose within him, bringing Laurent to his feet. There had to be some way he could send for aid, someone in Jamaica who would come to Spanish Town at his request. For himself, he cared not, but he would find some way to free Renée. She was innocent of all but her passion for him. For that she must not pay with her life! "Think, Lavasseur! Think!"

Renée stared out in misery at the aquamarine crescent of Royal Harbor, visible from the second floor of Government House in Port Royal. After three weeks, the dull pounding at her temples had subsided but pains still shot up through her neck when she moved her head too quickly. That did not disturb her as much as the thought that she might suffer a permanent scar above her right eyebrow. Absently she touched the bandage. It was hidden beneath a yellow silk scarf which she had tied, bandeau fashion, across her forehead to hide the ugly court plaster.

At any moment the door to the governor's office would open and she would be called forth as a witness. It was what she wanted, what she had pressed for from the moment the governor of Jamaica sent one of his assistants to fetch her from Spanish Town prison. Jamaica was not England, but not even here was the relative of a peer of the realm left to languish in prison, whatever her suspected crimes.

Renée shivered, remembering the terror of those first few hours. If she had not worn a gold bracelet, she could not have bribed the turnkey to send her message to the governor. Once her identity was made known, she was quickly released and brought to the governor's home as a guest.

The bracelet had bought her freedom and Giselle's. Now, by other means, she must free Laurent.

"Oh, Gweneth, I pray you are not the sole heir to the Valois family wits," she whispered to herself.

Before the door opened fully, Renée was on her feet, her hands balling into fists in spite of her resolution to remain calm.

"The governor will see you now," the uniformed soldier said.

Renée forced herself to walk slowly toward the man, a provocative smile of greeting forming on her features. As she neared the young man, she saw that his eyes followed the shape of her limbs, visible beneath the scandalously sheer fabric of her gown. She did not possess Gweneth's flair for words and common sense, nor her ability with a blade, but she knew the power of feminine beauty and flirtation and had chosen her dress with those prerequisites in mind. She was to be a woman in the company of males.

"*Merci, monsieur,*" she voiced sweetly, and touched the soldier's arm with a gloved finger as she passed him. His mouth fell agape, his cheeks growing vivid as his scarlet uniform as he fell instantly in lusty love with the exquisite French lady.

That tiny victory emboldened Renée's failing courage as she stepped into the office to find the governor flanked by half a dozen military officers. If the governor were as easily distracted by the sight of a pretty girl as the young enlisted man, things would go much smoother for her.

To her delight, she heard a collective intake of breath from the roomful of men as all eyes riveted on her scantily clad figure.

The governor was the first to recover himself, for he had had the pleasant experience of the young lady's presence at his dinner table every day for weeks.

"Mam'zelle Valois," he greeted warmly. "'Tis a villainous business we have before us, and I apologize for the need of your presence. However, you were a passenger aboard one of the captured vessels and your testimony may prove enlightening. We won't keep you long, that I promise."

"*Merci, Monsieur le Gouverneur.*" His ill-fitting wig was picked out like a bird's nest but Renée favored him with a smile that he returned with a degree that bared all his yellowed teeth.

Then, as if she had made some horrible mistake, her hand flew up to cover her mouth. "But I make a mistake. We must speak the English, *mais oui?*" The question was framed in purposely accented fashion, a deception, for her English was nearly as pure as her French.

"Yes, indeed, my dear," the governor replied with a besotted gaze. "Do be seated. Would you care for tea for the reading of the charges? No? Then let us begin."

The charges were short but deadly. The charge of smuggling leveled against Laurent astonished her. The charge of conspiracy to commit piracy and disrupt British justice left her appalled. What had Laurent been doing before they met? Was any of this true? If so, the man she loved she knew not at all.

"Call your first witness," the governor ordered when the reading was finished.

Renée listened with half an ear to the young lieutenant, a member of the crew of the British frigate which had captured them, as he gave a long-winded account of the engagement and ensuing surrender and capture. She was too busy dividing his audience's concentration by smiling sweetly and in turn at the lieutenant,

the governor, and various members of the all-
male company.

"Thank you, lieutenant." The governor waved
the young man away. "Next." Two more officers
gave various accounts of the naval engagement
in Bull Bay.

After a polite cough, Renée raised her gloved
hand. "Pardon me, *Monsieur le Gouverneur.*"
She rose to her feet at his acknowledgment. "I
do not understand. Your officers keep referring
to the *Christobel* as the 'French privateer's vessel.' Why does he say that?" Renée dimpled
prettily. "I confess that I am French, but I was
not aware that, by definition of English law, it
makes me a privateer."

"It does not!" the governor replied emphati-
cally. "We refer to the *Christobel*'s captain,
Laurent Lavasseur."

Renée gazed innocently at the governor, puz-
zlement creasing her brow. "Capitaine Lavasseur? You would not expect me to captain my
own ship, certainly? The *Christobel* belongs to
me, monsieur."

Renée smiled at the startled man. This was
clearly news to the governor, and she had meant
it to be so. Some instinct had warned her to
admit nothing to her host but that she was a
passenger until she learned the reason for the
attack upon the *Christobel.* Now she was glad
she had.

She reached into her reticule, withdrew her
ownership papers and placed them on the governor's desk. "I purchased the *Christobel* and

Capitaine Lavasseur's services in Tortola more than a month ago."

When he had inspected the papers, the governor seemed satisfied with their authenticity. "Let the man come forth who makes the charges," he demanded.

The officers murmured among themselves, the lieutenant stepping reluctantly to the fore. "Sir, there is a bounty on the head of Captain Lavasseur of New Orleans for suspected smuggling activities in the British West Indies."

Renée turned on the young officer a cold glance, but as she did so, her gown slipped, baring one lovely rounded shoulder, which the young man fastened greedy eyes on.

"Lieutenant, that makes no sense. Capitaine Lavasseur has been in my constant company since leaving New Orleans over two months ago, and . . ." She paused as a murmur ran through the crowd. "And," she maintained with a slight rise in the level of her voice, "I assure you, we have had no traffic with smugglers, pirates, or villains of any kind during that time."

She turned appealing eyes on the chief official. "Monsieur, you cannot suspect me of smuggling? The only French silks and lace aboard the *Christobel* are for my own personal use." She swept a hand over her gown, drawing all eyes to the shadow of her slim legs beneath the fabric of her gown. "Perhaps," she suggested coyly, "I do admit to a weakness for brandy. Does that brand me a brazen pirate?"

"No!" The word leaped from the governor's mouth before he could stop it, and his ominous frown did little to erase the impression of partiality as he added, "Of course, that proves nothing in Captain Lavasseur's case."

"Of course not," she agreed politely. "But you are convinced that the *Christobel* is innocent of carrying contraband and will therefore release her immediately into my charge?"

"Sir, I protest" the lieutenant said, only to redden under the disdainful glance of the beautiful lady. "Well, this is most irregular," he added defensively.

Renée held her breath. Clearly, in the past Laurent had angered the British authorities in some manner.

"Is there some problem, gentlemen?"

All heads turned toward the doorway at the question.

By his expensive dress, the man was clearly of some note. The fact was verified when the governor rose in respect as the man entered the room. "Lord Granger, welcome. Do come forth if you can shed light upon this matter."

Lord Granger took his time, stopping to make himself known to Renée. "My lady," he said, saluting the hand she extended to him.

He was familiar. Renée racked her brain. "Have we met, Lord Granger? In Road Town?"

The question did not seem to please the man, for he released her hand abruptly, albeit politely. "No, mistress. I would remember it. Delighted all the same," he said shortly, turning away from her to address the man in charge. "With your permission, sir, I would like to call Captain Adam Breedon forth. At the end of my questioning you will understand precisely the nature of the charges and have at your disposal all the proof necessary to hold Captain Lavasseur."

Renée tensed at the mention of the *Yanqui*'s name. She sensed that Lord Granger was a certain and present danger—and Breedon was the catalyst. She watched in silence as Breedon was led into the governor's chambers.

Only fear of calling undue attention to herself prevented a gasp of dismay from escaping her at the sight of the man. Breedon had been in a brawl. But unlike the results of the battle on the New Orleans dock, Breedon had now clearly been the loser. In sharp contrast to the clean shirt and breeches he wore, his face was a travesty of orderliness. One eye was swollen shut and multiple bruises so badly distorted the contours of his face that she wondered if his arms had been pinned while he was beaten. He walked with a limp, and even at a distance she could detect the uneven breathing of a man with a punctured lung.

"Stand forward and state your name," Lord Granger demanded when Breedon paused near the back of the room.

"Adam Breedon," the American replied thickly, and moved forward.

The nobleman smiled slightly. "Is that your full and legal name?"

"It is," Adam answered without hesitation.

"Very well. Please tell the governor what you

know of the clandestine activities of Captain Lavasseur."

Adam grinned for the first time, though it must have hurt to stretch those portions of his face. "That would be little less than nothing," he stated in a stronger voice.

Lord Granger frowned. "I ask you to think back a few months' time, Captain Breedon. Think very carefully and then answer the question again."

Adam's gaze was full of mockery. "I know nothing."

Lord Granger turned away, but he flung words back over his shoulder as his eyes came to rest on Renée. "Tell me, Captain Breedon. Were you not recently in New Orleans? Did you not meet two men there who offered you money in return for supplying them with certain information?"

Adam's easy stance did not alter. "I meet many hellhounds in my business. The particulars of most escape me."

Lord Granger's lips tightened. "Allow me to refresh your memory, captain. There is a tavern on the riverfront, the name is Azar's. In the rear of the courtyard, on the second floor, you met with two British agents."

For the first time Adam's gaze flickered to Renée, who stood absolutely expressionless. "I met two jackals slavering over the prospect of baiting a trap for an unsuspecting man."

"Indeed? Yet you were not averse to accepting their money. Five hundred pounds was your price, I believe."

Renée gasped aloud at those words. The *Yan-*

qui had taken money to betray Laurent. *"Bastard!"* she whispered.

"You haven't answered, Captain Breedon."

Adam's gaze stayed on Renée. "I accepted a sum of money to inform Captain Lavasseur that his ship was to be auctioned in Tortola. I agreed to see that he arrived in Tortola on time. I was asked to make his acquaintance in such a manner that if—and the word is 'if,' gentlemen—if Lavasseur were to be considering a smuggler's trade with the return of his ship, I should be apprised of the plot."

His gaze never left Renée as he smiled slowly. "I will swear on my dead mother's head that I never heard a word from Lavasseur that led me to believe he was involved in smuggling at any time since our meeting in New Orleans."

"I wonder, captain," his questioner mused, "if your mother were as saintly as you would have us believe?"

For the first time, anger flared in Adam's face. "Whoreson!" he said softly. "Filthy, coarse-grained son of a bitch!"

"That's better," Granger said, smiling now. "So, to the present matter. You accepted a bribe to spy on a man. You're a man of expensive tastes, I'm told." He eyed the American's battered face in mild disdain. "The addiction exacts a high price. You took the gold for that reason?"

The murmuring of those present rose slightly, but Renée kept her eyes on Lord Granger. Here was someone unmoved by her beauty, her coquetry. Here was a man who might mean the

266

destruction of all she held dear. Suddenly her palms were damp inside her gloves. She needed quick thinking to play against such an opponent, a commodity she was sorely afraid she did not possess.

"I admit nothing, sir. The men I met were sweating, brandy-soaked sons of whores. They steamed with deceit and stank of calumny."

"And yet," Lord Granger persisted pleasantly, "you went in answer to their summons in Road Town. You demanded the second half of your payment. And so a new plot was hatched. The trap was rebaited with the news that a half-dozen of the *Christobel*'s crew were languishing in Spanish Town prison. When Captain Lavasseur came here to release them, he would be arrested for abetting their escape."

Adam smirked. "You seem very well informed. Were you one of the masked cravens who mewed to me of the lost prize in Juan's Cove? You said you did not trust the competence of the British fleet to accomplish their goal. You devised that filthy plan to entrap a man only suspected of wrongdoing."

"Very well said, but lies will not help you now, Captain Breedon," Lord Granger remarked, admiration ringing in his voice above the rising dissenting voices of the officers present. "Or do I have it wrong? Is it not better to call you Captain Southey of Charleston?"

Renée saw Adam blanch. In the days since arriving in Jamaica, she and Giselle had talked at length of the men each loved. There were no secrets they did not share. If Lord Granger used that name, he knew Adam's secret and that it could hang him.

For an instant Renée held back from any action. Adam Breedon had deliberately set out to betray Laurent. He had seduced Giselle—no matter that the girl thought herself in love. His word could send Laurent to the scaffold and earn him the indebtedness of the British. And yet . . . the *Yanqui* was choosing not to collaborate in the charges against Laurent when it was obviously expected of him.

Renée looked up at the injured man as a coughing spasm brought a bloody foam to his lips. This was the man Giselle loved. She carried his child, she would be here to defend him now if she could. But because she was a quadroon, she could not even testify for him. Suddenly Renée knew that *she* must do something.

Words poured from her mouth without reason or plan. "Lord Granger, I recall that we were not introduced. Allow me to rectify the matter. I am Renée Valois, sister-in-law of the Earl of Mockton."

Lord Granger turned to her, his concentration on Breedon broken for the moment. "The Earl of Mockton's sister-in-law?"

Renée nodded, choosing her words carefully. "I have little knowledge of English law, but I imagine that the charge against Capitaine Lavasseur is deserving of a trial. In the meantime, a letter will be sent to my brother-in-law. He is a man of some consequence, his seat in

Parliament aside. I think he will find the case most intriguing."

"No need to alarm yourself, dear lady," Lord Granger returned, but the pleasantness had evaporated from his voice.

"I am not concerned, only surprised that the English must stoop to cheats and lies, hire spies and jackals to do their business," she returned, her heart beating high in her chest. It took every effort of will to withstand the cold glare from the nobleman's gray eyes, but at least he had turned back from the abyss of Adam's crime.

The man's smile was mocking. "Permit me to say, one seldom catches fish without getting wet."

Renée's chin lifted. "I was put more in mind of a quote about lying with dogs and rising with fleas," she responded, her eyes sweeping him meaningfully.

"Touché!" Adam murmured low, wondering if and when to speak. Something held him back: the suspicion that the tiny French girl might just be able to handle the Englishman.

The whispered words were heard, and Lord Granger turned back to Breedon. "You're wanted for crimes both heinous and abominable. The sentence was death, I believe—"

"One moment, monsieur!" Renée stamped her foot, aware of the scene she was creating. Her only thought was to stop the man's dreadful speech. "I cannot believe that you are so audacious as to accuse Capitaine Breedon of villainy because he refused to do your dirty work."

269

"Mademoiselle, he did not refuse. He is wealthier by two hundred and fifty pounds. Ask him."

Renée ignored this statement of the truth. For Breedon's betrayal of Laurent she could cheerfully scratch his eyes out. But for Giselle, she would do her best to save him.

She sought the governor's help. "Monsieur, I have been here three-quarters of an hour and nothing substantial has come to light." She shrugged elaborately. "As for this fantastic tale of spies and traps and baits, I care nothing. Capitaine Lavasseur made no attempts on Spanish Town prison. I suspect, considering present circumstances, he should prefer to break out rather than in. Furthermore, what do you English care for the crimes of a *Yanqui* committed in America?"

The governor, scrambling for a footing in the slippery crosscurrent of the nobleman's interrogation, found high dry land in the French lady's logic. "Damn! My thoughts exactly! There's been no proof of smuggling or villainy."

"Forgive me, sir," Lord Granger said with an arresting gesture. "You may release Captain Lavasseur, since our proof has vanished, but Breedon must remain. There are certain letters already en route to Charleston. Within the month, enlightening correspondence will reach the British courts concerning the man."

"This is ridiculous!" Renée cut in once again. "With no proof of wrongdoing, I demand that Captain Breedon be released immediately, into my custody if you desire it."

"Mademoiselle, I caution you to think again." There was a long pause while Lord Granger observed his opponent. "You ally yourself with thieves, liars and cheats who would sell their souls for gold. When certain matters come to light"—he stressed heavily the threat implied by the words—"you will not wish to be misunderstood."

Renée eyed the nobleman coldly. He looked as thoroughly impregnable as a king on his throne. He thought himself in control, inviolate. A man of immense power who would stop at nothing to gain his goal. A thought flashed through her mind, so absurd that she gave it voice before the audacity of it could silence her.

"Lord Granger, I believe you have lied, cheated and contrived to convict an innocent man of crimes in order to further some ambition of your own."

"The devil you do!" The superb self-control dropped for an instant so brief that none but Renée saw raw fury peek from behind the man's baleful stare.

In a twinkling it was gone, but the instant was enough. To see her wild stab strike him thus made her heart leap with fright. She had guessed correctly, but in doing so, she had gained the man's wrath.

Indignation fired her own anger. She was not so poor of heart as to back down from a dare. A clear and obvious trap had been laid for Laurent, and he had nearly stepped into it. "I wonder that you did not wait for Capitaine Lavasseur to act, monsieur, if you believed him guilty. Was it that you did not trust the word of your paid informers?"

Lord Granger looked at the young lady before him as if she had suddenly grown fangs. Then, with all the good grace of his breeding, he smiled. "Perhaps, Miss Valois, my fault was in the choice of ally. Had you been in my employ, I doubt not at all that Captains Breedon and Lavasseur would be hanging outside the iron-studded gate of Spanish Town prison even now."

Renée did not mistake this as anything other than a threat, and that did not bode well for the *Yanqui*. "Perhaps I cannot win Capitaine Breedon's release today, but you may be certain that my opinions of your conduct will be repeated often in any willing ear I find in Jamaica."

Lord Granger smiled. "You must do what you must, my dear. Spanish Town prison will house the *Yanqui* until word reaches us from America. That will be some time, I fear. And prisons are murderous places."

He nodded at her courteously, and though her knees shook so badly she was afraid she might subside to the floor, Renée turned to the governor.

"Monsieur Governor, I hope this ends the matter for the present. I expect Capitaine Lavasseur's release to be immediate. Will someone call a carriage? I feel the heat most sorely. I . . ."

She did not feel reality slipping from her. Rather the sound of the ocean's roar rose in sudden urgency until it encompassed all sound, even that of her own voice. And with it came mists—surprising, for she had heard that fog was nearly unheard of in these tropical climes. But sea and mist whirled up and over her until there was nothing but the not unpleasant sensation of slipping down into cool darkness.

Chapter Fourteen

"*Non!* Absolutely not! We will speak of it no more!"

Renée heard with growing impatience this beginning of yet another argument. She stared at her antagonist across the space of the small parlor which was part of the suite of rooms she had rented in Kingston. Her eyes followed the lean lines of his strong body displayed by his leather breeches. An open shirt revealed the golden cross which had lain between her breasts as they made love. Now he was striding up and down like a caged beast while she sat demurely on the settee. Less than a week ago Laurent had been released from Spanish Town prison, yet hardly a civil word had passed between them since.

"For a man whose life I saved, you seem deliberately ungrateful," she observed.

Laurent turned to her slowly, his own patience a rapidly evaporating commodity. "May I remind you, mademoiselle, that I have thanked you as much and as often as I have the wherewithal to manage at present. Once the *Christobel* is sufficiently repaired to make it possible for us to leave Kingston, I will sail you to England sans my pilot's fee."

Renée colored under his withering gaze. There. It was in the open at last. He still resented her ownership of the *Christobel*. Now, to add fuel to the fire, she had just thrown up in his face the fact that she, not he, had affected their freedom from a dangerous situation for which he was partially to blame. How that must chafe, she thought remorsefully. For a person who was determined to think only of others from now on, she was behaving rather badly.

"Laurent," Renée began placatingly as she rose to intersect his path and placed a hand on his coat sleeve. "*Chéri*, do not think unkindly of me. I was so worried when I thought you might hang." She lifted her face and leaned toward him, her lips parting in open invitation.

Laurent looked down into the exquisite face turned up at him, at her great dark eyes shining with the golden luster of love, at her sweet lips whose taste reminded him of wild strawberries, and wondered at his restraint.

From the moment she had come running across the floor of his cell and rushed into his arms with the news of his release, he had known that he loved her, loved her so much that he never wanted her out of his sight again.

But how could that be? He could not even protect her. He had been wholly impotent in her greatest hour of need. *She* had effected her own release from prison. *She* had found shelter for herself and Giselle. *She* had pleaded his case and won for him his freedom.

That was what gnawed at him, and the knowledge of his own attitude surprised him. If he had been asked a month ago if it would matter that a woman might prove more intrepid than he, he would have said no and meant it—because he would not have believed it possible. But now he had failed to keep the woman of his choice safe. Love her? Yes, that he did. Honor her? Of course. But he had failed to protect her. No, it was more than that. If not for him, for his own puffed-up arrogance at thinking he could snatch a part of his crew from under the eyes of the English, she would never have been in any danger at all.

Laurent turned abruptly away from her, his pride smarting from that realization. "Mademoiselle," he said, stressing the fact that he did not return the privilege of using her given name as she had his. "I think we would both benefit from putting the folly of Jamaica behind us. The *Christobel* will be ready to sail no later than the end of the week."

"That's not nearly soon enough!" Renée protested. She tried not to think of the hurt his turning away caused her. She tried not to think of the fact that she had offered him a kiss and been refused. She must think only of others, of Giselle and Capitaine Breedon.

Renée poked Laurent insistently in the back. "Attend to me, capitaine. I have a proposition for you!"

Laurent turned, with mild surprise on his features. With a hand, he raised her chin so that he could look down into her eyes. "Make your wager, mademoiselle. But I warn you, you have nothing that can make risking my life to free that *Yanqui* worthwhile."

Renée felt the anger in him; it communicated itself to her through the hard fingers embracing her chin, but she spoke in spite of it. "Nothing, monsieur? Not even the *Christobel? Oui!*" she confirmed as amazement lifted his brows. "I offer you the *Christobel* in return for freeing the *Yanqui* from prison. Tonight!"

Laurent thought himself incapable of fresh surprise after the events of the last days, but the emotion struck him anew. "You are asking me to break a man out of Spanish Town prison, the very thing that Breedon was paid to trap me into doing?" he asked wondrously.

"You appreciate the irony, *mais non?*" Renée encouraged.

In spite of himself, Laurent did. The hand on her chin softened its hold, becoming a tender caress. Absently his thumb began tracing easy circles on her cheek. "You are certain the wager is worth it? My inclination would be to kill Breedon rather than save his life." His voice was almost drowsy in nature, at odds with the harsh words. "What if I fail?"

Renée told herself to resist the seeping of desire through her limbs at his touch. She told herself that this was no time to distract him from the prize so nearly won. This was no time to recall kisses, caresses, the night when candlelight and shadow and a private bath had turned into a rapturous dance of love—no! She must think of a stick to go with the carrot of the *Christobel* she waved before Laurent's eyes, something he loathed as much as he desired the ship.

"Capitaine Lavasseur, you have something I want." The huskiness of her voice did not embarrass her. She wondered that she could speak at all. This new bold selflessness was quite daunting.

"Once marriage to you was my goal." She met his narrowing gaze as well as she could. "If you refuse to attempt to free Capitaine Breedon, then I shall announce to all of Kingston a demand that you marry me. I shall tell them that I have been your mistress. I shall brazenly lie. I will even say that you are the father of my unborn child."

"You would not dare!"

"*Mais oui*," Renée answered softly, using the same words with which he had once threatened her. "Do not force me to prove it."

Laurent regarded her a moment in cynical amusement. The pinched line of her lips betrayed the emotional turmoil inside her, and yet her wide coffee-colored gaze was unblinkingly clear. Poor girl, did she think he still despised the thought of marriage as much as he once had? Did she truly not believe in her own powers to persuade him otherwise? "What makes you think that I might not find marriage to you less abhorrent than risking my life for that miscreant? After all, I recall proposing, after a fashion, the night we were arrested."

Renée's hands clenched and emotions played across her face which she knew were read by that black, all-seeing gaze studying her. Of course he had proposed. It was natural that he would not want to think of himself as being as callous as the *Yanqui* where a woman was concerned. Laurent would marry her—for duty's sake, not love.

"Look me in the eye, monsieur, and tell me that you wish to marry me above all else at this moment."

Laurent muttered a deprecation under his breath and dropped his hand from her chin. Twice in five days he had ridden back and forth between Kingston and Bull Bay, where the *Christobel* was still moored in order to facilitate repairs. What he wished above all else at this moment was a good night's sleep. But that was not a very gallant declaration to make. However, he was not about to allow her to win him to wedded bliss that easily. He wanted the *Christobel* back, but was her offer a fair way to win it?

"Why should I choose between two evils?" he challenged.

Renée's heart lurched at the comparison, but she saw the glimmer of amusement in his eye and knew that he was close to relenting. "Think of it as an adventure. Did you not tell me only yesterday that the love of danger attracted you to smuggling?"

"Why do you care what happens to Breedon?" Laurent demanded wearily.

"I've told you, for myself I do not care at all. The *Yanqui* nearly caused you to be killed. For that I will not soon forgive him. But Giselle loves him, she carries his child. If she cannot have him, she will die of heartbreak."

"And what if Breedon should refuse to take responsibility for the girl once he's freed?" Laurent questioned quietly.

Renée stared at him as if he were mad. "But of course he will! You must make him promise to do so. If not, I will bring the *Yanqui* back to Spanish Town prison myself!"

The outrageous statement so astonished Laurent that he burst into laughter. Renée smiled, the dimple in her left cheek appearing for the first time in weeks. "I knew you would not refuse me."

Laurent shook his head. "Mademoiselle, I'm not at all certain why I find myself in complete agreement with you. But you must not misunderstand. If I fail, nothing will save me this time, not even the sight of you playing Lady Godiva on the main street of Kingston."

"Then you must not fail," Renée stated simply. "I do not much like riding horseback."

Laurent choked on his laughter. "What?" he roared. "Have you no plan, no scheme, no course of action at the ready?"

Renée gave him an elegant little shrug of complete feminine disavowal. "*Quant à ça,* you shall manage something. I absolutely believe it!" She looked around, spied Piper on her seat, and scooped him up to drape him over Laurent's arm like a scraggly orange-and-white muff. "Come, *mon cher,* sit and tell me what we must do."

Renée found it ridiculously easy to make friendly contact with the British soldiers who were stationed aboard the *Pelican,* still harbored along with the *Christobel* in Bull Bay. The trip from Kingston to the bay was accomplished cross-country. The morning of the day after Laurent's last visit to her rooms in Kingston, Renée and Giselle reached the shore of the harbor where the two ships rode anchor.

Two hours later, Renée was ensconced in the captain's quarters of her ship. As a gesture of goodwill, she was to offer the last of Laurent's imported French brandy to each of the officers aboard the *Pelican* and a keg of rum to be split among the enlisted men. Laurent had sent her to the *Christobel* to wait until he came. If he had been successful in freeing the *Yanqui,* they would have to set sail immediately and hope that the English were too lazy to give hot pursuit. That was her job, to distract the English holding the *Pelican* hostage so that they would be in no hurry to detain the *Christobel* if they became suspicious. That was a boring assignment, Renée thought sourly. Dispensing brandy and rum was the job of a butler. Where was the thrill of adventure which she had promised Laurent?

A scant half-hour after the delivery of the gifts, a note was returned, inviting her to dine with the officers aboard their trophy.

"Of course, you will not go," Giselle opined.

"But I must," Renée returned as she pondered the note. "It has just occurred to me, Giselle, that two ships are better than one."

Giselle raised her eyes heavenward. "What are you thinking, mademoiselle?"

"Oh, nothing," Renée answered absently. "It was just a thought."

Distract the English, Laurent had said, but stay away from them!

Renée could think of several ways to distract the soldiers, but all of them involved her boarding the *Pelican* for a short while. Laurent would be furious, of course, but he did not realize that she could not sail to England with him. After he had won back the *Christobel*, she would be forced to honor her promise to never again mention marriage to him. That meant she would become his mistress. She would be too weak to resist the temptation, and she knew it.

No, she would need other transportation to England, and the *Yanqui*'s ship was the quickest method. He would need to leave the Caribbean. She would be doing him a favor to offer him his ship in trade for passage to Europe, Renée reasoned, convinced that she was *not* thinking only of herself.

"Giselle, will you ask the ship's steward if we

have any red wine aboard, something dark and heavy, something that would mask the taste of a sleeping draft?"

"No, mademoiselle! You mustn't!"

"You must come with me. It wouldn't be at all acceptable behavior for me to go unchaperoned," Renée continued blandly. "Giselle? Did you ever learn the location of the *Yanqui*'s horde of laudanum?"

Giselle hung her head. In a moment of weakness she had confessed what she should not have.

"Oh, please do not misunderstand!" Renée pleaded, and put a friendly arm about Giselle's shoulders. "I want it to help give the English soldiers a good night's rest. I know the *Yanqui* will never need such stuff again. He has you now, *mais non*? And soon he will have *monsieur le bébé*."

"Mademoiselle," Giselle corrected.

Renée's fine brows rose. "A girl? You are certain?"

Giselle began to giggle, and soon both were doubled over with laughter.

"You will see, Capitaine Lavasseur will bring you your *Yanqui* this very night, and we, Giselle, will be able to give him back his ship!"

Three hours later, at nightfall, Renée, Giselle and a half-case of Laurent's best claret were being handed aboard the *Pelican*.

"Be careful, mam'zelle!" the *Christobel*'s boatswain's mate called after her, and Renée turned to wave him farewell. The plan they had formed together in the heat of the afternoon sun seemed a little foolhardy now, but "It just must work!" she mouthed to herself as she turned to greet her hosts.

"Messieurs, a toast to your health," Renée intoned with a dimpled smile as she eyed warmly in turn each of her six red-coated hosts. After a tiny sip of her wine, she added, "I am delighted to learn that it is not so."

"To learn *what* is not so, mam'zelle?" came the expected reply from the officer on her left.

Renée leaned toward him slightly, her lips parted in blatant flirtation. "Why, that the English are not the stiff-as-a-poker race that I've always believed them to be," she finished saucily, and transferred a kiss to the end of his nose with her fingertip.

The resulting laughter was inordinately loud, but then, thought Renée as the masculine noise jarred her, these six men had consumed two bottles of wine each with dinner and were now making great inroads into their brandy bottles.

Ma foi! she thought disparagingly, she did not understand how Gweneth could bear to marry herself to an Englishman, let alone be content to live in a country full of them. But she smiled until her cheeks ached, because whatever else, men were men and they were so pleased by her presence that they had not even objected to her suggestion that Giselle act as *sommelière* after dinner, thereby freeing their steward to join in the cracking of the rum keg on the deck.

Only once did Renée sneak a look at her friend, and Giselle's one slight affirmative nod made her sigh in relief. The laudanum was finding its way into the evening's libation, but the process was nerve-rackingly slow. If anything, the men seemed to become more rambunctious.

That thought was confirmed by the clamping of a hot sweaty palm on her knee under the table. Without hesitation Renée picked up her fork, and under the cover of conversation, jabbed the offending appendage.

The officer on her left yelped and jerked his right hand up to his mouth, mumbling something about biting his tongue.

Renée did not look at him, but as she placed the fork back on the table, she said, "My mother always said a lady could be told by her table manners. I think it is true of gentlemen, also."

When the first round of smothered yawns swept the table, Renée nearly wept with relief. "Messieurs, I must go," she announced a few minutes later, and rose. "Giselle, you will signal to our ship."

"That won't be necessary," the soldier on her right maintained.

"Of course it is necessary," Renée replied sweetly as Giselle went to do her bidding. "You English are men of many talents, but I doubt a soldier makes a good sailor."

The men agreed with hearty chuckles.

Renée had been amazed to learn that a portion of the *Pelican*'s crew was still aboard and that the English military consisted wholly of soldiers, not naval personnel.

Renée nearly threw herself into the boatswain's mate's arms when she was lowered into the boat for the journey back to the *Christobel*. "They're nearly asleep on their feet!" she whispered. "You know what to do."

"Aye, mam'zelle," the seaman answered. "That we do!"

Fool! Imbecile! Lovesick calf! Buffoon! Laurent ticked off the deprecations in his mind as he trudged back and forth in the small room on the ground floor of Spanish Town prison. He had given away nearly all the money Renée had provided him with and yet he did not know if the opening of the door would mean the release of Breedon or . . . his own capture.

Renée's ridiculous suggestion that the *Christobel*'s crew attempt to carry the jail by force seemed more reasonable with every heartbeat. Why had he allowed himself to be talked into buying Breedon's freedom?

"Because, you love-sotted bit of arrogance, you wanted to prove to the girl that you are worth her belief in you!" he muttered grimly. Of course that was it. He had failed Renée once; how could he refuse to help her now?

And there was something else, something he had never credited in her, though it had been staring him in the face practically from the first moment he had met her.

He shook his head. Renée's ability to shape her world to her liking was a truly frightening thing to behold. It frightened him still. He had thought her lovely but ineffectual, sweet but without sharp wits. At every point he had been shown to be wrong. Oh, yes, she was lovely, but she was not without effective power when defending someone she loved. As for her sweetness, she could be as bitter and vindictive as any man alive when wounded. Her wits . . . Well, perhaps they were not the ordinary sort; she certainly viewed the world through a different point of reference. She had talked him out of prison . . . and back again.

The footfalls in the corridor made him jump. Straining for sound, he heard a second, lighter tread follow the first. Tensing, Laurent reached for the short truncheon he had slipped into his pocket and pulled the hood of his cape up over his head. Two soldiers, he could probably handle without much difficulty.

The damp-rusted hinges seemed to scream in the near-silence, and then the door was opening on the bribed turnkey and Adam Breedon.

Adam paused in the corridor, uncertain of what to expect, and then he saw the man, weapon in hand. He fell back a step, and for an instant he seemed about to bolt. But then he shrugged and came forward into the room.

"Should have told me I was about to be beaten to death, turnkey. I'd have dressed for the occasion," he jeered hoarsely, like a man too long without water.

"Leave us," Laurent demanded, suddenly thinking better of simply running.

The turnkey shrugged. "'Tis a queer business, payin' to do what will be done fo' free afore daylight."

"What's that?"

The turnkey jerked his head toward Adam.

"Man was to hang come first light. Don't guess it matters if he's beat to death."

"Who ordered that?" Adam questioned. "There's been no trial."

The turnkey shrugged again. "I don't question them orders, just do as I'm told." His eyes passed back and forth between the two men, as if measuring them, and then settled on Laurent. "Ye want, I'll chain him for ye. Make things easier."

Laurent swore at him, and the man retreated from the room.

When he was gone, Laurent turned to Adam and threw back his hood. The American regarded him with a sardonic smile. "I knew you had won your freedom. I did not think to see you again. But then, neither did murder seem to be your style, Lavasseur," he said after a moment.

"Men often learn they are capable of many things they thought they were not," Laurent answered quietly, his eyes on the bruised face of the man before him.

Adam folded his arms across his chest, his eyes still on the weapon in Laurent's hand. "I won't promise not to try to kill you in return," he said. "But a sudden return of old scruples reminds me that I owe you an apology. I may have done you—and me—a disservice the night of our last conversation."

Laurent considered this statement for a long time before speaking. "I won't ask your reason for offering to play Judas for a man who once considered you a friend, but since Mademoiselle

Giselle has seen fit to forgive you all, I will defer to her judgment of your true character."

Breedon looked up, amazement in the sapphire eyes that locked with onyx black. "You won't believe your own ears, captain? Devil take me! You're a romantic! I hope I shan't find it necessary to kill you. At this moment, damned if I'm not inclined to tell you the full tale of my life over a shared bottle of brandy."

Laurent smiled at last and put away his weapon. "You may have that wish, provided a certain young lady can count on your protection for the rest of your life."

For the first time Adam came alert, his body tensing as he rose to his full height. "Giselle is nearby? You've come to free me?"

Laurent sighed. So Renée was right once again. *Mon Dieu!* The lady was a witch!

"Come, Breedon, let's leave before the turnkey decides my bribe was not sufficient."

Adam caught Laurent by the arm, his face turning the color that in any other man would have been a blush. "I . . . I want you to know I sent for the English."

Laurent's eyes narrowed. "I know."

"I thought you had taken Giselle as your *placée.* I was jealous!" Adam hurled the words as if they were insults.

Laurent's expression softened again. "That I did not know. Thank you for telling me that . . . *mon ami.*"

"*Mon Dieu!* Are you mad?"

Renée beamed up at Laurent's horrified face

in the early-morning light. She had not been able to resist being rowed ashore to wait for the men. After a brief hesitation as the two men came crashing out of the tropical forest, she had launched herself at Laurent and was caught up in a bearlike embrace.

"Mon cher! I knew you could do it!" She pressed frantic tearstained kisses all over his grimy face. *"Merci, mon cher! Merci!"*

Laurent swung her back to earth. "We must hurry. In another hour the tide will be at its peak, and the *Christobel* must be beyond the shallows before then."

"Do not forget the *Pelican,"* Renée suggested. She glanced at Adam, beaming. "Giselle is aboard the *Pelican.* We thought it would be better if one of us behaved with decorum."

The light which brightened Adam's face was beatific, and then he was racing across the sand toward the boats waiting to carry them back to the ships.

"What madness is this?" Laurent protested.

Renée spread her arms wide. "While you were saving Capitaine Breedon, Giselle and I saved the *Pelican.* Do not look so angry, *mon cher.* It was perfectly safe. We put laudanum in their wine. Puff, like that, they went to sleep, and the *Christobel*'s crew had only to tie them up and put them ashore." She pointed to a spot along the edge of the jungle. "They put the English back there somewhere. I don't know. I didn't ask. But we must hurry!"

Laurent allowed her to pull him to the water's edge before he stopped, jerking her to a halt.

"You are the most infuriating, imbecilic, frustrating women I have ever known! You could have been killed!" he thundered, and shook her until she sagged unresistingly in his arms.

A second later, he found himself kissing her as though it would save both their lives. The anger and fear that ran through him made his heart hammer loudly in his ears. When at last he dragged his mouth from hers, there were tears on her cheeks and a pain in her eyes that he had not seen since that night back at Bonne Vie.

"*Bon soir*, Laurent," she whispered as his arms released her, and she turned and ran into the surf after the boat that Adam had launched.

"What? Where are you going?" Laurent cried, starting after her, yet too angry to give her a real chase.

"To England!" she cried over her shoulder as she waded deeper. "The ship's papers are in your cabin! Be happy, my love!"

"Marry me!" Laurent called out across the water as he watched two burly seamen lift her out of the waist-high water and haul her aboard.

"*Je t'aime*, Laurent. *Je t'aime!*" Renée called, waving broadly as tears streamed freely down her face.

Chapter Fifteen

THE DRIZZLE OF EARLY MORNING HAD GIVEN WAY
to buttery sunshine just after midmorning, an
event that should have lightened the humor of
the single occupant of the hired coach. It did not.
As Laurent looked out over the gentle rolling
hills of Dorset's uplands, at the white dots of
grazing sheep across the soft green of spring-
time, he wondered anew if he were a fool to have
come to England.

From the moment the *Christobel* made harbor
in Southampton, he had been filled with an
eager anticipation that only wound tighter as he
neared Mockton Hall. Raoul Bertrand was his
oldest and best friend, yet he was not at all
certain he would be welcome. That is why he
had not written ahead to tell anyone of his
arrival. He could not chance that Renée would

disappear before he had an opportunity to speak with her.

What a fool I am!

Disgusted with his own nervousness, Laurent jerked the leather curtain closed over the sight of the lovely April day. It had been five months since Renée had waved good-bye to him from the deck of the *Pelican* as it sailed out of Bull Bay. He could scarcely believe that she had actually left him. In spite of everything, he knew she loved him. Why, then, had she again refused his proposal of marriage?

"She refused me!" he murmured. The thought was still incredible to him. It was the third proposal of marriage he had made in his entire life—all to the same lady—and she had refused him.

Laurent shook his head. He was mad. That must be the answer. Not quite ten months ago he had stood in his own *garçonnière* and flatly refused to marry Renée though her brilliant eyes begged him to reconsider. He had behaved in a contemptible manner in his quest to retain his freedom. She was the same lovely, desirable and passionate being who had, not a month later, lured him to breach every boundary and limit of gentlemanly conduct with the undeniable need to taste of her love. Yet, when she sailed out of his life for the final time in Jamaica, it shamed him to remember his relief as well as his sadness.

"I'm not the marrying kind," he had professed aloud.

But the protest now seemed so feeble he sneered at his reflection in the window glass. What sort of man *was* the marrying kind? Was it only those who found it necessary to carry on the family line? He had time for that still. He was the eldest son and heir to Bonne Vie, but his brothers were all married, Michael and Stephen each with a child. No, heirs were of no urgency. And yet . . .

Laurent closed his eyes, his mind's eye filling with the vision of Adam Breedon as he had last seen him in Haiti two months earlier. The *Yanqui* had changed so much in a few short months that he was hardly recognizable as the same man he had known for nearly two years. The gaunt, haggard look of dissipation had cleared from his face. The Atlantic crossing and return had seemed to blow away the dregs of the opium's ravages. By far the most noticeable change was his smile. Oh, the *Yanqui* grinned as much as ever, but there was now a tenderness that had once been lacking in the cutting edge of the self-mocking grimace he had worn. Once he had wanted all men to hate him as much as he despised himself. Laurent understood that now. Adam himself had told him of his past. He was a complex man who had been haunted by a past he could neither forget nor absolve himself of— until now.

Laurent smiled. He knew the cause of the change. Giselle. She had blossomed in the four months of their absence from the Caribbean. Adam would be a father before summer. That fact had made the final alteration in Adam's life—or his perception of it. The past was no longer a specter to haunt him. He was a man full of plans for his new little family.

Breedon had Renée to thank for that. At her encouragement, her brother-in-law had sent a letter to Charleston, apprising the authorities of the death of Adam Southey in Spanish Town prison. Adam Breedon, under the protection of Lord Avernon, Earl of Mockton, had been given a charter from Bertrand Merchant Ships, Ltd.

Renée would be delighted to know that Adam and Giselle were married, Laurent decided, a service performed by himself as captain of the *Christobel*. The marriage was not legal everywhere, this union of a quadroon and the *Yanqui*, but Adam said his country was the deck of the *Pelican* and there he made the laws.

They would be happy. Just the way Adam reached for Giselle at every turn, the way his hand curved possessively about her expanding waist, anyone with eyes knew they were bound by a love that had the power to heal and nurture, and that they would thrive against all odds.

"You're jealous!" Laurent said aloud, startling himself with the sound of his own laughter. Had he not compared and envied Gweneth's and Raoul's love in just such a fashion? Was that not the real reason he was on the road to Mockton Hall—and to Renée? Did he not hope that, with her, he would possess the same all-encompassing love that twice he had witnessed?

What if she will not have me?

The thought sobered him considerably and he fell into a silent brooding quite unlike himself.

But then, he felt quite unlike himself. Renée Valois had turned him from a carefree Creole privateer into a brooding, restless man mooning over a tiny, brilliantly alive butterfly. Did he possess the lure to capture her once and for all?

"We shall see, *mon chaud papillon*. We shall see!"

"No! I will not! I cannot! Gweneth, *soeur*, look at me! What will he say? What will he think?"

Gweneth Bertrand, Lady Avernon and Countess of Mockton, eyed her only sister's figure with misgiving. "He will think, perhaps, that you're eating too much," she suggested lightly.

"Oh! Do not tease me. This is serious!" Renée cupped both hands around the swelling beneath the bodice of her sprigged-muslin gown as diamond-bright tears beaded up in her lashes. "Why did he not wait a few months more? Why did Laurent choose now to come to England?"

Gweneth put her arms around her sister's shoulders, amazed that Renée had burst into tears. In all the time since her arrival at Mockton hall, never once had Renée shown the slightest concern about her condition, nor would she name the perpetrator of the deed. But now, with the news of the unexpected arrival of Laurent Lavasseur, Gweneth's suspicions were confirmed.

"Renée, *chérie*, do you not think it time that the father know of your child's expected arrival?"

Renée's head jerked up. "Father? Monsieur

Lavasseur has nothing to do with . . . with"—
she made an eloquent gesture to indicate her
belly—"with this!"

Gweneth's brows arched in disbelief. "Shame
on you, Renée. You always were a terrible liar.
Of course Laurent is the baby's father. *Morbleu!*
Do you think me a simpleton? You forget that I
know what it is like to lie in that Creole's arms
and receive his kisses."

Renée's moan made Gweneth regret her indis-
creet remarks. "Forgive me, *chérie*. I only wish
to make you realize that I know the temptation
offered a woman when a man like Laurent
begins making love to her. If not for Raoul . . ."
She smiled the secret smile of a woman who is
perfectly content with matters the way they are.
There was Raoul, and that's all there was to
that!

"Why did Laurent come now?" Renée murmured again.

"To see you, perhaps?"

Renée shot her sister a dark look. "No. He
could have come anytime since the day I left
Jamaica. He must have business in England. We
are just a side trip."

"Then we shall be perfectly genial hosts,"
Gweneth responded, tired of fencing with words.
"Finish dressing, Renée. He asked most particu-
larly to see you."

"I can't see him. You don't understand!" Renée wailed.

With a mutter of exasperation, Gweneth
caught her sister by the shoulders and turned
her around. Her jade eyes were stern and yet

compassionate. "Then explain to me, Renée. Tell me why you cannot see Laurent. Is he the father, or was there someone else? Is that why you and Laurent did not marry?"

Renée's mouth formed a stubborn knot of silence.

Gweneth took a deep breath, striving for enough self-control to keep from slapping her stubborn sibling. "For months I have patiently waited for you to confide in me. Do you think I do not care that my unmarried sister grows round with a child and there's no man to press for a marriage ceremony? *Mon Dieu!* When Raoul found out, it was all I could do to keep him from sailing off to Louisiana to find out the truth. And Benoit? When our brother returns from France you will not be able to hide it from him and he *will* go after Laurent. Do you not care that your silence may be the cause of a duel and someone's death?"

"Let me be, please!" Renée broke from her sister's grasp and ran across the room to fall weeping upon her bed.

"What folly!" Gweneth exclaimed as she threw up her hands in defeat. "If *you* will not tell me, I will ask Laurent!"

"No! Please come back. I will tell you everything!" Renée cried, struggling to a sitting position on the bed.

Gweneth turned on her heel at the door. "You will tell me the truth, the whole truth?"

Renée nodded, wiping the tears from her cheeks with her fingertips.

"Very well, then." Gweneth crossed the room

and sat down by Renée and put her arms around her. "Out with it."

A few minutes later, Gweneth was chewing her lower lip thoughtfully as Renée ended her story. "You must see, the baby changes nothing. I tried to trap him with my love. I faced the truth of that when he accused me of being too preoccupied with myself to see Giselle's troubles. That's why I left him and came to England. Laurent is a man who needs his freedom. My love was not enough to make him wish to give up his liberty. Yet, now that there is a child to be considered, I do not doubt that he would do the honorable thing by asking me to marry him."

"That would be the fourth time," Gweneth observed dryly. "For a man who is singularly uninterested in matrimony, he is very free with his proposals."

"You're making fun of me again!" Renée cried indignantly.

A compassionate smile blossomed on Gweneth's lips. "I will tell you what Benoit told me when I was too foolish to believe in my own attraction for Raoul. I think your greatest fault lies in your pride. *Oui*, I said your pride. We all spoiled you shamelessly when you were little: Papa, Philippe, Benoit, Adolphe, Madame Bourgeaux—all of us. You were our beautiful porcelain *petite*.

"Well, you are no longer our favorite, our live doll. You are a woman with all the passion and pride of the Valoises in her blood. If you want this man, you may have him. And, believe me, he will be glad to be gotten by you."

"I do not know," Renée replied, but the trembling of hope was in her voice.

"Of course not! You believe that if he loved you, he should have felt and recognized that love from the very beginning and been helpless to even seek to strive against it. After all, you are the beautiful, exquisite Renée Valois. How dare a mere colonial be in doubt of his love for you!"

Renée blushed to the roots of her hair. "Do I sound that conceited? No wonder Laurent thinks of me as a foolish butterfly."

Gweneth laughed. "As what? A butterfly?"

Renée's skin pinkened still more. "He called me his passionate butterfly, to be exact."

Gweneth shook her head of glorious cinnamon curls. "And you wonder if the man is smitten. Renée, *petite,* I think you should go below and put the poor man out of his misery."

Renée placed a protective hand on her stomach. "I don't want him to marry me because he feels obligated."

Gweneth stood up. "Did he make love to you because he felt obligated to you?"

"Certainly not!"

"Then I doubt he will be overly dismayed at the results. But I urge you, marry him quickly or your honeymoon will be delayed several months, and I do not think Laurent will care much for that!"

"Where is he?"

Gweneth helped Renée to her feet and brushed a wisp of ebony hair back from her sister's face. "He is below being interrogated by Raoul and the twins. No doubt Raoul learned the truth long before I."

Renée's eyes widened. "You don't think Raoul will challenge Laurent, do you?"

Gweneth chuckled. "And saddle himself permanently with a sister-in-law and her child? Silly girl! Go and wash your face. I will choose the perfect gown for you. Go! Quickly!"

Laurent watched in perfect amazement as the Earl of Mockton balanced the pair of one-year-olds, one on each knee. It was rather disconcerting to see their father's cerulean gaze reflected in two such different faces. The girl, named Philippa after Gweneth's brother, was of the same coloring as her mother, fair-skinned with fine blond hair whose reddish gleam promised to darken into rich red-gold with time. The boy, named Jason after Raoul's father, was dark-haired and possessed already his father's prominent features of nose and brow.

They were a handsome pair and, doubtless, would be the cause of much spirited courtship and adventure when grown to an age for such things. Now they merely contented themselves with pulling the knot of their father's lace jabot and drooling upon his knee breeches.

The most amazing thing was to hear Raoul himself cooing to them in his rich deep voice, as if afraid his quarterdeck volume might frighten them. His dark head was coiffured in the latest London fashion and his clothes reflected the meticulousness of a feminine hand.

Here was the only man Laurent ever thought twice about insulting, looking more like a British nobleman than the bombastic English privateer who had sailed the Atlantic like he owned it and claimed from that very ocean his bride.

"Amazing," Laurent murmured aloud.

"So." Raoul raised his head when satisfied that his charges were content. "What brings you to Mockton Hall, Lavasseur?"

The sapphire stare that met Laurent's black gaze was more reassuring than anything he had witnessed thus far. It was direct, steel-edged and knowing. It was the gaze of the captain of the *Cyrene*.

"To see you, of course, *mon ami*. What else?" Laurent answered with a warm smile. "And look where I find you, in the nursery. Ah, Bertrand, who would have believed it?"

Raoul smiled slowly. "And you, do you not long to set up your own nursery?"

Laurent shrugged. "I have yet to find a wife. First things first."

"Sometimes," Raoul murmured. "But last I heard, you were engaged. Mademoiselle Renée Valois?" he prompted when Laurent did not readily reply.

A slow thick pounding began in the place where Laurent's heart lay. "But . . . she is with you, *non*?"

Raoul's face revealed nothing. "Is that what you thought?"

"It's what she told me. *Mon Dieu!*" Laurent sprang from his chair. "You do not mean to tell me she's not here? She left Jamaica months ago!

Adam Breedon saw her as far as London. Could something—?"

Raoul's immodest laughter startled Laurent, but his children did not even move, apparently accustomed to the volume of their father's amusement.

"Be seated, Lavasseur. Renée is here, safe and sound. But your interest intrigues me. Why all this sudden concern for a lady you allowed to leave you months ago?"

Laurent realized at once that he had given himself away. He sat down and smiled his chagrin. "So tell me, what is it like, this business of marriage?"

Raoul grunted as a tiny hand tugged the hair just above his left ear. "Heaven and hell," he muttered, and shifted his son into the crook of his left arm. He looked up smiling. "And I wouldn't trade it for anything on God's green earth! So suppose you tell me why Renée has been here for months and you are only just arriving."

Laurent crossed his legs and made a steeple of his fingertips. "I do not understand it myself. But I will tell you a story. A man makes a perfectly logical judgment, unclouded by passion or greed or even fancy. He thinks to himself, 'I'm happy. I have no desire to change my life. Why should I change it? No! I won't change it.' Logically, he goes to free himself of an entanglement with a perfectly lovely lady whom, in a moment of sentiment, he made the mistake of thinking he might marry."

Laurent sighed, his brow furrowing. "The

young lady is informed that no marriage will take place. There is no question of dishonor—then," he added under his breath, uncertain of how much Raoul knew. "The lady is furious, you understand. It was to be expected. They part on bad terms. He thinks never to see her again. But the fates, they are lying in wait for him. He and the lady are thrown together until even the lady loses sight of her hatred and dislike."

Raoul waited for the man to go on. When he did not, Raoul said gently, "It happens to most men sooner or later."

Laurent shook his head. "You do not understand. Renée is so . . . so unpredictable," he complained, giving up his pretense of a story.

"One moment I want to wring her neck and the next she does something so incredibly wonderful I want to kiss her breathless. One instant I think I understand her, I think I know what she wants, but then she makes me so angry I . . ." Laurent raised a bewildered gaze to his old friend. "I think I have gone mad. Desire, I understand, I am acquainted with. But this is madness!"

"Oh, my friend!" Raoul answered with laughter. "You once thought me a fool to be so in love with Gweneth and then to treat her so shabbily. I was so afraid of her love that I nearly killed us both before succumbing to the inevitable. I now know why I struggled so hard, so I will save you the exercise of puzzling it out. A woman like Gweneth, like Renée, demands all that a man can offer. She becomes everything in life to him—what he wants, what he needs, what he would die for. It's terrifying and it's wonderful. You love her, Lavasseur. It's that simple."

"I hope it is me you are discussing," Gweneth said as she swept into the room. "Laurent, *chéri*, how wonderful to see you!"

Laurent caught her up in an embrace that lifted her off the floor. *"Ma chère!* You look more beautiful than I remember," he murmured against her cheek just before he bent his dark head and snatched a kiss from her.

"Laurent, you never change," Gweneth replied breathlessly when he released her.

Laurent gazed down into her sea-green eyes and said, "But you do, *chérie*, and I think your husband had better be careful. If your sister will not have me, I shall have to spirit *you* away!"

Gweneth reached for her daughter as Raoul came up beside her. "I fear I must disappoint you, monsieur. I have prior claims on me—three, to be exact."

Laurent looked at the four happy faces before him and felt a pang of jealousy. Would he ever be so blessed? Until this moment he had never thought much about wanting a family. Yet, it felt right. Perhaps Raoul was right. Perhaps he had been caught all along and simply did not know it.

"Well, will you not ask about Renée?" Gweneth chided.

"Where is she?" he responded without hesitancy, and Gweneth pointed to the room across the hall.

Renée listened in quaking uncertainty as a man's steps rang on the marble floor of the hallway and then the doors to the music room opened. He was silhouetted against the brighter light of the hallway, his tall masculine form achingly familiar. She was reminded of the night she had watched him bathe, and of the splendor of his wet naked body, and of the passion that had been shared between them. The sweet aching burned through her now, the aching that was need and desire and love.

He stood perfectly still, as if listening for her too rapid breath, and she clutched her knitting between her hands, unable to pray for either his departure or his entry. She must not encourage him in any way, she told herself. He must decide for himself.

Then he saw her and smiled and came toward her. *"Bon soir, mademoiselle,"* he said.

That was all, a salutation made a thousand times a day by thousands of people.

Renée stared up into his face until the sight dissolved before her eyes, obscured by tears of joy she dared not shed. "Monsieur Laurent," she murmured faintly.

Laurent looked around. "Why sit in the dark, mademoiselle?" He reached for a tinderbox on a nearby table and struck a spark. A feeble thread of flame nibbled at the lamp wick, growing steadily brighter until the room glowed.

Then he turned to her and all else ceased to exist. There were only he and she, and the distance between them. That space seemed to shrink and then yawn wider as Renée studied his beloved face.

"I have missed you," Laurent said after a

moment, his voice sounding deep yet quiet in the room's stillness.

"I, too, have missed you," Renée replied, discreetly rearranging the knitting in her lap, hoping to disguise the bulge that was not quite so obvious when she was seated.

Laurent did not move toward her. "Why did you run away?"

Renée made a disclaiming gesture. "I did not run, monsieur. I gave up."

Laurent cocked his head to one side. "I asked you to stay," he reminded her gently.

Again Renée made a movement of denial. "You only did what any gentleman would. We were beyond civilities. That was my fault." She looked up at him.

Laurent took two steps toward her, pausing when he came under the spell of her golden-flecked dark eyes. The months of separation seemed to recede, and with them the last of his doubts. All the joy and the anguish of love's discovery came back to him until there was nothing but its power.

"If I had been wiser, *mon coeur*, I might have saved us these last months. But then there would not have been a night like the one aboard the *Pelican* when I played knight-errant to a poor frightened maiden and discovered a passionate woman in return. I might have spared you the tedium of Tortola, but then I would have spared the sweet agony of those days we shared my cabin and the night—do you remember?— the night you lured me from my bath and into your bed." The expression on his face was both infinitely tender and hotly passionate. "I learned I loved you that night, *mon coeur*."

He reached out to touch her cheek, caressing the petal softness. The glorious reality of her skin beneath his fingers, the subtle fragrance of her perfume, the golden pools of flame that caught and reflected his image in their depths, all of it combined to feed the rising tide of emotion within him—a swelling of love that he no longer sought to break free of. "Do you remember?"

"Yes!" It was a whisper of admission that Renée breathed against his lips as his mouth claimed hers.

His touch held her spellbound with the knowledge that she would never be rid of him, nor of the weakness that made her flesh, full with his child, awaken in welcome to the slightest graze of his lips. It was no simple irritant of momentary passion. This all-consuming yearning stemmed from a love starved for the sight of him, a love that in the intervening months had sunk roots deep into the fertile ground of her being. The selfishness of love had metamorphosed into a selfless wish to see the man she loved thrive. That hunger fed on the softening of his eyes as he moved back from her, the undisguised return of that love borne in his taut features.

Laurent's hand at her chin trembled as his other hand came up to entangle itself in the heavy black silk of her hair. "This is why I came, *mon coeur*."

He bent and began placing feather-light butterfly kisses at her temples. "This is what I ran from and yet could not escape. It is not only your weakness but mine. We're irrevocably bound, I know that now."

"Oh yes, Laurent!" Renée cried softly, placing her hands on either side of his handsome face. "I love you so, and have for so long!"

It was all so simple, Laurent could not imagine why he had once been so afraid of love.

"Au revoir, liberté" he mouthed softly against her lips. *"Vive le bonheur!"*

And then he began to laugh, the happiness he wished "long life" bursting free from any restraint of doubt. He scooped Renée up, and as her arms went around his neck, he swung her about, his joyous laughter filling the room.

"Monsieur Lavasseur! You must be more careful!" Gweneth admonished as she pushed open the music-room door outside which she and Raoul and the Bertrand children had stationed themselves in shameless eavesdropping.

Laurent swung around to face them, Renée still in his arms. "We are to marry, and quickly!" he said by way of greeting.

"That would be wisest, *mon amoureux,*" Renée responded, and deliberately lowered her eyes to the bulge rising prominently beneath her gown.

"You're . . . you are with child!" Laurent's expression of stunned amazement drew laughter from his soon-to-be in-laws.

"I hope this is proof enough, Renée, that Laurent is not marrying you out of pity," Gweneth chided mildly as she reached out to encircle her husband's waist.

"Oh, no!" Renée exclaimed with a satisfied smile as she nuzzled Laurent's neck contentedly. "I knew from the beginning how it would end."

About the Author

Moth and Flame is Laura Parker's eighth novel. Her credits include contemporary romances as well as her first love, historical romances. Thanks to three understanding children and a terrific husband, Chris, Laura finds life "hectic, hard work, and wonderful."

If you enjoyed the passion and adventure of this book...

then you're sure to enjoy the Tapestry Home Subscription Service℠!

You'll receive two new Tapestry™ romance novels each month, as soon as they are published, delivered right to your door.

Examine your books for 15 days, free...

Return the coupon below, and we'll send you two Tapestry romances to examine for 15 days, free. If you're as thrilled with your books as we think you will be, just pay the enclosed invoice. Then every month, you'll receive two intriguing Tapestry love stories — and you'll never pay any postage, handling, or packing costs. If not delighted, simply return the books and owe nothing. There is no minimum number of books to buy, and you may cancel at any time.

Return the coupon today . . . and soon you'll enjoy all the love, passion and adventure of times gone by!

HISTORICAL *Tapestry* ROMANCES

Home delivery from Pocket Books

Here's your opportunity to have fabulous bestsellers delivered right to you. Our free catalog is filled to the brim with the newest titles plus the finest in mysteries, science fiction, westerns, cookbooks, romances, biographies, health, psychology, humor—every subject under the sun. Order this today and a world of pleasure will arrive at your door.

 POCKET BOOKS, Department ORD
1230 Avenue of the Americas, New York, N.Y. 10020

Please send me a free Pocket Books catalog for home delivery

NAME _____

ADDRESS _____

CITY _____ STATE/ZIP _____

If you have friends who would like to order books at home, we'll send them a catalog too—

NAME _____

ADDRESS _____

CITY _____ STATE/ZIP _____

NAME _____

ADDRESS _____

CITY _____ STATE/ZIP _____

368